Children of the Goddess

Michela Scheuerman

To Sandra
with gratitude
& love!
Michela Scheuerman

ISBN: 1-894936-65-5 Complete 9781894936651
Copyright © Michela Scheuerman 2006
SAGA BOOKS
sagabooks.net
Cover Linda Macfarlane

In loving memory of
Dean Scheuerman,
who always believed in me.

Chapter One

Awakened by a foreign presence in his bedchamber Cano's eyes opened abruptly, the king saw Rhiannon's grinning face hovering above his. She was so close he could feel her breathing. Startled, he jerked into a sitting position waking Liban, the queen.

Urien slapped Liban when she screamed and Cano leaped to Urien's throat and called out for his men. Rhiannon laughed, and with a single pass of her hand Cano fell back on the bed unable to move.

"Where are the guards?" Liban cried out.

"I put a spell on all your warriors and made them mine," Rhiannon said. "They will only obey my commands, and Urien's. All we had to do was ask them to open the doors of the palace and they obliged; they led us to your bedchamber."

As Cano and Liban begged to be spared, Rhiannon stabbed the king's bare chest with her talons and excised his heart. At the same time, Urien cut Liban's throat from ear to ear. Blood spewed over the bed, spurted on the furniture and on the walls and stained the assassins' clothing red. The metallic odour of the blood was like a drug to Urien; he relished it and drew vital vigour from it. Rhiannon replenished her spent energy by feeding off the strong vibrations emanating from the red colour of the blood. She was the alchemist, the brains behind the planning of the storming of the town of Aileach.

***

Amergin and Kalos were the soon-to-be-parents of twins. With Airmid, Amergin's mother, the three were Druids at the court of Cano and Liban. Airmid divined, early in the pregnancy, that Kalos was carrying fraternal twins. Prophetic dreams and the sacred runes predicted that the children were the ones that a well-known prophecy spoke of and, since the king and the queen were childless, they had promised Amergin and Kalos that their children would inherit the throne.

Amergin was tall and slender. He wore his sunset-red long hair parted in the middle, and thinly braided around the contours of his face. He had a closely cropped goatee which, defying the tradition of Druidism, he was determined never to grow too long. His skin was light with a pinkish cast to it, his eyes green and mellow, and his lips often parted in a smile.

When he had been only a Druid apprentice, he travelled to the Greco-Roman world in search of new wisdom. At the time, the Roman Empire had fallen and Christianity was slowly replacing Paganism in the Mediterranean. Kalos and Amergin met after she had fled Rome.

Kalos' father, a Roman aristocrat who had converted to Christianity, commanded Kalos and Selenia, her mother, both High Priestesses in the temple of Isis, to abandon their underground practice of witchcraft and to become Christian. When they refused to comply he, enraged, repudiated them and banished them from his home.

Kalos and her Greek mother lived like beggars in the streets of Rome, where Selenia contracted pneumonia and died soon after.

Kalos returned to her father's house to claim the gold that was rightfully hers; it had been passed on to her from her mother and it was supposed to be her dowry. Instead, she thought she would use it to live an independent life. Julius, her father, outraged at Kalos' insolence ordered that she be flogged. She took the punishment and afterwards she faced her father with the same request.

"You are no longer my daughter! How can you claim 'your gold' if you are dead to me? Be gone, witch, be gone for good; the fact that you still live shames me!" Julius shouted as he slapped Kalos and pushed her towards the door.

Kalos, blinded by anger and by pain, called out an invocation to Isis and her father was suddenly struck dead. The servants, who had rushed to the room in which father and daughter had been arguing, believed that Kalos had murdered their master. Kalos put her ear next to Julius' chest to confirm that he was dead and, when she discovered that he had no heartbeat, she cried out aloud.

"I loved you! Why did you make me hate you?"

She ran to her bedchambers, took the ivory box which contained her gold and left, knowing that she had to flee the city because soon guards would be looking for her and would make her pay for the murder she did not commit. It had not been her intention to kill her father.

Amergin met Kalos, whose name meant "beautiful" in Greek, in Gaul, where she had settled, feeling she would be safe. They fell in love with one another instantly.

She was short and thin, perfectly proportioned, and carried herself with a posture and a dignity which many mistook for haughtiness, but nothing could have been further from the truth.

She had the kind of black hair which cast blue reflects in the light. It was wavy and flowing down to the small of her back, but she often wore it braided and pinned behind her nape. Her face was an oval graced by a dewy, ivory complexion and large, dark-brown eyes which attributed a certain melancholy to her expression. Her lips, pink and soft, were delicately full. Amergin had loved the fragrance of jasmine and lotus which enveloped her at all times.

She told him all about herself, fully trusting him. He gave her his heart and told her all about himself. Soon, they travelled to Amergin's native Ireland, where they married.

Chapter Two

At dusk in Aileach, at the cottage where the king's Druids lived, far away from the castle and close to the grove, Amergin and Airmid had nursed Kalos since morning through her heavy labour pains, but the babies would not come. Kalos uttered something in Latin; Amergin was quite sure she was invoking the Goddess' name so that she would grant Kalos the strength to endure the tremendous and still unfruitful pain.

"Soon the babies will come, love," Amergin spoke, while Kalos' mind was too clouded by pain to take notice.

"I know I am going to die," she reasoned, remotely surprised at the fact that the thought of dying, right then, seemed rather reassuring.

She let out a scream which Amergin thought was too wild and animal-like to have come out of one of the most beautiful creatures on Earth. Amergin squeezed his wife's hand.

"Ah!" Airmid said excitedly. "A little head is crowning; push Kalos, push love...soon the pain will disappear." Driven both by nature and by desperation, Kalos gathered up enough energy to push, huffing and sweating profusely, trying to catch a breath between one contraction and the next. It finally happened! The first of the two babies gushed into Amergin's welcoming paternal arms, while Airmid fetched a fresh wet cloth which she wrapped caringly around Kalos' head, so the young mother was refreshed enough to work on the second delivery.

"Wife, we have a beautiful girl," Amergin whispered to Kalos.

"Bring her close to me," she muttered, "so I can see her."

She gazed upon her daughter. As she pushed once more, she managed to smile, and then tilted her head back, closed her brown eyes, and her thick dark hair hung down the back of the birthing chair that Amergin had built out of solid oak.

Another wild scream, followed by a sigh, vibrated the room and a son was born. Both infants cried the cry of life. Airmid took the baby girl out of her father's arms so he could hold his other child. Amergin was elated.

"I want to see my babies..." Kalos whispered, exhausted, while she tried to sit up straight. She looked into her lover's eyes and felt the intensity of the power of creation in the complicity of their love.

Amergin and Airmid helped Kalos off the birthing chair to clean her and the twins up, and then they laid her on a soft sheep-skin pallet warmed by the fireside.

The girl-child was named Morrigan, and the boy was named Lugh. They had been born during Samhain, the period marking the ending of the old year and the beginning of the new one.

November, the month of the Birch. This was a propitious time to make contact with one's ancestors. The curtain separating the world of the material from that of the ethereal was being lifted on Samhain. Children born under such auspices encapsulated some of the knowledge and the wisdom of the spirits who sent them to the world of flesh and fire with special missions.

Once Kalos was comfortably resting on the warm skins she was handed the babies, each gently swaddled in supple lamb skins, flushed and crying healthily. They lay by Kalos' side, gazing at their mother with their tiny but alert eyes, demanding love and nourishment. She gazed back at them with infinite tenderness.

Amergin washed the golden sickles with which he had cut the children's umbilical cords. This was the same instrument he used to cut the sacred heather and mistletoe.

He walked across their bedroom and knelt by his wife's side, they both cried. Amergin looked at her flushed, transparent skin as she began breast-feeding the babies, starting with Morrigan, the one who cried the loudest. Kalos was so small that Amergin found it remarkable she had been able to safely give birth to twins. He caressed her raven mane.

"I am the happiest and most fortunate of men," he thought.

The grey-haired Airmid came back into the bedroom to make sure that mother and babies were doing all right.

"Let her rest now," she smiled at her son. "I shall cook us a special meal." Amergin thankfully smiled back at her. He could not understand how Airmid could possess such seemingly boundless energy as an elderly woman while he, a man in his early thirties, felt unquestionably exhausted.

He gently removed the children from his sleeping wife's side and set them each in their own birch cradle. He had worked on the cradles during their months of waiting.

"Birch is for good beginnings," he whispered as he lay down beside Kalos. By the time that Airmid's meal was ready, it was dark outside and the young family slept.

Chapter Three

Kalos was blessed with an extraordinarily keen gift of second-sight, which manifested itself most incisively through her dreams. She was having a very disturbed sleep. She dreamt of a man, dark and tall who, with a blonde woman by his side, and soldiers, stormed their peaceful Aileach during the sleep of its unsuspecting people. Urien was the man's name; she heard it whispered throughout the dream. His hounds pillaged, raped, killed, enslaved and turned the town into a nightmare of fire and blood. King Cano and his wife were slain.

Kalos woke abruptly. The sound of the fighting outside broke her spirit, as she suspected that her dream had been a forewarning. She splashed some water on her face, ran to the window and screamed when she saw the town burning, and soldiers moving erratically in the distance.

In a flash of psychic insight Kalos saw that, by virtue of a rare and powerful talisman, Rhiannon, Urien's blonde accomplice, had discovered who the children of the prophecy were, and where they would be born. Since that revelation, Rhiannon blocked Kalos' powers of second-sight and enhanced her own. Kalos could not have averted what she did not know, but when Rhiannon and Urien were so close in Aileach, a psychic path opened within Kalos' mind through her dreams, and she knew that she and her family were in danger.

Amergin and Airmid woke in a panic, and so did the children. Kalos sobbed, until she found the composure to explain that her nightmare was taking place outside. Amergin and Airmid witnessed the commotion as well. Airmid ran to the cradles, picked up the babies and tried to quiet them.

"They have died..." Kalos said, alluding to the king and his wife.

Amergin understood. "There is nothing we can do but leave. We are next."

They all began to prepare for teleportation. They were westbound for the town of Dooey, ruled by king Ossian, Cano's brother.

Danu's power, the power of the ancestral mother-goddess of Ireland, was summoned. The three gathered close, cradling the newborns among them, stilled their minds and let them merge with one another's until they synchronized into one thought frequency.

The spell began to flow through their minds:

"The energy that spun all life in motion,
the Universe is not a big, black box.
Tenax, tenax vox.
We are because It is, It is the Energy

that spun our Universe in motion. Open your mighty
doors to our frail human emotions...
Tenax, tenax vox, the Universe is not a big, blank
box."

As the spell reached completion, they all dematerialized.

**

The usurpers of King Cano's throne finally reached the Druids'
dwelling. Urien kicked its door open and the piercing, steel blue of his
eyes avidly searched in the dim light of a few candles for the family of
the Druid he had longed to meet.

"Where are you?" Urien howled in frustration and
disappointment.

The rooms in the house were searched. Dark corners were lit,
oak trunks burst open and curtains were slashed by sharp sword blades.
Tapestries were yanked off the walls, all in the hope of finding behind
them the existence of some hideaway.

Finally Rhiannon, who had been standing motionless at the
centre of the house trying to gather the vibrations of the people who had
lived in it, spoke.

"Stop searching. There are no secret passages in this house. The
Druid and his family teleported themselves. Where? I do not know.
Damn them...I cannot see...." She brought a hand to her forehead.

Urien kicked the fur pallets on the floor and proceeded to tear
the rest of the house apart out of anger and disbelief.

"Only a handful of Druids in the whole of Ireland have the
power and knowledge to teleport themselves," Urien said while shaking,
and maniacally tugged at his black, short beard.

He knew that Amergin was a seeker of peace and wisdom and,
by virtue of that, Urien had mistakenly assumed that Amergin and Kalos
could not possess such high powers, as he perceived power only as a
destructive force.

"They must all perish," Urien stated as Rhiannon nodded, and
they both left the dwelling.

Chapter Four

Amergin and his family materialized outside the castle where they lay exhausted, until king Ossian's soldiers, guided by the babies' cries, found them and brought them inside the palace in the presence of Ossian and his queen, Arianrhod. Kalos explained her dream, and with her husband and Airmid, described what they had witnessed in Aileach.

Ossian and Arianrhod were well acquainted with Amergin, Kalos and Airmid. Devastated by the news of the death of Cano and Liban, Ossian promised himself that he would not let any harm come to Amergin's family.

They were given hospitality at the palace for the night and, in the morning Ossian would find a suitable dwelling for the small family. He and his queen had the utmost respect and trust for the three sorcerers. In the dim, soft candlelight of their bedchambers, Amergin and Kalos put the babies to sleep and lay down to get some rest themselves. Kalos, tired after having nursed the children, fell asleep.

"Kiss me," she whispered in her husband's ear. "I am falling asleep. See you in the morning." He turned his face towards hers and kissed her lips tenderly. "I love you Kalos," he murmured. Her lids were closed, but she smiled and drifted off.

Amergin could not sleep. He was, like anyone else involved, still in shock at what had happened in Aileach, yet eager to know who the usurpers of Cano's throne were. Amergin was happy and grateful to the goddess that they had been spared, but did not feel safe. Then, upon him came the realization that he had two children, and the comfort of knowing that, no matter what, he would protect his children's lives even at the cost of his own.

Hope fired up his mind. Thoughts of joys to be shared with his family surfaced and delighted him. Amergin began to imagine Morrigan and Lugh as they might look at the ages of six or seven, sitting before him under a mighty tree. He was going to tell them about the proud past of Ireland, about its heroes and about its gods.

His imagination grew so intense that he rose from his bed and, very quietly, approached the cradles and began to speak to his children.

"Once upon a time, there was no time, and it was then that the gods ruled the Earth in all their splendour. It was a remote time of deep magic during which gods and humans lived side by side, a time in which all wonders were a reality.

"Since time immemorial, two races fought over our fair emerald isle: the Tuatha De Daanan, or tribe of the goddess Danu, and the Fomor, an amphibian race of half human, half animal-looking beings who were more ancient than the Daanan, and who lived in the abysses of the sea.

"The children of Danu, the humans, had their capital city in Tara which they also called Drumcain, the "beautiful hill." It is said that the Daanan came from the sky. Although the Fomor chose the bottom of the sea as their permanent abode," Amergin gently stroked the cheeks of his newborn children, "they had an island outpost which they called Balor's Castle. This was a glass watchtower they used, to keep track of the Daanan's movements.

"Balor was the name of their terrifying and most powerful god" Amergin said. He sat on the bed by the cradles, smiled at the mental image of his children, older and attentive, and continued.

"...Over time, the children of Danu and the children of Balor fought many battles. Often the Fomor had won over the Daanan by unleashing on them unknown and unspeakable diseases. But in the battle of Northern Mag Tuireadh, the Children of Danu, aided by the formidable Morrigan, were able to repel the Fomor back into the realm of Annwn, the aquatic underworld. The Morrigan, the Great Queen, was the most powerful of five Daanan goddesses. Morrigan had the power to shape-shift, to turn herself into the prophetic Raven, but, most important of all, during battles she appeared with wild fury hovering above the Daanan soldiers and, in such manner, she terrified the enemy as she incited her warriors to fight majestically and to win."

Amergin was getting tired of whispering, of talking all together, but his mental journey needed to continue, narrated by the softer voice of his mind. He lay on his back.

"Lugh was the splendid, powerful and many-skilled sun-god. Do you know that there would be no life on this Earth of ours without the sun? For your names and their meanings, you must be proud."

"Father," the children would ask perplexed. "You said that the gods Morrigan and Lugh were. Are they not gods, still?"

"They are still gods and they always will be. When I said that they were, I meant that they no longer come among us humans, lest we summon their presence with good... with good...cause." Amergin yawned, the last images in his mind slowly faded into sleep, tucked under the weight of his eyelids.

Amergin had not had a chance to talk about Balor, but he dreamt about it. A gigantic monster stood before him. Balor, the creature, was trying to focus his one, infected eye upon him, so that its venomous gaze would annihilate him, but the eye, thwarted by Amergin's will, was not able to fix its gaze. Yet it kept trying, terrifying the wizard who tossed and gasped in his sleep.

Chapter Five

In Aileach the days were blemished with violence. At first, Urien and Rhiannon's men did the ransacking and the killing. However, many people had lost everything and often everyone in their family, so they stole from those who still had something. Some children wandered around parentless and many died from neglect and exposure.

Urien had further plans for the people he had attacked and massacred. He had taken material possessions from them, had subjugated their bodies and now he planned to enslave their minds and their wills to fear, fear to rebel against him and his rule.

The rumour of Rhiannon and Urien's sorcery spread quickly out of Ulster to the rest of the country.

In the very beginning, other Irish rulers thought of Urien's takeover of Aileach as a transitory and short-lived act of bravado. Although they were aware of the fact that King Cano and the other members of his family had been murdered, they chose not to intervene.

In the meantime, the rulers put their Druids to work on the background of Urien and Rhiannon to understand their magic, their psychology, their strong points, and the weak ones, so that successful plans of attack would be devised.

Within weeks after the occupation of Aileach, everyone in Ireland knew that the invaders had managed to enslave the senses of the King's warriors to their will, and realized that, unless stopped, Urien and Rhiannon would become a permanent threat to them all. However, not all rulers felt confident enough about their Druids' magic to challenge Urien and Rhiannon. Amergin and Kalos had the potential to develop magic powerful enough to deal with them on equal terms.

At King Ossian's castle, his Chief Druid, Dylan Buarainech, seemed surprisingly knowledgeable about Urien and Rhiannon's background, and offered to reveal it to the king in the presence of Amergin and Kalos.

"How is it that you came to know about them?" Ossian enquired.

"Many years ago I had to deal with them. They first came to me seeking knowledge of the magical realms and, very gradually, they gained my trust, which they betrayed. I had in my possession the extremely powerful Egg talisman, a milky-looking, oval-shaped crystal which was passed down from generation to generation in my father's family. One morning I woke and found that Urien and Rhiannon were gone, and so was the Egg. In truth, without it I had not enough confidence in my own magic to pursue them and get my talisman back."

"...So cryptic." Kalos thought, feeling that there was more, but did not dare say so, not even to Amergin. Her mind had met a gloomy curtain in Dylan's mind and soul, which frightened her away, discouraging her from looking deeper. She only knew that she sensed danger from what appeared to be the most frail and genteel of men.

However everyone felt about Dylan, it was apparent that he was willing to disclose precious, if limited, information about the enemy.

Dylan began to move across the assembly chambers with his usual humble, almost viscid pose, slightly hunched and walking slowly, clothed by a white robe, which seemed to overpower his small frame.

He held his clammy hands cradled in each other and, as he stopped next to Kalos and began to speak, his ice-grey eyes squinted and appeared watery. Dylan's soft voice was anything but pleasant for it was a childlike squeal artfully modulated into a soft hiss.

The closer Dylan was to Kalos, the stronger were the feelings of uneasiness and coldness she received from him, and he was aware of it.

"Urien and Rhiannon," Dylan said, "are the two only children of a Briton Chieftain who, having discovered his son and daughter's incestuous involvement with one another, cast them out of his house and his village and warned them never to return. As far as he was concerned, they were dead to him.

"So Urien, at the age of seventeen, and Rhiannon at fifteen, found themselves homeless and completely alone in the world. Little by little, they wandered from village Druid to village Druid, gathering a knowledge of magic that they must have planned to misuse to suit their own purposes.

"They chose to come to Ireland, they told me, because they knew the Druids' magic is widespread and powerful here, and there was much to be learned. That's-how-I-met-them," Dylan concluded in a flat staccato.

All listeners asked him to go on. He did because he relished the suspense he was creating, and the undivided attention he received.

"I was living in the south of Ireland when they came into my life and I remember one very peculiar thing about them. They had given each other nicknames; Urien wanted to be called Thetra, and Rhiannon wanted to be known as the Pythoness."

"Pythoness...after the Sybilla of Cumae..." Kalos thought, surprised that the Mediterranean seer's fame had reached even Ireland. She and Amergin were listening very attentively. Kalos even felt compelled to do so as if her life, as well as the lives of those she loved, would come to depend on it.

Ossian, wearing an expression of concern so deep it cast a grey shadow upon his face, said "Thetra – that is the name of a Fomorian death deity. Why would he choose such a name?"

Dylan fingered his robe. "I noticed that Urien gradually developed an interest in Fomorian history and became obsessed with it. Once he even said he wished he had Balor's power."

Chapter Six

A robust fire was burning in the royal chambers at Caer Balor, which was what Urien and Rhiannon had renamed King Cano's palace.

Urien, clothed in black, stood by the fire admiring its capability for destructiveness and wished he possessed it. His hair, cut bluntly at the jaw-line, was wave-less and dark, with a streak of gray at the forehead, and he wore it swept-off his face, except for a chunk which seemed to want to cover his left eye.

Eventually, he was sure he would get to rule Ireland once the Fomor's power on the surface of the island was restored. But things were not happening fast enough.

Deep in thoughts of power, he involuntarily cracked the walnut he held in his left hand so forcefully that his palm bled.

The Pythoness, voluptuous, entered the room, wearing crimson from head to toe. Her thin and usually pale lips looked warm and full when she carefully outlined them and stained them with red from wild berries. Though she looked very different from her brother, the traits they shared were their tall physical stature and a lust for power and wealth.

Her skin, transparent and delicate, had blushed with much passion during her life and her very blonde, straight hair conferred to her rounded face a childlike quality, which excited Urien. Her aqua-blue eyes looked clear enough to hide all the lost innocence.

Hearing Rhiannon come in, Urien turned around and stared at her.

"We have much work to do. We have to plan our every move and word if we want to rule this land in the name of Balor," he said.

"That's why I came," Rhiannon replied smugly.

Urien's thin frame shook nervously. He ran his hand through his hair and short thin beard, which was so scant it barely framed his angular pale face. He looked into nothingness intensely, with narrow and widely spaced eyes heavily framed by dark eyebrows, which met above the bridge of his perfectly straight nose. His lips, looking bloodless and thin, parted in awe at thoughts of whom or what he might become.

"Twins will be born, who shall restore the age of Danu," Rhiannon quoted the prophecy.

"Time to stop dreaming and to start living our greatness, remember?" She mocked Urien and snapped her fingers right before his eyes. Urien grabbed her fist swiftly, stopping the clicking sound.

"I know what needs to be done!" He shouted as he shook her.

"You are hurting me Urien. Let go!" She yelled pulling her wrist out of Urien's hand lock. "You know you need me. Don't you forget that I am the seer and the alchemist. Never forget that! I could stand alone if I wished it; you could not."

Urien's face reddened painfully with rage and fear. He knew she was right and stormed out of the room furiously kicking the door open on his way out.

"Still a little boy playing power games," Rhiannon whispered to herself, smiling. Seeing him so full of passion had always excited her. She followed him to their bedchamber, where another fire was providing more than comfortable warmth. He was sitting at the edge of the bed.

"What do you want?" He was still annoyed yet he knew the answer. They had always been addicted to each other's bodies and that was the force that bound them.

She moved close to him and kissed his lips with a softness and sensuality that seduced him each time as if it were the first. She let her robe and her tunic slide off, grasped his head in her hands and cuddled it between her breasts.

He pulled back to disrobe himself quickly because he knew he had to take her and while undressing, he began to tongue and nibble at her reddened nipples.

Exuding lust, she kissed him deeply, stepped forward and sat in his lap facing him, her legs spread apart and let herself be entered by him, and they enjoyed each other as they always had.

***

In the darkness of the castle's damp dungeons lay the very first sketches of their enterprise. They had drawn what was to become a pure gold statue of Balor and its venomous eye. Heaps of precious metals and gems that the soldiers had taken from the people sat nearby, piled into glittering mounds of rings, necklaces, torques, broaches, belt buckles, earrings and many other valuable objects of beauty.

Chapter Seven

It was night time in Dooey, but Dylan Buarainech could not sleep, engrossed as he was in thoughts of greed and deceit.

"I could propose a trade to Urien and Rhiannon: Amergin and Kalos' children in exchange for my Egg." He clenched his fists and quivered with excitement.

"This is the perfect opportunity to claim my power over the maggots I now must bow to," he thought, enraged at the fact that he, the great Druid Dylan Buarainech, should be a servant to whom, he thought, were weak rulers.

"Just like Cano, Ossian, too will perish because of his soft heart. No human sacrifices, no forcing of virgins and such permissiveness towards women, who are allowed to gain and maintain equal power with us...such nonsense!" His eyes blazed with rage and consternation. "Such foolishness..." he hissed under his breath.

"The age of Danu is over, and the rightful male claim to the power of magic must prevail; I shall devise a plan to deliver the children into Urien's hands, and the Egg back into mine." Hours went by, filled with sordid thoughts and schemes. Then he came to a resolution, which made him feel ready to communicate with Urien and Rhiannon.

The Druid lay on his back at the centre of the floor of his chambers, lulled by ebbs of different states of consciousness. He had ingested a liquor which altered his perceptions to a state of being suspended between dream and reality. He saw fragments of future scattered in his mind in the form of symbols, sounds and images to be pieced together into a coherent whole.

He saw himself reclaiming his Egg and his power. He felt that pain would come along with that power, but he was determined to endure the suffering as long as he could reap the rewards.

Dylan was motionless, his cold eyes, dazed and languid, fixed upon the ceiling. His body began to convulse and his facial muscles to spasm. Astral projection had always been a difficult, rare and unpleasant experience for him, but he learned to cope with its roughness as he experienced it.

His fingers involuntarily clenched the fur upon which he lay, and he finally felt himself detaching from his physical body and gently floating above it. His astral body felt comfortable and warm, the sensation of weightlessness was both delicious and frightening.

Dylan's will powered a command to his astral body to move at the speed of darkness to propel itself to Aileach, travelling at a dizzying rate of velocity through the layers of time and space.

He suddenly appeared, preceded by an explosion of white light ripping through the darkness of Urien and Rhiannon's bedchambers.

"Dylan!" Rhiannon cried out, startled into wakefulness by the appearance of his astral body.

"Urien!" She yelled, frantically pushing on her lover's shoulders. "Wake up, wake u..."

Urien opened his eyes and sprung into a sitting position with a look of stupor and disorientation on his face, as he saw the image of their father standing before their eyes.

"What on Earth are you doing here? What the hell do you want?" Urien spoke loudly and with the intensity of a deep anger in his quivering voice.

"I came to reclaim what belongs to me."

"...And how do you propose to do that?"

"I can trade you Amergin's children, as well as his life and his wife's, for my Egg." Dylan was sure he had struck a chord, for silence followed his proposal. Then Urien broke the stillness of the moment.

"You know where they hide?"

"How did you come to know them?" Rhiannon asked avid to know.

"They sought refuge in Dooey, under king Ossian's protection. You two fools were not even aware that Cano had a brother, and a powerful one," he muttered while shaking his head and pointing his right index finger at them. "We are getting sloppy, aren't we? Apparently, taking over a town is not as easy as stealing your own father's dignity, is it?" Dylan chewed bitterly on each word.

"In exchange for my Egg you will own the twins to do with them as you wish. Think of the possibilities. You could raise them in hate, train them to serve your purposes by using their inborn potential for magic, or you could kill them to make sure they will not grow up to use their powers against you.

"On the other hand, if I do not receive the Egg, I shall make sure to protect, raise and train those children to become such a powerful source of destructiveness to you, that you two maggots will suffer unheard of pain, and such losses that you will wish you had never seen the light of day."

Dylan's image was undulating in the ecstasy of his delirious ravings about things to come, glorious events that would avenge his trespassed honour.

Urien and Rhiannon, mute with disconcert, could do nothing but stare at the image of their father with more hatred than their hearts had ever carried for him. There was nothing left to say, but "You will have the talisman in exchange for the children."

Urien and Rhiannon assured Dylan that they would send two emissaries to Dooey within the passage of three moons.

"Very well," Dylan replied. "I shall be awaiting them at the banquet which I am going to persuade king Ossian to offer in honour of his distinguished new guests.

"I shall hold the children in my arms, and swiftly trade them for my Egg. Do not even contemplate sending me a replica of it. I shall know and chastise you accordingly."

Rhiannon spoke up. "You will not be disappointed, old sack of rotting bones. You will receive your talisman. How will you account for the presence of our emissaries at the banquet?"

"I shall tell the king that the two new guests are my nephews, come to seek my patronage in their endeavour to study the magic arts and follow in my footsteps. By the same token, how can you be sure that the emissaries can be trusted to carry such precious and powerful cargo?"

"All of our soldiers are under our spell. They are completely in our power and do whatever we ask without even being able to expect, or demand, any reward. They exist in a state of 'living death'" Dylan's daughter explained.

"Very well," Dylan said. "I shall be waiting to reclaim my Egg. Do not disappoint me. You will be sorry for it, more sorry than you could imagine. Should I convince Amergin to cooperate with me to destroy you, you will not stand a chance for survival, not even if you use the power of the Egg. It will not serve you well if employed to challenge the both of us, united." Dylan disappeared as fast and as abruptly as he had appeared.

***

He regained consciousness in his room, a few minutes after he had evaporated from Urien and Rhiannon's presence. The entire experience had been so stressing to his system, that he had drifted into sleep the moment his astral body had slipped back into his physical one.

So much planning awaited him. It was not the thought of lying to Ossian and Arianrhod that troubled him, but rather the possibility that he may not be convincing, or arouse suspicion of some kind.

"...But why should they doubt the sincerity of my intent to celebrate the arrival in Dooey of the 'great' Amergin and his prodigious family?"

Chapter Eight

In the warm and safe atmosphere of their new dwelling, Airmid and the young family woke, but Kalos' day began in sadness.

"Something is wrong," she told Amergin and Airmid, who gathered around her, sitting at the breakfast table. "I felt something, something strange happening while we were asleep. I sensed a threatening presence."

"Who was threatened?" Airmid asked.

"I felt a great deal of negativity, directed towards us, from Dylan. I feel powerless. Ever since the night of our escape from Aileach, it is as if my ability to 'see' has been stunted, and I hate it. We must find out how Dylan is connected to what happened in Aileach," Kalos said, looking in her mate's eyes with much despair.

"I won't let anyone harm the children. This I promise you," Amergin said as he held her hands in his.

"There is emptiness behind his eyes, and a lot of darkness," Airmid said of Dylan, and Amergin nodded in agreement.

That same morning, while Kalos and her loved ones were discussing their perplexities about Dylan, the old Druid was phlegmatically on his way to present his proposal to king Ossian.

"Great Ossian," Dylan began while entering the intimate 'blue' chambers in which Ossian and his consort held their conferences with the Druid.

"I thank you for agreeing to see me so early in the morning, but this meeting concerns an urgent matter."

"Wise Dylan, you are very welcome to confer with myself and with the queen whenever you deem it necessary. Sit, make yourself comfortable." Ossian pointed one of his large hands in the direction of a comfortable and sturdy-looking chair.

"Ossian, Sire, I have just received news of the imminent arrival of two of my nephews from Leinster, my sister's sons. You see they have expressed a desire to come under my tutelage so that they too may be trained in the magic arts. To their request, I have taken the liberty of consenting. They shall arrive in two moons, counting tonight's."

Both nodded in assent, but Arianrhod spoke, her bright, green eyes sparkling against the transparency of her skin and the red of her flaming mane.

"It is done now, and so be it, but I cannot help but wonder why you did not feel free to come to us before you accepted your nephews' request. Rough times lie ahead of us all in Ireland. We must rely on our Druids entirely for their expertise to fight the villains who so brutally usurped King Cano's throne, took his life and that of his queen, and are now possibly moving towards us." She kept her composure in spite of her indignation.

Dylan swallowed hard and painfully, feeling the pressure of his blood rise and flood his face. He knew he had to conceal his feelings; he knew that what he thought was overdue to him would come if he remained patient and cautious.

"The horrible wench," he thought." She senses something, or maybe she is merely being her usual clever self. Nothing worse than an opinionated wench. She'll pay, by the gods of Annwn, she'll pay dearly for inconveniencing me so." He found it hard to hide the shortness of breath that his anger caused.

"I must admit, my queen is right," Ossian spoke. "I agree with her thoughts regarding the matter. However, it is also true that you are our oldest and most trusted friend." Dylan bowed his head subtly, smiling a bittersweet smile. "And, even in such perilous times as these, you do still have a right to live your own life, provided it will not impair the quality of your service to your sovereigns, and to your Mother Ireland.

"I trust that you will manage to train your nephews discreetly without letting the matter of their education distract you from your duties as Chief-Druid of this community."

"Kind sovereigns," Dylan spoke tasting bile. "You have my most solemn word that I shall not let my private matters interfere or hinder my duties as Druid.

"This brings me to another part of my request. This matter is mainly a mutually beneficial proposition," He took a deep breath.

Ossian and Arianrhod showed genuine patience and interest in hearing him out.

"You see, I was thinking that it would be nice if, pending your approval of course, we could give a banquet in honor of our much distinguished guests. It has occurred to me that, given the dramatic circumstances in which they arrived here, and amidst the grief for the death of your brother, King Cano, and his queen, we have not yet had the opportunity to welcome them to our town, and to show them proper hospitality.

"Furthermore, I would consider it a great honour if I was allowed to cooperate in my duties with Amergin and Kalos, and I am sure that it would also be immensely beneficial for my nephews if they were allowed to meet such prodigies."

Stunned at such magnanimity, that they believed it to be both sincere and sensible, Ossian and Arianrhod needed only to look in each other's eyes to know that they both accepted Dylan's request.

"Dylan," Ossian spoke. "Your proposal is welcome. It does appear to be kind and beneficial to all involved. I shall order the servants immediately to prepare for the arrival of your nephews as well as to make all the arrangements for the banquet to be given upon the night of your nephews' arrival."

Dylan knelt humbly at the feet of his sovereigns, expressed his deepest gratitude to them while mentally plotting their deaths. He spoke once more.

"If I may be so bold as to ask for one more thing: the presence of Amergin and Kalos' children at the banquet would be both welcome and honouring to us all. After all, it is a known fact that children bring blessings and joy wherever they go."

"So be it," Arianrhod responded, smiling. He had appealed to her unfulfilled but very much alive maternal nature. The Druid had been able to get through her curtain of cerebrality and to reach masterfully into her feelings, which were most tender where children were concerned. She even thought of his request as surprisingly sweet.

"In his old age, our tough, old bird must be growing in humanity," she thought.

***

"He is up to something! Help me, help our children!" Kalos cried out to Amergin, who stood at the centre of their bedroom, cold and motionless, struck dumb by the magnitude of what was about to happen. He knew the women were right. He trusted their intuition with his life and now, this invitation was the sign that the old Druid was indeed maliciously involved.

Amergin moved towards his wife. She was shaking, looking very white and overwhelmed with panic. He took her trembling hands in his.

"I promise you the safety of our children. No harm will come to them as long as I live. Our magic, combined, will protect the babies and us. We are both aware of the limits of Dylan's magic." He smiled faintly and caressed her face. Airmid approached them and hugged them both.

"My magic is simple, but ancient. I cannot claim the ability to accomplish amazing feats of magic, but I know enough to be convinced of the fact that I can help. The children will be safe. Should something happen to the two of you, rest assured that no one will even be able to come close to Morrigan and Lugh. I shall vanish with them. They'll never find us, never find us!" Her eyes welled up with tears, and Kalos rested her head on Airmid's shoulder.

"I cannot see what will happen at the banquet, but I feel with all of my being that we shall die Amergin," Kalos said.

Airmid cried out in agonizing pain; she knew it too.

"But I also know that Airmid and the children shall live. I don't know if happily, but they shall live. Maybe we are fulfilling our destinies; maybe this has to happen." Kalos said as she looked exhausted, but filled with a new strength.

"How can it be?" Amergin cried out in frustration. "All our magic, our hope to change the future, how can it be? I swear I shall keep you safe!" He promised through their unstoppable tears, and he believed he would.

"I love you," he whispered, holding Kalos tightly in his desperate embrace. "Let us run away. Let us go somewhere where they will not think to look."

"They'll find us anywhere," Kalos said.

"So, what are we to do? Are we to walk into our death-trap without even trying to save ourselves?" Amergin was frustrated and angry, but his anger was not directed at his wife, nor his mother, for they only talked of what they felt and saw.

"There's always the possibility that you might be wrong, isn't there?" He speculated.

"My love," Kalos said, "there's always that possibility." And, while speaking those words, she and Airmid did know that there might be a chance for error.

"This is the plan," Airmid announced, resolute and self-confident, as she felt that her personal power was strong at that moment, and that her words would be wise.

"You two accept the invitation. Refusing to go would disappoint and surprise Ossian and Arianrhod, and it would infuriate Dylan who, sooner or later, will manage to get you and your babies to that banquet at last.

"He might even accuse you of treason and convince the sovereigns of such nonsense. Ossian and his queen are wise, but these are times of deep fear, of betrayals and distrust. If they so wish, Dylan, or Ossian, shall get to us eventually, should we decide to disappear." Silence enveloped the room for a brief moment of contemplation.

"This is what you will do. You will attend the banquet. Just before it is time for you to go, I shall make the babies cry and look ill. Don't worry. I shall not hurt them of course, but we'll just skip one feeding or two before you go, and they'll cry out of hunger."

"Kalos, you will express some milk for them and I shall feed them right after you leave. I am sure that, knowing that the children are ill, will be a good enough excuse for leaving them at home. You go and watch Dylan's every move and rely upon your intuition and your listening skills to figure out how he is connected to Urien and Rhiannon. If and when you two see definite danger, towards yourself or your children, mentally combine your energies and your magic. If Danu wills it that you live, your gifts are definitely powerful enough to let you fight back. We shall handle the future as we go along. What's important is your survival. Dylan will be exposed, sooner or later, after you react to him." Airmid's blue-gray eyes glimmered with love and deep conviction.

Chapter Nine

Three moons had gone by; the emissaries arrived in Dooey, and the banquet hall was prepared sumptuously, brightly illuminated by large torches and many candles. The light warmed every piece of furniture, the multi-coloured crystal wind chimes hung at the windows' arches, and fire illuminated the faces and clothing of the guests.

At home, Kalos, Amergin and Airmid were nervous but kept their minds as clear as possible. They needed to rely on their own inner-strength, and to show Dylan neither suspicion nor fear.

"Here!" Airmid applied some beet juice to the infants' cheeks to make them look feverish. "Now all we have to do is miss a feeding, and by the time you two have to go, these lovely babies will be crying heartily!"

Kalos retired to her bedchambers to express her milk and was not looking forward to hearing her children cry, but she knew it had to be done in the more than likely case that Dylan would drop by their cottage, to make sure they were taking the babies to the banquet.

"I hate you!" Kalos kept repeating to herself while thinking of Dylan. She cried hot tears. She felt as angry as she had been at her father, and she felt scared because she knew that they were all about to face a turning point in their lives.

"As long as nothing happens to the children, I can take anything." In that thought she found strength and she dried her tears. She finished expressing her milk. She had just started to dress when she heard a knock on the door.

"Dylan Buarainech!" Kalos heard her husband say in a stern voice. "How may we help you?"

Dylan, clothed in a silver robe, dragged his minute frame slowly into the cottage where he sensed, and relished, the fear and nervousness that all were trying to conceal from him.

"I came to make sure that you'd remember to take your babies with you, children are such an inspiration! My nephews are looking forward to meeting all of you."

Kalos entered the room where Dylan had been received, and they both sized up each other's dislike very politely.

"While it is extremely kind of you to want our children to be with us tonight, I fail to see how their presence could possibly enlighten your nephews. After all, they are just infants." She placed the emphasis on the last four words.

Dylan was now sure that Kalos and Amergin suspected something. He felt betrayed by the power he thought he had, to completely prevent Kalos from intercepting his feelings and intentions.

In response to Kalos, Dylan said, "I agree with you, but I believe that the mere presence of your children at the banquet would be a delight to our eyes and our ears. The presence of children and of the innocence they carry with them is a great inspiration in itself."

"Old bastard!" Kalos thought so intensely, that Dylan almost heard it.

"Thank you," she said, bowing her head slightly to Dylan, trying hard to stay poised.

The babies finally began to cry. Amergin and Kalos took a breath of relief. Airmid, purposely looking concerned and a bit surprised, rushed to the cradles and, in turn, felt each baby's forehead.

"They feel very warm!" She gently rocked the cradles.

"Let me see," Kalos said. She put her hand on one baby's forehead, and then on the other's.

"Your mother is right," Kalos told Amergin. "It looks like our children are sick."

Amergin walked to the cribs and took one of the babies in his arms.

Dylan was livid. He felt he really could not push further without compromising himself entirely, but could not afford not to have those children at the banquet. He finally resolved to walk to the cribs to check the infants for himself.

They did feel hot to his touch, because Airmid and Kalos had mentally transferred heat to the babies' foreheads when they touched them earlier. The infants were certainly screaming and looked flushed. Dylan hoped in a miracle.

"I am certain that they will be all right at the banquet, if we provide a nurse to take care of them there," Dylan daringly proposed. Airmid quivered with outrage.

"I shall stay here and take care of my grandchildren!" She stated firmly, looked straight into Dylan's viscid eyes and he felt a small electrical charge course through his head, then the symptoms of a strong headache appeared. He knew that Airmid was causing it, and he realized how much he had underestimated her powers.

He did not have any other recourse, so he frantically began to think of other schemes so that the emissaries would have the chance to come into contact with the infants later that evening.

Suddenly, Lugh ceased crying. Somehow, he seemed tired of crying and of being hungry, and just drifted into sleep.

At the moment, it was as if the same burden was lifted from Dylan's shoulders and was dumped onto Amergin's and Kalos.' Airmid was still convinced that they would be able to sway the Druid from his absurd idea.

"Well," Dylan exclaimed with an audible pitch of jubilation vibrating in his voice. "It looks like we shall be able to be honoured by the presence of one child, at least!"

"It is very kind of you to want our children at the banquet, but you must realize that the fact that Lugh fell asleep does not mean that he is no longer sick." Amergin stayed as calm as he could while he visualized himself disintegrating Dylan.

Dylan, acting as if he had not heard Amergin, approached Lugh's crib and picked up the sleeping infant.

Kalos stepped forward as if to stop Dylan, her heart pounding in her chest. Airmid stood by the cribs, petrified, unable to say or do anything short of throwing the Druid out and so upsetting the entire plan, and further endangering them all.

Amergin swiftly grabbed Kalos by the waist, preventing her from confronting Dylan, who had not noticed her lunging towards him. She was so scared she could hardly swallow her tears, which Dylan, turning to face her, saw.

"Now, now," Dylan said while looking in Kalos' direction. "It is not as if we were going to sacrifice this little one to the Gods!"

Kalos gulped audibly and began to sob openly. Amergin and Airmid tried to break the intensity of the moment by explaining to Dylan what a protective mother Kalos was, as most new mothers should be.

"It will be all-right dear," Airmid said while touching Kalos' arm. "I shall take care of Morrigan and you and Amergin will take care of Lugh." She looked into Kalos' eyes sending strength and faith that all would turn out well.

***

The banquet hall in Ossian and Arianrhod's palace was enormous and lavishly beautiful. Ancient and colourful tapestries hung from the tall stone walls. The solid, polished furniture, some of which was built out of oak wood, and some of which was made of cedar wood, was artfully crafted and weighed down by gold and often jewel-encrusted ornaments.

A large, long table overflowed with all kinds of food: mutton, beef, roasted fowls, a variety of vegetables, especially corn, and fruit, custards, breads and great amounts of ale.

Large crystal wind chimes which hung from the many arched windows, told ancient tales of glory with their lilting sounds. They had graced the banquet hall for centuries, reflecting the light of the sun and that of the moon, glorifying that special room which had hosted many sovereigns, and many feasts.

The strong light coming from the high, blazing torches enshrined between the building blocks of the room's walls, shone like miniature suns and warmed the colours of the people's clothes and of their precious stones. A very large hearth held the majestic fire which warmed the chilly air breezing from the windows and through the stone walls. Jewelled veil curtains softly wafted off the eerie, ancestral windows.

Ossian and Arianrhod moved towards Amergin and Kalos to greet them. They felt very cheerful.

"Oh my! There's your beautiful little boy!" Arianrhod's eyes beamed with joy and tenderness as they set upon Lugh, the sight of whom made the queen not notice the absence of Morrigan.

"May I hold him?" She humbly asked Kalos, extending and cradling her arms to receive the infant.

"Of course," Kalos whispered, attempting to smile while her eyes, when they met Arianrhod's, seemed full of fear and sadness.

"If you only knew what we know," Kalos thought looking at the queen, who appeared so joyous and carefree, already enjoying the anticipation of what she thought was going to be a memorable evening.

The banquet hall slowly but steadily became filled with people, among whom Urien's emissaries and Buarainech, who accosted Amergin and his wife while they were talking to Ossian and Arianrhod.

"Let me introduce to you my nephews, Liam and MacRoth." Dylan smiled ceremoniously while introducing the tall and serious looking young men to those present.

"We are honoured to be in your presence," Liam murmured in a monotone, speaking also for MacRoth.

After having taken a good look at the young men, Kalos and Amergin looked into each other's eyes and attempted to communicate telepathically for the first time in a long time.

"They are in a trance," Kalos said mentally to Amergin.

"Yes," he replied, "their breathing is slightly irregular, and their gazes are unfocused. They must be under a spell."

"...Urien and Rhiannon's," Kalos disclosed to Amergin who took a step back from the emissaries, and noticed they were carrying daggers. Everything was clear to him and to his wife in that instant.

Kalos had been able to see through Urien and Rhiannon's thick curtain of treachery. She and Amergin knew that Buarainech's involvement with the two impostors made him a traitor.

"What to do?" Kalos and Amergin kept asking while each glanced meaningfully into the eyes of the other.

Amergin coughed loudly trying to create a diversion, and walked away from the company to attract the attention of the royals who, in fact, crowded around him, concerned.

"What is the matter?" Ossian asked Amergin while patting his shoulder.

"...Huh...I desperately need to talk to you, alone," Amergin implored under his breath, while Arianrhod moved closer to him to hear him more clearly. In the meantime, Buarainech's suspiciousness reached an apex and he made his way towards Amergin, but Kalos, approaching him with the warmest, most seductive smile she could conjure up, in a gesture of friendliness rested her right hand onto Dylan's left arm, suddenly bringing him to a halt.

"What is the matter, lovely Kalos?" Dylan asked her as the colour of her face grew paler by the second.

"Nothing is the matter, Dylan. I just caught the opportunity to have the wisest Druid in Dooey to myself, in the hope we could strike an enlightening conversation. I am certain that you could teach me much," Kalos smiled feigning calm.

Dylan knew she was stalling him and rudely pulled his shoulder away from Kalos' touch and walked quickly towards Amergin and the royals.

Amergin grew quiet at the approach of Dylan. He had not been able to tell Ossian and Arianrhod much; the king and the queen looked very perplexed and confused. All they had understood was that Amergin and Kalos were having a problem, and that they needed to discuss it with them alone, definitely without Dylan present.

"I am sure that whatever it is, it can wait until after the banquet," Ossian said to Amergin, and walked away with his queen towards the centre of the banquet hall, greeting and mingling with their noble guests.

Amergin stood shocked, stunned by Ossian's ability to shrug the matter off so easily. He knew there was more depth to Ossian.

"Good magic, ah?" Dylan said impudently while looking at Amergin, obviously claiming to be responsible for Ossian and Arianrhod's uncharacteristic behaviour.

Amergin grinned. "What do you want of us?" He grabbed Dylan's robe at his throat. Dylan remained unshaken.

"You have no choice but to let your destiny unfold. Ossian and Arianrhod are under a powerful spell I cast on them, poor, helpless worms that they are. Nothing you can do or say will save you, or your family. You'll find yourself pleading to Ossian for help, and he will cordially offer you a mug of his best ale in reply."

Kalos, close by, stared at them stunned at what she was witnessing.

"Take me, take my life, but let my family live. They will go away from here, wherever you want to send them, but please, I beg of you, let them go," Amergin said, trying to maintain as much dignity as he could. He was aware of the fact that Dylan was operating above his own magical potential.

"He must be in possession of a magical talisman," Kalos and Amergin thought synchronically. She saw Amergin cry as he released Dylan from his grip and she moved closer to them.

Dylan, who walked away unaffected by Amergin's plea, had earlier risked taking the Egg from the emissaries, fearful that offering them one child would invalidate the agreement. Although he had been able to get the talisman unbeknownst to Liam and MacRoth, he had decided that he was going to follow the plan anyhow, because he thought he had much to gain by doing so.

The banquet hall resounded with the music of harps, fiddles and drums and the guests were dancing, unaware pawns in Dylan's cruel game. Kalos and Amergin went to a nearby room to collect their child from a nurse with whom the sleeping Lugh had been left earlier, and walked back to the banquet hall to take their place at the table.

They saw what appeared to be carefree people dancing, faster and faster in the merriment of the feast which would be their death scene. Looking at the people move swiftly and quickly gave Amergin and Kalos a dizzying feeling of disorientation.

Sounds, colours, images and aromas were blending much too fast and seemed to be unnaturally heightened. Ossian and Arianrhod headed towards the table and everyone else did the same. Lugh, tightly bundled in his mother's arms began to cry, but feebly, almost gently. Kalos looked at him and felt her death coming from within. The thought of having to wait helplessly for Dylan and whomever else to harm her little boy, maybe her entire family, ate away at her stomach and her heart as if a slow, malicious insect were gnawing at them.

She remembered Airmid's last look, the look that made her feel that they would all find a way out, that all would be right. Tears filled her eyes as she realized it would not be so, and the image of her little daughter's face flashed in her mind, with the bitter realization that she would not see her again.

Amergin's senses felt strained; he was closely monitoring every movement and sound in the hall. He pushed his hearing to the limit in order to catch something even remotely useful in the conversations that went on around the table, but nothing made sense, nothing felt real.

Ossian and Arianrhod stood up quite unexpectedly.

"Noble guests," the queen said. "The king and I want to express our gratitude to you for honouring us with your presence tonight."

Then Ossian spoke. "The reason we are all gathered here tonight is to extend our welcome to the family of Amergin and Kalos

32

MacDohbar, who are not only outstanding practitioners of the magic arts, but innovators in that field as well, and the parents of two wonderful children, a boy and a girl born on Samhain."

Everyone lifted their glass to them and cheered. "Long life to Amergin and Kalos' family!"

Amergin and Kalos sat motionless and murky, incapable of maintaining a front of serenity in the face of the grotesque situation they were experiencing. Lugh was whimpering softly. He was starving; it was more than past the time for his feeding.

Dylan rose and spoke. "Blessed be Kalos, Amergin and their small family, the part which is present, and that which awaits at home." The people cheered again, then everyone continued dining.

Amergin and Kalos had no appetite, but there was nothing else to do but eat. Kalos excused herself from the table to go and nurse Lugh.

Ossian and Arianrhod smiled graciously at Kalos as she stood up to walk away from the table. Before going, she whispered into Amergin's ear, asking him to focus and attune his thoughts to hers while she would be nursing the baby. Maybe they could think of a plan.

As Kalos exited the banquet hall Dylan became agitated. He had kept his eyes on her the entire evening, waiting for the right time to get to hold Lugh and finally slip him into Urien's men's arms.

Dylan rose and excused himself from the table as well, and met an unexpected puzzlement in Ossian's look which put him in a position of embarrassment and nervousness and, in spite of himself, Dylan felt compelled to sit down again.

Amergin and Kalos' plan was working. They telepathically joined their wills to open a path of awareness in Ossian's and Arianrhod's consciousness. Soon Kalos returned to the table. Lugh had been fed and she continued to synchronize her mind with her husband's. The plan would continue to work regardless of their exhaustion, provided they were not distracted by others trying to engage them in conversation.

As soon as Dylan noticed that Amergin and Kalos were neither speaking or responding to anyone, he spoke to them from across the table, drawing everyone's attention to the three of them.

"Kalos, Amergin, I was wondering if you would be so kind as to let me hold your little one; after all, this feast is also meant to honour your beautiful children and, although I am regretful that little Morrigan could not be here, I would very much like to hold Lugh and to get acquainted with him."

"May you rot in the depths of Annwn," Amergin and Kalos thought while giving him a piercing look of hatred. Dylan walked around to where the couple was sitting, and that gave them enough time to fuse their thoughts once more.

The old Druid was finally close to Kalos, who cradled Lugh tightly to her breast. Dylan sensed that something was happening but could not divine what, and that drove him mad.

As Dylan put his arms forward and looked into Kalos' eyes to let her know he was ready to receive her son, she pulled Lugh closer to her chest, closed her eyes and she and Amergin simultaneously recited the incantation necessary to breach a passage into the parallel world of the Sidhe, where they knew their child would find shelter.

Suddenly, Lugh became suspended in mid-air; Dylan stepped back yelling curses. Some of the guests screamed, others simply stood up quickly, staring at the scene in amazement.

"What is happening?" Ossian yelled, standing and banging his fist on the table. He was obviously out of Dylan's spell. Dylan was too distracted and too angry to keep control over the situation.

"Guards!" The queen ordered. "Remove the Druid Dylan Buarainech from this room!"

"Why you miserable worms!" Dylan yelled at them, shocking everyone in the banquet hall. "This is only a little complication on my way to glory!"

It was hard to sort things out in the commotion, but it was clear to everyone that the Druid was a deceiver. They saw Liam and MacRoth reach upwards for the baby, still suspended in a vacuum between their reality and that of the Spirit world. Lugh was prevented from breaching-through by Dylan's talisman, which he drew out in everyone's presence pointing at Lugh's cradling air bubble.

At the sight of the Egg-talisman everyone cleared away. Even the guards would not touch him, yet, in spite of the Egg, Dylan had been upset by Amergin and Kalos' impromptu plan. He hated what he could not anticipate and fully control.

As the emissaries had become close to Lugh, their hands went right through the bubble and they grabbed the whining child. Amergin and Kalos cried at the top of their lungs while lunging forward to retrieve their son, but to no avail.

Because of the talisman, when they came close to Urien's men a back draft blew them away and they ended up crashing into the edge of the table. People were screaming. Those who tried to help Kalos and Amergin were blasted away.

Ossian himself stepped forward in Lugh's aid, but Dylan pointed the Egg at him and then at Arianrhod, piercing them through the heart with a beam that the talisman emanated.

Amergin and Kalos gathered what strength they had left and lunged once more towards Urien's men in a last, desperate attempt to retrieve their screaming son, but their bodies met with the sharp blades of Liam and MacRoth.

As the daggers sank deeper into their writhing bodies, Amergin and Kalos looked in each other's eyes with infinite love and each stretched one arm towards the other's, until they finally grasped fingers that locked forever in the greatness and nobility of their love for one another, and for their children.

While the banquet hall was in an uproar and Dylan was laughing hysterically out of the pleasure he was receiving from witnessing Amergin and Kalos' agony, the two, for the last time, synchronized their fading minds into a single image: that of the children and Airmid, and they both implored Danu to protect them.

As unbelievable as it seemed to them, Amergin and Kalos realized that they had indeed come to the end of their lifecycle on Earth. They promised one another they would watch over their children from the world of the Spirits and held that thought until the end, until death drew the final curtain of blackness over their minds, where all thoughts were extinguished and consciousness was put out like the flame of a candle.

Chapter Ten

At the exact moment of Amergin's assassination, Airmid was shaken by an unbearable pain to her stomach, which caused her to collapse onto the floor while she barely had the breath to cry out for pain.

As her body crashed against the cold pavement her mind flashed with the images, relayed through Amergin's eyes, of what was taking place at the banquet hall.

"No! Danu don't let it be so...no, let them live...." Airmid cried out when she felt her loved ones slipping away. She saw Dylan laughing and she knew, she knew that he had killed them, and that the young men were mere executioners.

She began to sob desperately, uncontrollably, and an overwhelming feeling of wild anger possessed her and she wished the Druid dead.

She had also seen Lugh being snatched by the young men's hands out of the bubble, and disappearing with the child into the unknown. Airmid did not know who those men were and where they were taking her grandchild. And the Druid, who was going to kill her and Morrigan next, had no idea that Airmid was telepathically witnessing the slaughter of her son and of his wife through Amergin.

The link to Amergin gave Airmid an enormous advantage over Dylan. She knew she had to put her grief aside for a while and put all her energy into escaping, and bring Morrigan and herself to safety as far away as possible from Dooey.

She went to the crib, picked Morrigan up and wrapped her tightly into soft lambskin, then she put the baby in a sack with strings. Airmid positioned the sack onto her chest and part of her stomach, and tied the strings around her trunk twice, and she did it all frantically hurried as she anticipated the appearance of Buarainech.

All the while she was sobbing, and vowed to vindicate the death of her loved ones and to find her Lugh one day.

She had strapped her granddaughter to herself because she was going to attempt teleportation on her own, for the first time, and she was afraid that, while jumping into the vortex of timelessness, she might lose her.

She ran outside in the chill darkness ripped by the silvery light of the moon, and she positioned herself directly beneath it, her heart racing with her breath, as she felt Dylan and his men coming closer with their blades and black hearts.

While sweating profusely and concentrating on a mental image of her destination, her native island of Iona, off western Mull, Scotland, she recited the incantation she had learned from Kalos and Amergin, unsure that it would work for her.

When Dylan finally broke into her dwelling he found it empty and felt a rage the intensity of which he had never experienced before. He tore the Egg pendant off his neck and clenched it in his right hand, grinning his teeth bitterly in the knowledge that the talisman could not have stopped that which he had not had the wit to anticipate.

***

Airmid and the granddaughter she held tightly to her breast landed on the shores of Iona, greeted by a few seals. A powerful moon illuminated the beach and made the slow waves, which undulated languidly in and out of the larger body of the sea, shimmer with pearlescent hues.

The impact of Airmid's body against the sandy surface of the beach was hard, but not painful. Airmid had landed on her back and, immediately, as her senses became whole again, she checked Morrigan, who was asleep. Airmid placed the palm of her left hand under Morrigan's nose to make sure she was breathing, and felt very relieved to have confirmed to herself that she was.

Soon Airmid realized it was very cold. A chilly wind seemed to have breezed right through her bones and she shivered, holding Morrigan tighter yet, in the attempt to keep her warm with her body heat.

The woman looked up and discovered that it was a starry night and proceeded to walk towards the interior of the island, to the village she had left behind many years past, when she had wedded Amergin's father, Conor MacDohbar, and left with him to live on the mainland.

On her way towards the village, something happened that to her seemed miraculous: she saw an elderly man, a Druid, judging by his long, white beard and by the way his head had been shaved only in its middle, from ear to ear. He was trying to run and behind him, a man and a woman carrying blankets.

Airmid knew they were coming to help her, but how did they know? She was certain the goddess must have sent them, and she cried tears of joy and gratitude.

When the three were finally close to her, she almost collapsed in the Druid's feeble arms, but the young man caught her in his, while the woman was trying to get Morrigan untied from her grandmother's chest.

"Be careful with the baby..." Airmid uttered while she tried to get back on her own feet, then wrapped a blanket around herself, and one around her little Morrigan, who began stirring and crying for hunger.

"She is hungry," Airmid stated.

"She will be fed; there is a woman in the village who has recently given birth and she offered to nurse her," the woman said. Airmid took a sigh of relief and marvelled at the villagers' foresight and kindness.

"I am Sandda," the Druid said. "And these are my son, Finn, and his wife Sionann. We came here to help you; we were expecting you."

"How did you know we would come?" Airmid asked, bewildered.

"Do you see that star up there, the one which is shining so bright and so blue?" Sandda asked Airmid, pointing his finger to the sky which was sprinkled with thousands of stars.

"I am not sure I see it..." Airmid replied candidly.

"No matter," the Druid said. "That star signalled to us that a woman and a girl-child would come on the first night of the full moon, and that they would be a gift to us, as well as a responsibility."

"In which way are we supposed to be a gift to you?" Airmid enquired, genuinely perplexed.

"The crystal spheres have shown us what happened in Dooey, and the runes have revealed your identity to us. You are Airmid, mother of the assassinated Amergin; grandmother to Lugh and Morrigan, and like a mother to the lovely Kalos. You are very special."

"In what way?" Airmid enquired. "As far as I can see, we just came here to seek shelter, I am not sure we have very much to offer, other than my skills as a healer and magician, which are indeed very modest. All I know is that my boy grandchild was taken and I do not know where he is. This other one is with me, parentless, by the hand of the Druid Dylan Buarainech," Airmid sobbed with as much dignity as she could muster.

"Airmid," Sandda said. "Do you not know that your grandchildren are being sought out because of the prophecy?"

"Yes, I know about the prophecy, but I do not know about the children's fate..." said Airmid.

"Two children will be born, breaths apart from one another on the night of Samhain, who will restore the age of Danu.' This is the prophecy, so you must trust that, no matter what has happened, the children must survive to adulthood to fulfill their mission," Sandda reasoned.

"How can you be sure of such things? How can you be sure that they'll live?"

"The runes and the stones in the sacred circle divined this truth, and you must accept it. The runes and the megaliths do not lie!" Sandda replied with some indignation woven into his soft voice.

"Forgive me," Airmid apologized smiling at Sandda. "I merely meant to express my surprise...Lugh, who has him? Is he alive?"

"Your Lugh is alive and safe, for the time being, in the hands of Urien and Rhiannon." Airmid began to see that they must be connected to Dylan.

"They will try to raise him as their own child you see, all the while training him to find his sister and to kill her. Urien and Rhiannon believe that they have the power to challenge fate, and to alter it," Sandda explained.

"Can they? Can Urien and Rhiannon change fate?"

"That will depend on the inner-strength and will of your grandchildren. Raise Morrigan to be a follower of the goddess and a servant to the people, and she will not fail.

"As for Lugh, he shall be raised among lies and deception, violence, and in the absence of love. He shall have to be very strong within and trust his intuition as to what to believe to be the truth, and act accordingly."

By the end of Sandda's elucidation they had all reached the village where the stone-walled houses looked so grey and so cold, out there in the moon-lit darkness of that most eventful night.

"Let us go in," Sandda said looking at Airmid and showing her inside his home.

A warm and fragrant waft of air from the inside of the Druid's dwelling enveloped everyone. A robust fire released heat and provided light to the room cluttered with roasted chestnut shells, familiar looking jars and cruets, crystals, stave-grimoires, a cauldron and some less familiar looking celestial maps and astronomical instruments of observation and measurement. There was a crystal sphere, and runes scattered almost all over the soft, hide-covered floor.

Somehow Airmid felt that all that would be her responsibility some day, and the thought of it frightened her.

There, on her native Iona, Airmid found some peace and security after all. Living arrangements were made for her and for her infant granddaughter: they were to live with Sandda, close-by the family of Fionnualla, the woman who had offered to breast-feed Morrigan. Airmid and the baby were to dwell with Sandda until Morrigan was at least one year of age, and no longer in need of woman's milk.

During the period in which Airmid lived in the Druid's house, she would be trained in theoretical magic and metaphysical matters. Afterwards, she and Morrigan were to move into a cabin in the woods where Airmid would have the opportunity to practice her magic freely, and have enough privacy to begin raising Morrigan in her new knowledge and wisdom.

After Sandda's death, Airmid was to become Druid of Iona, and was to take Sandda's dwelling as her own.

Chapter Eleven

Many years had gone by since Airmid and Morrigan's arrival to Iona. Airmid was in her sixties and Morrigan was about fifteen years of age.

The Druid, in his mid-seventies, was still lucid but extremely frail, plagued with arthritis and an asthmatic condition.

By then Airmid had discovered, through her now sophisticated prowess in the art of divination, that Dylan Buarainech, who had underestimated Urien and Rhiannon's resources, had been murdered by Urien himself, who took the Egg talisman back and added Dooey as a satellite-city within his orb of power.

The veil of darkness descended over Iona and over Airmid and Morrigan's humble dwelling in the forest.

Morrigan had blossomed into a beautiful girl to whom Kalos and Amergin were vibrant characters vividly and lovingly dreamed up by her grandmother's imagination. But she did know that they had once been very real, real enough to give life to her and to the mysterious brother with whom she had not had the opportunity to grow up.

The young girl was consumed by curiosity and a longing to meet Lugh. She wondered whether he looked like her, or perhaps completely different.

"I'll find you one day," she often repeated to herself while thinking of "her" Lugh.

Morrigan knew no other mother but Airmid. There was a stronger bond than the parental one between them, because of the circumstances in their lives. To Morrigan, Airmid was mother, grandmother, teacher and friend.

Airmid loved Morrigan deeply, just as deeply as she loved life and all living creatures.

"Grandmother," the girl said while she was helping Airmid fill some jars with healing herb extracts, multipurpose elixirs, and vegetable ointments.

"Yes love," replied Airmid lifting her gaze from the cruets she was filling up, to her granddaughter's blazing brown eyes.

"I love you!" The girl answered cheerily while winking at Airmid, who burst out laughing and shook her head, thoroughly pleased and amused.

As time was advancing further into the night, Airmid put aside the many bottles and potions and exhorted Morrigan to do the same.

"Love," she said to the girl handing her a steaming cup of chamomile tea she had been brewing. "This will soothe your cramps."

Morrigan reached for the cup, smiling gratefully, while Airmid found herself looking at her child with unusual intensity.

"Morrigan," she began. "Today is a very special day. With the arrival of your first moon-blood you enter womanhood but that, in itself, does not make you a woman. There are certain beautiful mysteries concerning womanhood and becoming a whole person that you need to know about, and which will help you along in your growth."

Glancing outside at the moon, entranced by its magical light, Airmid grabbed a patchwork blanket and two shawls and asked her granddaughter to follow her outside.

"Let us go sit on the grass, in the moonlight, and we shall talk."

Morrigan felt a flow of dizzying excitement starting at the pit of her stomach and bubble up to her head. Such a whirling of emotions bordered on pride, for the privilege she realized she was being granted, to share into Airmid's wisdom.

"Let's go!" Morrigan announced excitedly, slipping her arm under her grandmother's, and pulling her close to her.

"You have grown so beautiful, love; I can see both the austerity of your father's looks and the loveliness of your mother's in yours. I love them so, I miss them so...You would too if you had known them. They were truly remarkable people, and are... will be forever, souls sparkling with love and courage," Airmid remarked.

Morrigan felt what her grandmother did. She could sense, distinctly, as her mother could, what people were feeling.

Once outside, far into the grove, Airmid spread the motley quilt on the silvery grass and they both sat, Morrigan balancing her tea cup while trying to sit down.

"I love the moon, and I love the heath," the girl said while looking around, bewitched by the dimmed but not diminished beauty of nature cloaked in semi-obscurity.

"I'm happy to hear that," Airmid responded. "But I have to say that I am not surprised."

Morrigan looked her grandmother in the eyes and she knew what she meant.

"You know how you experience dreams of things that come to pass?" Airmid asked.

"Uh, uh," Morrigan nodded

"...And those strange, strong feelings you receive from people you talk to, that reveal to you a bit of their hearts...?" Airmid continued. "Well, you are a true child of the moon."

"I've always felt I belonged to it."

Airmid always knew that about Morrigan; she, a creature of the night, would not easily yield to the demands of the daytime. She was never lazy, but her energy level rose at night, especially during full moons as if the old, argentous sphere were feeding her with its light, which coursed through the girl's veins with her blood, firing up the body's activity, and her imagination.

"The moon is the seat of very powerful forces. Look at it. She is the originator of all emotions; all life vibrates within it, just as her colours, white and silver, contain all colours in a primordial state.

"She is The Female, the mysterious three-faced goddess who embodies and governs the three stages of all life: Birth, Life and Death. Rebirth, signalled by the rising of the new moon, marks the beginning of her phases, of life's phases, all over again. And this is how the universe works, on these simple principles. But the universe in itself, and life, are not simple realities."

Morrigan listened enthralled, in devotional silence, eager to learn more and to ask Airmid many questions.

"You see love," Airmid continued with a smile that was targeted at breaking the intensity of the topic. "The moon is raw emotion; it is an impersonal force which buries itself deeply within our hearts. She is responsible for piecing together one's dream world by drawing upon the deepest recesses of our souls.

"Images, feelings, sensations, thus appear within us so strongly that they cannot be ignored and often need to be interpreted, explained."

Morrigan felt flooded by a feeling of anxiety originating in the fact that, she thought, she was being invested with far more wisdom that she could manage. If the moon was so powerful, and if she was a true child of the moon, that must mean that she must learn to harness the deep, raw emotions and powers within herself very artfully and effectively.

She was a wild force of nature which needed to focus and modulate its eruptiveness in order to become purposeful and beneficial to herself and to others. She knew she was the child of the prophecy. She knew that there would be evolving and fighting, and that she would have to leave behind the peace to which she was accustomed, at some point in her life. She lived in waiting of her call, in the wake of her becoming.

"Morrigu," she thought while visualizing the wild berserker, the mythic inciter of the Dannan's warriors, who also was her namesake. "I will never comprehend her fury."

Chapter Twelve

With the arrival of puberty in Morrigan's life, came the heightened manifestation of her psychic powers. It was one thing to have a vague perception of such inner-forces, and another having to face them in their full-blown expression.

As she began to hear the leaves speak, the stones murmur and water whisper actual words to her, reality became an enhanced experience. It was not unreality, but rather a super-reality.

Once she overcame the initial shock and the feelings of fear and disbelief, knowing that nature was indeed alive became acceptable. Discovering it was conscious was both unsettling and wonderful; she realized she had been given the key to unlock the doors which lead to a deeper understanding of existence.

Morrigan was completely fascinated by and drawn to water, as if it were the source of nourishment for her soul. When she was not in the mood to sit on the beach and look at the sea, she found her way to the forest's crystal clear stream and looked at her image reflected into it. She imagined what it would feel like to truly be immersed in it, and one day she tried it.

She carefully went from sitting on the stony and mossy bottom of the stream, to lying down on its green and slippery surface. She felt the cold water rise and lace the contours of her face. She blinked and breathed faster then she held her breath, closed her eyes and slid completely under, keeping her eyes shut. But she wanted to know whether she could see through the water if she opened her eyes, so she did.

The water stung her eyes mildly, and she could see nothing but a white blur of bubbles which disoriented her. She involuntarily took a breath and instinctively rose out of the water coughing up fluid profusely, and rubbing her reddened eyes.

On quiet and gloomy days, she looked at the fish in the stream and at the birds circling above her.

***

Quite early in the morning, Airmid and Morrigan were awakened by a frantic knock on their door.

"It's Brian Ilbreach," Morrigan mumbled half asleep but matter-of-factly, leaving Airmid perplexed on her way to opening the door.

"Brian Ilbreach!" Airmid muttered in amazement, realizing that, perhaps, that was not a guess, that maybe Morrigan was not only empathic, but also clairvoyant.

"What can I do for you?" Airmid asked Brian.

"It's our eldest boy," the tall, husky man answered trembling and looking so vulnerable in spite of his size.

Airmid understood that the boy might be in danger and told Morrigan to fetch their medicine bag, their shawls and to follow her and Brian to the village.

"While their mother and I were still asleep," Brian Ilbreach explained, "our boys got up and somehow began fighting with one another. Our youngest, Luibra, brandished a knife and stabbed his brother quite deeply in his right thigh.

"Their screams woke us. Luibra ran outside and we don't know where he is, or why he did such a thing! Nyssien has been crying out for pain and moaning all along, so he has not been able to explain what happened yet.

"Neither myself or my wife touched Nyssien before consulting you...you have to help him. You realize that with the Druid being ill, I tried to run to your cabin as fast as I could and I hope I made it in time for you to be still able to help Nyssien."

"We shall certainly do our very best to help your boys: they both need our help and understanding. Nyssien's wound does not sound like a particularly bad one," Airmid reassured him while lightly squeezing his arm.

"As for Luibra, bring him to me after you find him. We must understand the reasons behind his actions and we must discipline him accordingly, but lovingly. Don't be too harsh with him; he's too young to be evil, but old enough to learn how to control his temper and to take responsibility for what he does, the good as well as the bad."

As Airmid and Brian walked towards the village, Morrigan's limber frame was following behind, hauling the hefty healing-bag. When they reached Brian's dwelling they heard Nyssien whimpering and saw him lying in a small pool of blood. His mother, Fionnualla, was sobbing quietly so that she would not frighten her son, and was holding his hand. Morrigan went to hug the woman who had been her wet-nurse, and she hugged her back.

"He's burning up," Fionnualla almost whispered while the tears kept streaming down her face.

Morrigan immediately took a handful of dried poppy leaves out of a jar from the medicine bag, and set a pot of water to boil in the fire-pit at the centre of the floor.

Airmid was looking at the knife, observing how it had penetrated the boy's thigh. She gently cleaned the blood off the skin surrounding the wound, and wiped the knife at its base, to better expose and prepare the area on which work needed to be done. She reassured the parents.

"He is going to be fine. It was very wise of you not to touch anything. Had you pulled the knife out yourselves, you might have caused the wound to bleed profusely.

"We are going to make him drink some poppy-leaves brew which will dull his senses for quite some time. This will allow us to pull the knife out without letting him perceive the pain too sharply. While the knife is being extracted, you'll have to hold his arms and legs down.

"Morrigan!" Airmid said.

"Yes, Grandmother...."

"You are going to pull the knife out. I know you can do it."

Morrigan's heart beat fast and she looked breathless for a second, but she knew she was ready to commence practicing what she had been learning from Airmid by watching her at work, and by listening to her words of knowledge.

Due to his fever and to shock, Nyssien had not been able to speak and had been subtly shifting in and out of consciousness. This helped the brew that was administered to him to work more effectively. Once he looked sufficiently sedated, Morrigan felt more confident that she could handle the task.

Brian and Fionnualla looked anxious about Airmid's decision but did not dare say so out of respect for their healer, who sensed their uneasiness all the same.

Airmid moved close to the boy's parents and hugged them.

"It's all right! She is really ready, trust me."

They smiled at her, embarrassed but relieved, and she smiled back.

Morrigan was doing well, considered she was working under the keen eyes of her master and of Nyssien's parents. She had been the one who had dissolved honey in the poppy leaves infusion and who fed it to him, patiently, and pulled back the eyelids to look at Nyssien's glassy blue eyes, while transferring to him a sensation of warmth and protection.

She covered his chest with the aqua blue blanket she and Airmid carried in their healing bag; colours had the power to soothe and to help in the healing process. Aqua blue was the colour that she knew would ease one's pain.

Because she could not lift Nyssien to completely wrap him in the blanket, she did it mentally, holding in her mind the image of Nyssien wholly embraced by a luminous blanket of blue light.

Morrigan scrubbed her hands and forearms and was ready to begin. She knelt by the boy, he was asleep. She looked at the knife, grabbed its dark handle steadily with her right hand, while applying pressure around the wound at the base of the knife with her other hand.

She concentrated for a few more seconds, then quickly pulled the blade out, seized the medicated bandage which she had pre-soaked in antiseptic rosemary-leaves extract, and firmly pressed it on the wound. The hands that had worked so precisely up to that point were now shaking at the sight of the blood showing through the bandage.

"That is normal," Airmid intervened to put Morrigan at ease.

Morrigan heard and regained control over the situation. She doubled the bandage and held it down while keeping mental count up to a certain point, following which she checked the wound underneath and discovered that it had stopped bleeding.

With Airmid's help Morrigan prepared to suture the small incision.

She poured some witch hazel over the wound to disinfect it once more, and Nyssien moaned feebly while his mother kept wiping his sweaty face with a cloth.

Cautiously, Morrigan began stitching up Nyssien's wound under Airmid's scrutinizing yet guiding gaze.

"You are doing well," Airmid reassured Morrigan, whose face was crimson and covered with perspiration.

When Morrigan first pierced the boy's flesh with her needle he let out a muffled cry which chilled her blood. Startled, she composed herself and kept on working.

Airmid, tall and beautiful with her greying blonde hair woven back into a thick braid, looked with pride upon her granddaughter's work with her slate-blue eyes. Her pink lips were slightly parted in an expression of admiration that she did not care to hide.

Morrigan was almost finished, but looked uncomfortable. Her grandmother wiped her forehead and she gathered the girl's long auburn hair away from her face.

Morrigan felt the relief of the cold wet cloth, and felt a light breeze softly blow through her face and nape.

She was done; the wound had been sutured and, although it had only taken minutes, to Morrigan it seemed to have lasted much longer.

She wiped the stitched wound once again with an antiseptic-soaked bandage and proceeded to tightly wrap a dry dressing around Nyssien's thigh. She told his parents to lay their son down on his bed and to give him vervain brew to drink to keep him pain-free.

"He'll probably sleep until sunset," Morrigan told Fionnualla and Brian while scrubbing her hands clean and putting all tools and potions away, save for one jar.

"This ointment here will help keep the wound from festering and will speed up its healing over the next few moons," Morrigan explained while handing the jar to Fionnualla, who could not thank her and her grandmother enough.

Brian also felt much gratitude and went to the part of the house which was their bake-shop to fetch some bread to give to the two women. He came back carrying several loaves and blushed as he handed them to Airmid. "I am sorry they are a day old," he apologized.

The sight of that big man timidly showing his gratitude with a simple gift moved Airmid. She never took payment for performing what she considered her duties to the community, but she would not dream of turning down such a genuine gift, such an earnest expression of thankfulness.

Morrigan, too, felt love for the people and a growing sense of devotion to them as a healer. "Thank you for the good bread," she said, speaking also for Airmid, whose arms were being literally filled with golden loaves.

When they left, Morrigan felt joy and satisfaction about having completed the new task successfully, but most of all for having been a part to the healing of another.

Morrigan took some of the loaves from her grandmother's arms. Airmid's heart swelled full of pride. "What a good girl you are," she said, looking at her child while her eyes filled with tears at the thought of all the pain that would come to Morrigan.

"...But pain makes us stronger," Airmid kept repeating to herself, looking for solace in those few words of popular wisdom. But solace was hard to come.

Chapter Thirteen

The people in the village were getting ready to celebrate the Autumn Equinox with the fire festival of Alban Elved.

"Fire festivals," Airmid told Morrigan, "are festivities which mark the turning of seasons and honor the Goddess. They are four, and happen in-between the major festivals."

Morrigan always listened attentively to her grandmother. It was her desire to grow as knowledgeable and as committed to serve the people as Airmid was.

One day, it would be her responsibility to assist women in childbirth, to lay out the dead, to work the weather, raising the winds for the fishermen and calming them down for safe travel. She would gather herbs and act as healer, as counsellor and diviner for the people of Iona.

Once every two moons, Airmid and Morrigan went down to the village, to the Gorsedd, or meeting place, a low hill by the sea where they taught children the sacred Ogham. The Druidic alphabet was based on the knowledge of the trees, and was invested with magical properties. Airmid answered the children's many questions while Morrigan was their storyteller.

Airmid, like Sandda, was determined to carry on a new way of teaching which, one day, would produce a generation of peace-loving human beings.

There was to be no blazing wicker-man loaded with sacrificial victims on Iona, to celebrate Beltane. There was no need to feed the gods human or animal blood.

"The goddess feeds on our love for one another," Sandda had always maintained and taught the young people in the village. That way of thinking and living needed to be kept alive, and eventually propagated beyond the boundaries of Iona. On the mainland, this process had begun with Amergin and with King Cano, who both upheld and practiced their belief in the transfigurative powers of human love for truth, nature and one another.

The island itself, since its beginnings, had had no ruler and it was meant never to have one. A council made up of the people and arbitrated by the Chief Druid, deliberated on different issues concerning the common well being and prosperity of the small community, as well as regulating all private disputes among the islanders, and their spiritual matters.

***

Although Morrigan spent a fair amount of time at the village, and had always had the opportunity to play with children her age, she always had trouble fitting in.

As a young girl, as much as she sought the company and the acceptance of her peers, she found herself being rejected somehow.

She spent most of her time wandering in the forest, her home. She loved the woods, so green in the spring and summer; mustard and russet coloured in the fall, and white in winter.

"The tree branches are so weighed down with snow that they look as if they are going to break..." she recalled commenting to Airmid when she was just a little girl.

Morrigan loved the sea, and water, above all else. On stormy days she went to the shore to look at the waves crest and shatter like thin glass on the dark sand beach, but she loved the enhanced smell and blue colour of the sea in the summer.

She walked along the beach sandal-less; she had the intuitive knowledge of the fact that her feet had been made to be bare, and to mark the shore's soft sand with their prints.

Often she sat on the flat rocks protruding into the sea and thought about the beauty of life and the peacefulness of her existence. There, crouched on those timeless, solemn rocks dense with matter and impenetrable knowledge of the Universe, she felt inspired to sing melodies ancient and haunting, brimming with longings that often were her own.

At times, words surfaced to her mind which filled her heart with the elation and excitement of a bard weaving lyrics into music beautiful beyond beauty, and as she sang those words, she cried.

Sometimes her tears were tears of happiness, sometimes they were tears of sorrow. She wanted the love of a stranger who would emerge from those waves and who would accept her wholly, and they would hold one another in the eternal rapture of their love.

> "I dream of you, yet I don't know you,
> I feel your beauty, yet you're a faceless stranger
> You hold my hand, and you'll be in danger
> Yet I still long for the sight of you..."

As silly as she thought she sounded to herself, the melody of the songs still brought tears to her young eyes. She seemed to have this unappeasable need to cry.

On an unusually warm autumn morning, Morrigan decided to go back to the stream in the forest and to finish what she had started earlier on. When she reached the brook, she looked at her reflection in the water and watched it being crinkled by a soft breeze that she enjoyed immensely.

She stood still in the wind, closed her eyes and tilted her head back while taking a deep breath. She felt purified of all ill feelings, and energized.

Slowly, testing the temperature of the water with her toes, Morrigan shuddered at its coolness but she loved the regenerating effect it had on her, and walked gradually to where the creek slumped deeper, and lowered herself down to sit at its bottom. Her heart was racing with trepidation and excitement.

"What will I discover if I go under and breathe in?" Her mind kept repeating, while she knew full well that the only logical consequence to such an action would be drowning.

"Come, come into my embrace, you will be safe," she heard the rushing waters murmur. She was sure that was what she heard, but could she trust the brook's voice? Didn't Airmid teach her to be cautious and not to be deceived by appearances, or by the many voices of nature and its spirits?

"You have to trust your intuition as well as your intellect," Airmid had taught her.

She took a deep breath, a breath that was meant to last her long enough for her to have time to slow her heartbeat down and to still her thoughts.

As she slid under the crystalline waters of the stream her brain felt as though it were on fire. The sound of the rushing water, the flight of the birds above her, the wise stillness of the trees silhouetted against the endless sky, were slowly fading, muffled and blurred by the water which was flowing briskly over Morrigan's pale face.

When she was completely submerged she held on to that breath that she had inhaled so mindfully, and felt her soul in tumult with the burning curiosity to know, to test her own limits.

She slowly exhaled under water. She opened her eyes: she could see clearly, and, in the extremely brief interval between the moment she had exhaled and saw her breath turn into tiny bubbles, and the flash of time when she felt she had to breathe again, she had to decide instantly whether to do it in submersion or to give up, and breathe the blessed air.

She knew then that she would not turn back. Her hands painfully clasped over her stomach, feeling the pressure of the wildly pulsating blood course through her veins, she closed her eyes and breathed in. The water flooded her lungs, but she felt as though her whole being had been filled with water, she was struggling with the water, her body sliding on the mossy bottom of the brook, unable to stand up. She coughed out in a jolt of panic and regret sure she was going to die. Airmid would be devastated.

As she fathomed the worst, the unbelievable happened. The coughing ceased, the sensation of drowning faded gradually and she found herself breathing the water as though it were air. An intense feeling of joy vibrated through her, body and soul quivering in a thrill that had no equal among her previous experiences.

"I must try this in the sea." She realized how beautiful it would be to be able to move and dance under marine waters.

Once Morrigan came out of the stream, she discovered that reversing to inhaling air was as traumatic as it had been to inhale water. She folded over and coughed up large amounts of liquid, her face red and congested, and she felt her eyes burn.

Then the novel breath of air came, welcome and fresh like that of a newborn. She felt alive and happy among the shivers. She noticed that the dim, autumnal hues of nature looked so vibrant, and she let out a scream to release the tension that the excitement of it all had accumulated inside of her.

At home, Morrigan shared her experience with her grandmother, who acted surprised but was not, and responded to her granddaughter's story with the weighty subject of creation, as it had been told her.

"In the primeval magma of creation, contained within her womb, the goddess, suspended in space in total stillness, bore the Earth and her children over an unknowable stretch of time, sleeping her fertility away, yet dreaming of her children to be. They would name themselves and the things of their world.

"On the birthing day, light illuminated the dark space, now scintillating with life. And the goddess screamed. The children cried, creating lightning and thunder, which echoed and resounded in space.

"It was thus that life began. Danu gifted us all equally with thought and feeling; she gave us blood and nourished us with the sweet, warm milk of her breasts then, when harmony was the rule of new life." Airmid's eyes were shut and she looked as though she were in a trance.

Morrigan, breathless with awe, touched Airmid's hand and felt her grandmother's reverence for Danu.

"How is what you told me connected to the experience I just shared with you?" Morrigan asked.

"...Because of your experience, you will be now able to access very remote states of being. I'll try to make myself clear, child, but bear with me, because this is a difficult matter to explain."

Morrigan nodded and promised to listen carefully and patiently.

"However," Airmid continued," what I am trying to tell you is that, now that you have experienced breathing water, you don't necessarily need to be submerged to recall the experience, not unless you choose to. You can train yourself, by shifting into a state of trance, to experience that feeling over and over at will. When you have mustered that much, you will be able to regress to your foetal stages."

"I can recall the experience of being in the womb?"

"Exactly," Airmid confirmed. "And you may accomplish such a feat by travelling back with your cells: your body remembers the primordial just as well as it remembers the prenatal. Millions of consciousnesses make up your unconscious. Just as you can reach your subconscious mind, so you can access your unconscious by regressing with your cells."

Morrigan was speechless, feeling crushed, once again, by the magnitude of the events to unfold. She felt the solitude of her responsibilities and bore the anguish of it in silence, for she had to fully accept that which was her destiny.

Chapter Fourteen

Morrigan was coming from gathering some herbs one afternoon, and when she arrived home Airmid said: "I need to speak with you."

"What about?"

"Well, I spoke with Luibra Ilbreach and he told me what happened before he stabbed his brother. He claims that, early that morning, he caught Nyssien stealing two coins from their parents' store and when he threatened to tell their parents, Nyssien flew at him, grabbed him by the throat and told him not to breathe one word of what he had seen.

"In fact, as Nyssien heard that their parents were being awakened by their fighting, he stuffed the two coins down his brother's shirt. Partially out of anger, and partially out of fear to be caught with the two midin on him, as he heard Nyssien call out to their parents, Luibra grabbed one of the knives kept in the store and stabbed Nyssien in the thigh. Having realized what he had done, he ran away in a panic."

"Did Luibra tell his parents what happened, and did they believe him?" Morrigan asked.

"Yes, Luibra told his parents, but they did not believe him because, he claims, they have always implicitly trusted his older brother. Apparently, Nyssien has abused his parents' trust before, but they have never known about it. Up until now, Luibra has been covering for him.

"He came to see me because he wants his parents to know the truth, once and for all. I need you to come with me to see the Ilbreach family today, and you'll be able to tell me which one of the two boys is lying, and I'll decide what to do accordingly."

Morrigan agreed and they began walking towards the village. When they arrived at the Ilbreach's dwelling, they were warmly greeted at the door by Brian and Fionnualla.

Luibra and Nyssien sat in the background, the first looking eager to begin the talks, the second looking visibly cross and not too happy to see the two women who had healed him.

"Please, do sit down," Brian said while Fionnualla was busy pouring some warm milk and honey for Morrigan and Airmid.

"I would like to come right down to the business at hand, if you do not mind," Airmid said frankly but respectfully.

Both boys cast their eyes down, knowing that their moment, good or bad, was coming. Morrigan sat next to them and closely monitored Nyssien's conspicuous body language, which seemed to betray quite openly a certain nervousness and defiance.

She sensed that he felt he should not even be in the position he was; how dared they, parents and outsiders, question his trustworthiness?

Airmid discussed the matter of Nyssien's stabbing with Brian and Fionnualla as seen from Luibra's perspective. Luibra nodded at every step of Airmid's accurate rendition of his account. His parents looked at each other to check with one another whether or not to express their doubtfulness of Luibra's words to Airmid. Fionnualla nodded at Brian, he stroked his beard and cast his eyes down as his wife began to speak.

"Airmid, with all due respect, we must let you know that we have heard Luibra's version of what happened, but our eldest has assured us that things happened the other way around, and he has always been the most level-headed and obedient of the two."

Morrigan and Airmid felt a simultaneous flash of anger at Fionnualla's pre-conceptions about her sons, but Morrigan being the young one, had to bite her tongue and let Airmid speak for both of them.

Airmid swallowed hard, she tried to control her outrage so that she would not sound too aggressive, but she had to make it clear to the boys' parents that they were being shamefully partial to their eldest son, and were not granting their youngest even the benefit of the doubt.

"Can you not you hear your prejudice towards Luibra in your own words? You have come to misjudge both boys based on their differences assuming, mistakenly, that the most open and imaginative of the two must always be the trickster, the liar, the one with something to hide.

"I am not saying that I know without the shadow of a doubt that Nyssien is guilty, but if I were you I would open my eyes to the possibility. Have you ever tried to really question him about this matter?" Airmid concluded all in one breath, feeling as if rocks had been lifted off her chest.

"Nyssien has always been so obedient, so truthful with us. Sure, in all your wisdom, you cannot tell us you know our own children better than we do," Brian rebutted, becoming quite passionate as he heard his own words. Fionnualla touched his arm to call him back to a more controlled demeanour.

"We think we are being fair in our assumptions because over the years we have seen Luibra get into trouble many times, and then admit to his guilt. Nyssien has not given us so much grief," Fionnualla explained.

"As far as you know you have not had trouble with Nyssien, as far as you know," Airmid added. Nyssien's blue eyes lit up with hatred for "the old hag's insinuations."

Morrigan felt his turmoil, and Luibra's heartbeat eager for a justice he hoped would be done, for once in his "wretched family life."

"What do you mean, Airmid?" Brian enquired, Fionnualla looking sad at the remote possibility that Airmid might be right; maybe they had always taken their children at face value, without looking deeper. Now, it was hard to look deeper within herself as she felt the weight of guilt crush her heart.

"I mean that both your children are human; they both, from time to time have gotten into mischief, but only the unruly one has been honest enough to admit to his shortcomings, while the other never had to deny them, since he did not reveal his faults to you.

"Luibra has told me, and I have reason to believe the boy, that he has often covered for his brother. No one ever covered for Luibra, and when caught he confessed his guilt."

For the first time tangled in the crafty web of doubt, Brian turned towards Nyssien and asked him, "Is this true?"

"It is not," Nyssien replied confidently. Regardless of his young age, he had always taken advantage of his parents' trust and poor judgment, and had consciously moulded himself into a consummate liar. But Morrigan touched his arm in a way that compelled him to turn towards her and to look straight into her eyes. He felt violated by her probing gaze, and he knew that she knew.

"He took the two midin, was caught by his brother and then blamed the whole incident on him," she stated fluidly, with no hesitation in her words.

"How can you be so sure, where you there?" Nyssien yelled springing to his feet, showing his parents a side of his nature that he had artfully concealed from them.

"Son, you shame us with your behavior!" Brian admonished, believing more and more that they might have been blind, all those years, and so unfair to Luibra.

Yet, Nyssien had the impudence to ask Morrigan the same question, in the attempt to intimidate her.

"How do you know it was I who stole the two midin?"

"Your eyes told me; you cannot deny it."

Luibra stood up and spoke in his own defence, then reminded his brother that he was speaking so rudely to the very person who had taken care of his stabbing wound.

"Stay out of this, you, miserable snitch; you had to tell, didn't you?" Nyssien shouted.

Brian and Fionnualla looked petrified from the shock of hearing Nyssien practically confess his guilt.

"How many times have you deceived us?" Brian yelled at Nyssien, whose anger he directed towards Morrigan, and he neglected to answer his father's question.

"Witch!" Nyssien cried out pointing a finger at Morrigan, who was fighting within herself to remain calm.

"It is all your fault, I hate those eyes of yours, evil witch!"

Brian asked Nyssien to stop. Fionnualla cried tears of shame, of bitter disappointment and of guilt, thinking of how unjust they had been to young Luibra, for so long.

Airmid watched everything, looking collected on the outside; someone was insulting her child but she could not, and would not, interfere. Rather, she closely watched Morrigan's reactions to Nyssien's verbal assaults.

"Who do you think you are, uh?" Nyssien continued, impervious to his parents' rage and disappointment. "You and the old hag healed me: so what? Your duty and only purpose in life is to serve others."

Those words burned deep within Morrigan's mind; it was true, one of her duties was to be a healer, but that was not her only purpose in life.

"The fact that I help people does not make me anyone's slave. I want to help people, it is my choice," Morrigan rebutted, and in the heat of their argument no one had the chance to interfere, least of all Nyssien's parents, who appeared to have been struck dumb by their son's outrageous rudeness and disrespect for Airmid and Morrigan.

"High and mighty Morrigan," Nyssien rambled on. "The child of the prophecy, ah! No man will ever come near you, witch. Who would? You have no sweetness, and you are strange beyond words. Most of the young men and women in the village fear you for it.

"Go, go hide in your forest and never come out; you need to get accustomed to loneliness, for no man will have you, and no woman will befriend you!"

Brian struck his son across the face as Fionnualla screamed and lunged towards her husband, holding him back from hitting Nyssien again, begging him not to. Brian was furious, but he came to his senses and realized that, if he had allowed himself to be carried away by his anger, he could have seriously harmed Nyssien.

Nyssien's words had struck a chord deep inside Morrigan's lonely soul and, feeling that she could no longer contain her outrage, she sprang to her feet, lunged at Nyssien's chest and fiercely clasped the collar of his shirt and wound it so firmly around her fist and under his chin, that he felt he would not be able to breathe if she did not loosen her grip, but she was relentless.

She pulled his face close to hers and she did notice that, although Nyssien had always looked bigger than she, he did not seem quite as strong in the position she held him.

He tried to fight back by kicking her in the knees, but he found them as sturdy as rocks.

"Look at these weird, evil eyes well Nyssien, because you are never to forget them. They shall burn in your memory like your cruel words burned into my soul." She loosened her grip, grabbed and pulled back at a handful of his hair in the back of his head.

"I do not need anyone, least of all a boy the likes of you, or those others out there that you call friends. For years I tried to blend in; now I would never want to." She spit in his face.

"Morrigan!" Airmid admonished. "That was uncalled for!"

Morrigan stood proud, stared at Nyssien one last time then she stormed out.

Luibra followed her every movement enchanted, almost in worship of her. He had never seen a girl behave quite so fiercely, even in a land of proud and courageous women.

She had spoken her mind so forwardly and powerfully, he could only wish he were a few years older, but then, "...That girl has made it clear that she doesn't need anyone," he thought.

Airmid excused herself quickly and, among Brian and Fionnualla's apologies, she promised to help them tie up loose ends as soon as she could. The major breakthrough had occurred. She ran after Morrigan.

"Slow down, will you? I can run, but I cannot keep up with you!" Airmid yelled while chasing Morrigan who did stop, in spite of the fact that her legs wanted to keep moving and take her away from that place.

"What do you want from me?" Morrigan cried back, begging her grandmother to leave her be. Airmid finally caught up with her, panting.

"My! Either you are a really fast runner, or I am getting old! I bet it is a combination of both, what do you think?" She asked Morrigan, while supporting herself by holding onto Morrigan's shoulders, but the girl was unusually unresponsive and kept turning her eyes away from Airmid, who caressed the side of her face.

"It's all right to cry in front of your old hag!" Airmid said, and they both found themselves bursting into laughter upon recalling Nyssien's name-calling.

"He was so unkind and so cruel," Morrigan cried out under her breath, so ashamed to show Airmid that Nyssien's words had really wounded her.

Airmid hugged her.

"You did well, standing up for yourself; you will need that grit in the future, Danu knows you will need it...But did you have to spit?" Airmid said, with a hint of humour in the tone of her voice.

Morrigan stared at her grandmother. "What would you have done in my place?"

"I would have broken the little bastard's legs!" Airmid replied with such seriousness that they both could not help bursting into yet another roaring laughter, as they started on their way home.

"One cannot be a hermit, at least not forever," Morrigan pondered in regard to her loneliness. In a brief epiphany, she realized that, until love came, she had to learn to fill her inner void by reaching deep for love within herself, for herself, and that love would always be there.

Airmid had taught her to be self-sufficient, and had often stressed the importance of learning to enjoy one's own company because some day that might be all one has.

Chapter Fifteen

Samhain, and with it, Morrigan's sixteenth birthday came. She woke to a treat that Airmid had prepared: Morrigan's favourite pudding of pureed boiled chestnuts and milk, all sweetened with honey and anise seeds.

After breakfast, Morrigan stood by the window, mystified by the beauty that the gloom of near winter could hold. She was not particularly looking forward to joining the celebrations of the festival of Samhain to be held at the village in the evening.

She did not want to see any of her peers, not after Nyssien had so rudely confirmed what she suspected all along about the way they felt about her.

She clenched her fists till her nails hurt the palms of her hands and the pain pulled her out of those sad thoughts. She knew that all she would worry about, from then on, were her physical and spiritual training. Her body, her mind and her soul needed to align within an equal, unwavering condition of strength.

Suddenly, a shattering headache burst inside of Morrigan's skull. The pain was unexpected and intense. The girl, impaired by it, wobbled to a chair and sat, holding the weight of her head in her young hands.

Airmid stopped and looked at her granddaughter realizing that the coming of such headaches marked Morrigan's openness to any influences from the Otherworld.

"Love, do you know what this pain means?" Airmid asked, too excited to express the compassion she felt.

"Yes," Morrigan replied dryly, "It means that I hurt!"

Airmid laughed. "Morrigan, I am so sorry! Of course I care that you are in pain, but your suffering will be rewarding; I can teach you things now that I could have not before this moment."

Morrigan understood; she knew Airmid was right.

"I am ready for your teachings," Morrigan said, pulling herself together and looking her grandmother in the eyes.

"Can you give me anything that will dull the pain?" She asked.

"You will find that the pain will disappear in the middle of the exercise I am about to teach you," Airmid said, recalling Sandda's words, when he had trained her.

In the peacefulness of the misty autumn woods, surrounded by some tall birch trees which where naturally arranged in an irregular circle, Morrigan and Airmid stood, immobile, facing each other.

They wore black, one-piece gauze-like garments which adhered to their bodies, leaving room for the greatest freedom of movement.

"What you are about to experience will, at first, make you feel disoriented and perhaps a little apprehensive. When the motion begins and your heartbeat rises, remember to breathe rhythmically and from deep within your belly. No matter how frightened you may feel, once the motion has begun, there is no turning back until completion, therefore, you must control the panic and conquer it, confident in the knowledge that you will return unscathed from this experience.

"I shall be moving synchronically to you. This is an exercise that requires two balanced energies to work. Are you ready?" Airmid asked, her tone very solemn.

"I will be when you explain to me the purpose for such exercise," Morrigan answered almost flippantly, nauseated by the headache.

"You will know its purpose when the need to apply what you learn from it arises," Airmid replied sternly, making it clear that not all questions will have immediate answers.

"She must learn patience and purpose," Airmid pondered.

"Then, I am ready," Morrigan said.

They both began to shift into the slow, deep and rhythmic mode of breathing of which Airmid had spoken. It was of the outmost importance that they both were in synchronization. Their eyes were open and their consciousnesses in full state of awareness while they slipped in a state of deep relaxation. Morrigan felt her headache fade, then disappear. She felt strong and centered.

Then, for the first time in her life, she "heard" her grandmother give her commands telepathically, and what felt more unsettling, was finding herself responding to them in the same way. She never knew she could hear and speak with the voice of the mind.

"Look deep into my eyes: our gazes must lock before we can close our eyes," Airmid directed, and Morrigan obeyed.

As their gazes locked, their eyes were entirely darkened by a vitreous-looking onyx glaze. Morrigan was aware that her eyes had become "closed" without having shut them.

Her heart began to pound, as Airmid had anticipated. Morrigan intensified the rhythm and the depth of her breathing, and felt her body levitate.

She was floating still, in a vertical position, a short distance above the ground, and a mental picture appeared and informed her that Airmid's status was the same as hers.

"Slow you heartbeat down. Slowly, very slowly!" Airmid commanded. Morrigan complied. "Now, let your mind follow my mind into a state of rest." They both entered the state of awareness existing, normally, between wake and sleep, and felt their bodies turn, ever so slowly, into an horizontal position, while simultaneously shifting from facing each other to laying beside each other, one's extremities parallel to the other's head. Then they felt their bodies float higher.

They hung in mid-air facing the limitless grey sky. Slowly, again, the bodies of the two women each began to rotate in space, one counter clockwise the other.

Morrigan, who had up until then channelled her mind into a blissful state of sedated awareness, felt herself being vacuumed out of her own body with extreme rapidity. She was being pulled out of her body so fast and so high into the sky that she felt she would never be able to stop and, in the rapidity of the moment, she did not notice that her grandmother was having the same experience.

Everything else seemed to have ceased to exist: her soul was in a state of deep silence, suspended in a paradoxical sensation of static ascent. She could see her body, and Airmid's, becoming smaller and smaller while still rotating next to each other.

"Morrigan, take my hand," she heard Airmid think, the voice in her mind sounding muffled and intermittent. Morrigan intuitively turned to what she perceived as being her right side, saw a light, and she knew that was her grandmother.

She looked down at her own lower-body which she felt, but discovered it was not there. Yet, she could see, she could hear, she could feel and she could move better than in her body of flesh and blood. In that condition, she did not feel she missed it.

She felt complete and not at all alone, in that apparent solitude. She tried to extend her hand towards Airmid's and saw a limb of light protruding out of the mass of brightness that she was, and watched it blend with Airmid's. When they touched, they felt infinite joy and gratification, feeling closer than they could ever hope to be.

The light of their souls illuminated the immediate darkness around them. Then, once again, Morrigan felt pulled higher, towards a light that seemed to be at the core of the universe. All she saw were beams flashing by at dizzying speed and she felt the sensation of that velocity down the depths of her being, which she identified to herself as the pit of her flesh-and-blood body's stomach. It felt as though someone was blowing right through it; it felt like a block of air was weighing down and then rising up off her solar plexus.

Morrigan and Airmid remained attached throughout the rapid suction of their ethereal bodies into the light.

"Morrigan, behold the Creatress of all," she heard Airmid say, and she slowly turned to discover the most awe commanding sight.

She had turned to look towards a corner of the universe where the light dimmed and, emerging from that crepuscular glow, was the silhouette of a gigantic woman's head.

It looked transparent, at first, but definitely three-dimensional, as if sculpted out of crystal. All they saw was the back of the head, and only a hint of what the front looked like, as seen through the transparency. But the head had begun to turn, majestic and breathtaking, and as it turned it assumed colour.

What they saw was the outline of the profile of a gorgeous and austere black Isis, mother of all, Creatress of Time conceived by her within the mystery of eternity.

As three quarters of the face were visible, Morrigan felt she recognized it in a memory of the Mother, not her mother, but The Mother. She was beautiful, in the shape of humanness that she had chosen to show herself, in a way that defied description.

When the gorgeous Ishtar faced Airmid and Morrigan they felt hurled into a deep sensation of peacefulness, utter acceptance and majesty.

The austerity in the look of the creatress' face did not stop her infinite love from flowing freely from her, right through her daughters' souls.

In the twilight, the creatress' skin looked as honey-hued and as transparent as amber; her eyes, large and doe-like, were as black as the surrounding space, but vibrating with the tenderness of an aqueous glaze resembling tears.

Her lips were full, sensuous and ripe with the desire to create, endlessly, and to kiss each one of her creations.

Her cheekbones were high, round and regal, and the root of her nose began with a slight depression, and flowed downward to create a thin bridge which, in turn, spread into wide but graceful nostrils, through which the air that the universe breathed was exhaled deep from within her powerful but invisible lungs. A cascade of a thousand tiny, mahogany braids graced her noble and proud face.

As Au Set's head began to turn again in solemn slowness, the face's appearance of youth began to shift into that of old age: she was indeed Au Set, the ancient creatress, her expressions of wisdom forever engraved in the deep grooves of her olive skin.

The magnificent head kept moving in slow motion, and the profile of the red-haired and young Danu appeared.

Her nose was straight and proud, the visible part of her iris a primordial ocean green, her thin lips looking soft and crimson. Her skin was transparent, the angular face rounded in the cheeks and was framed by unruly waves and thick red locks. Then, just before the head turned

63

completely out of sight, Morrigan and Airmid saw the waning profile of a very young, very innocent looking blue-eyed, fair-haired girl.

As the ever-changing image of the creatress disappeared, engulfed in the crepuscular light from which it had emerged, Morrigan felt drawn into an extremely rapid descent towards her body, which she entered rather abruptly.

As Morrigan and Airmid re-entered their bodies, their minds eased into the rhythmic mode of their bodies' motion, which slowly arrested, and resumed the original standing, face-to-face position.

The women's eyes returned to their normal appearance. Morrigan had to blink quite often in the attempt to soothe hers, which felt dry and strained. Airmid was used to the discomfort because she had felt it all before.

Morrigan felt as though she had woken up from a disturbed sleep and a wondrous dream.

"How do you feel?" Airmid asked Morrigan while stroking her child's cheeks and smiling.

"I cannot quite describe it: it feels like a dream, but I know that it was real. I have seen the goddess, and I cannot accept that, I cannot believe it really happened," Morrigan confessed.

"It is natural for you to feel overwhelmed; this sort of thing does not happen everyday, and not to everyone. I mean, eventually everybody returns to the goddess, but you have had the privilege to be chosen to restore her age and her power into this world, and you could not do that if you had not seen her. Understand, though, that what you and I saw was not the goddess, but only a series of images of herself that she chose to project to us."

"What does she really look like?"

"No one among the living, in this world of flesh and fire, knows what the divinity looks like. It may have no gender, and I have come to believe, from my experience of being outside of my own body, that you do not need a flesh body out there."

"I decided I will keep referring to the divinity as a female entity," Morrigan told Airmid.

"I think it makes sense. Looking far back in time, and then at the present, it is plain to see, between man and woman, who the slayer has been and still is. And, after all, we are the ones who bear and birth the children. It is our instinct to fight to protect those we love. Men's instinct seems to be to fight for what they want, and what they want is power.

"Look at the practice of slavery. And that of human sacrifices that male Druids have instituted over most of our fair country, and which still goes on outside of Iona. They find it easy to kill to serve their purposes; such acts scare people into subservience and raise Druids to the stature of demi-gods not to be disobeyed, challenged or irritated. They are the law makers, you know, kings are mere puppets.

"Your father was different because he is a special soul, and because of my teachings. He managed to extend his philosophy to king Cano and his queen, Liban, who both proved very receptive and supportive of a system of government based on justice and respect for human life. Look what happened to them."

"Grandmother, who gave you the awareness you passed on to my father?" Morrigan asked.

"Child, I was very fortunate to have been born on Iona. In remote times, a group of Druidesses from all over Ireland and Scotland, tired of being looked upon as perpetual apprentices with no real power, no final say, and sickened by the inhumanity of Druids and Kings, with their wars, their slavery, their rapes, their human sacrifices, developed an underground network of communication which lead to their escape from anywhere on the British Isles to Iona.

"These women called themselves Korriganed, witches, whose goal was to educate future generations in such a way that, eventually, the original universal harmony would be restored. Love is the force that binds us. Without it, we shall wither away and ultimately self-destruct."

Morrigan was curious about the Korriganed, a heritage of which she felt proud.

"When the Korriganed came to Iona, were there other people here? What kind of men did they choose to be the fathers of their children?" The girl asked.

"Yes, Iona was scarcely populated back then, by Irish and Caledonian folks. The Korriganed mated with good, simple men, true human beings: shepherds, fishermen, farmers, artisans, whose dreams were to share with the woman they loved in providing lifelong security, and devotion for one another and for their children.

"Men with pride and dignity, so different from some of the pompous aristocrats on the mainland. These men on Iona seemed to have had their dignity and sense of value moulded by the very toil most other men would shun. I am proud to say that it is from this stock of special men and women that you and I have had the fortune, and the honour, to descend. I have lived on the mainland, I have seen a very different world from the one we live in, and you will too. That is why you must be prepared," Airmid concluded with a sombre note in her voice.

Morrigan's mind was ablaze with pride and a new charge that gave more meaning to what she knew she must achieve.

Chapter Sixteen

The evening, the anticipation of which had been so loathed by Morrigan, came. She and her grandmother had to go to the village and partake in the celebration of Samhain.

The village, nestled between many hills and the sea, appeared misty and phantasmagorical. The bonfires lit were large enough to be seen at great distance from the village, and they filled the air with amber light, as the aroma of smouldering wood suffused warmth into the bracing surrounding air.

"The sight is enchanting" Morrigan thought, rejoicing. All around people bustled joyfully, some roasting meats and chestnuts, boiling large pots of corn-ears, others dancing to the music of harps and bagpipes, waiting for Sandda to call them to gather around one of the bonfires, to teach the young and remind the old of the reasons for celebrating Samhain.

Morrigan looked at the stockades that had been filled, for the winter, with all the animals. She felt sad at the thought that many were going to be butchered because, during winter, shortage of grain meant that not all livestock could be kept alive.

She also knew that people had to eat. It consoled her to think that, at least on Iona, it was forbidden to hunt game for reasons other than sustenance. She could not conceive of hunting for sport, for trophies, yet she heard it was common practice in most of the known world.

The crowd came to a stillness of movement and sound at the sight of the approaching of Sandda. He had been ill, the old Druid, and had fought hard against his cold and his latest arthritis spell in order to speak at the gathering for the celebration of Samhain.

He was a sight, dressed in his ceremonial black robes rimmed with silver. Bent over and frail, Sandda walked with dignity, carrying the staff of white hazel wood that was the emblem of peace and friendship.

His white beard, long and split in the middle, attracted the attention of the little children, who came close to touch it, and he kindly obliged each and every little one.

Bards followed Sandda in a respectful and slow procession, playing soothing harp music and singing the glories of the victory of the Children of Danu over the Fomorians in the very ancient cosmic battle of Mag Tuireadh, which was being recalled and celebrated on Samhain as a good auspice for the beginning of the new year.

As the children of Danu had overcome the horrific Fomor, so the children of the island would forever protect and fight for the independence of Iona from the deteriorating influences of the outside world.

People gathered around one of the bonfires, Sandda stopped in front of it and coughed a dry and old cough residue of his cold. When he began to speak, he held everyone's reverent attention in a spell of absolute silence.

"The time of the year is upon us again, when we are blessed with the opportunity of leaving the old behind, and to start fresh with new ideas, new plans for the advancement in the life of each person, family and the entire community.

"The goddess is retiring underground to sleep now, but there is no need to grieve, for she is among us at all times, and will awaken, rejuvenated and strong, to initiate the blossoming of spring.

"This is also the time in which we commemorate and honor our dead; as you know, the sacred doors of the parallel world of the Sidhe are opened to let the souls of the dead walk among us. We, too, must open our psyches to be able to properly receive the spirits of the bodiless ones."

As he had said that Airmid, who was standing beside him, pulled a fistful of dried night-shade leaves out of a large pot and threw it into the fire, which, on contact with the herb, produced a puff of smoke and a crackling sound. The incense so produced was going to open people's minds and souls and make the invisible reality visible.

After years of training, Airmid and Morrigan could shift into such state at will, but the incense made it easier and more powerful to alter their perceptions.

The small children had been sent home to be watched by some of the older children, so that the young ones would not be harmed by opening themselves to the souls of the dead. Not all souls roaming the village would be benevolent, and an adult could better cope with the dark ones.

Sandda and Airmid's task was to exorcise the presence of evil spirits who may infiltrate their people and may possess their bodies. On the night of Samhain, no one would dare walk around far from the protection and the wisdom of the Druids.

As the fumes of the belladonna's burnt leaves began to work, men and women broke their silence. There was moaning; some seemed to be living a nightmare of sorrow, upon seeing again the shape of a long-gone loved one.

Others would laugh, in conviviality and happiness, conversing with the dead. Everyone's pupils were dilated, staring at an apparent nothingness, but seeing so much, and so vividly.

Morrigan resisted the trance; there, among so many others, it gave her a feeling of loss of control and vulnerability to which she would not allow herself to be abandoned.

Airmid who, like Sandda, was able to keep a certain level of ordinary awareness within the state of trance, walked close to Morrigan and whispered in her ear: "Go to the sacred circle of stones on the hill that slopes by the sea." Morrigan obeyed at once, without her usual enquiries.

When she had reached the circle of stones she realized how marvellous the sight of the megaliths was there, at that precise moment in time, illuminated by the crisp light of the full moon.

She walked through the menhir and the dolmen and, although in a daze, she did notice that there seemed to be a few new stones. The massive size of all the megaliths humbled and overwhelmed her with reverence and mystery. She felt her heartbeat with the rhythm of the frothy sea waves, and with them break up on the shore with a remote rustling sound that evoked in her feelings unidentified, but deep and captivating.

"The stones are like us," she thought, laughing a second later at the realization of how absurd that thought was.

Morrigan, feeling cold while she stood there by the two new stones, backed up into them seeking shelter from the wind that was whipping her hair around, blinding her, making her feel at the mercy of the elements.

In a moment that felt to her as slowed down and happening outside the bounds of time, she felt the arms of two people protrude out of the stones and hold her close, but gently.

She could see human hands clasping over her abdomen and she knew she had to turn around and look, fighting the terror she felt with all the strength she had.

"Baby..." she heard a soft, woman's voice whisper with the tenderness of a mother, and she knew. She turned around, and as she did so, the embrace loosened and when her turn was complete, she was in the presence of those who she instinctively knew were her birth parents. She stared at them speechless, and saw the same love in their eyes that she did in Airmid's.

"My child," Amergin said proud while stroking Morrigan's cheek with his hand, as she noticed that his touch had a certain softness and an almost static quality to it.

"...We have watched you and your brother grow, from the Other Side, but to touch at least one of you, what a wondrous gift," Kalos said.

"Did you visit Lugh?" Morrigan asked.

"We would love to," Kalos explained. "But he knows of us, not about us, therefore has no desire to see us. His soul has to call to us for us to be allowed to be seen by him. Your soul called us so loudly, we knew you must be ready, and we came."

Morrigan, struck by the beauty of her mother and the majestic appearance of her father, had no comments to make, no more questions to ask. She felt the void inside of her which their absence had created and, in an attempt to fill it, to make up for all the lost years, she simply spread her arms and embraced them, burying her lowered head onto her mother's chest, while gripping tight her father's shoulder. She cried all her tears and all her pain within the safety and the warmth of that magnificent hug.

As Morrigan stood there, cuddled in her parents' ethereal arms, Kalos and Amergin lovingly hushed her while caressing her hair. Time did stand still, Morrigan knew that for a fact. After she had felt her parents' lips kiss her head, she raised it, and she saw she was embracing the cold stone. But she knew, she knew that encounter had been real, and it could not have lasted forever, and that thought helped her not to feel despair. She wiped her reddened eyes and made her way back towards the village, whose orange bonfires illuminated the night.

She walked as if on air, each step faster towards her grandmother. "I saw my parents," her mind kept repeating in the anticipation of breaking the news to Airmid, and she heard each step sound out her thought.

The village was a sight. Most people had come out of the trance, while some were just beginning to come out of it. Bards and musicians were singing and playing harps, drums, flutes and bagpipes into masterful harmonies which wrapped and lead people into a frenzy of dancing and euphoria.

Sandda could not dance, but he honoured the festivities by sitting and watching his people being happy, celebrating the start of a brand-new year.

Airmid danced and danced until she could no longer, out of breath and energy, and collapsed on the ground panting and dripping with sweat. She felt that was the best time she had had in a while, and the knowledge that the new year held much promise overjoyed her.

Morrigan laughed at the sight of Airmid, who was lying spread-eagle on her back, trying to catch her breath.

"You missed a good dance!" Airmid said between one breath and the next. Morrigan bent down by her grandmother's head.

"Tonight, I danced with the spirits," she said, but Airmid remained composed. She sat up, looked into Morrigan's eyes and said, grasping Morrigan's arms with her strong hands: "I know you did; I sent you there." They embraced.

"How did you know?"

"A witch knows these things..." Airmid teased.

"But I am a witch also, and I...," Morrigan protested and before she finished her sentence, Airmid argued.

"I am an older, much older and wiser witch than yourself," and concluded her argument as she playfully poked Morrigan's forehead with her index finger.

Morrigan smiled and did not pursue the matter further; Airmid knew how to keep a secret.

As Sandda tried to stand up again, the dancing and the music gradually faded and everyone kept quiet to witness the unfolding of the most awaited event of Samhain: the tossing of the runes. They would divine the single most important event which would affect the community in the new year so that, bad or good, the people of Iona could prepare for it.

Sandda stood very still and closed his eyes, calling upon the goddess' power to let him "Toss runes in his head." In fact, he was visualizing all twenty-four marked stones in his mind, checking to make sure he was not missing any.

The hard part was to toss the runes and let them fall, free from the influence of his will, so that he could provide a glimpse of the future and not of his own wishes or fears.

When he felt he had achieved the complete detachment of his will upon the outcome of the runes, the projected image of them whirling in space, high above the fire, became enhanced in size, visible to everyone.

Those runes which did not fall into the bonfire, but rather bounced off the ground around it, would be the ones that Sandda divined.

The eyes of the crowd were held up, then plummeted following the fall of the runes, punctuated by a common "...Uh!" Which sounded so powerful, "...As the synchronization of human voices usually does," Morrigan reflected, feeling the goose-bumps on her arms.

Sandda raised his arms, the left hand still clutching the staff.

"This is the beginning of the year in which the Children of Danu and the Fomor will engage in their final cosmic battle. One side will be completely annihilated. The outcome is in the hands of Danu, but the runes tell me that our chances to survive are high.

"Our consciousnesses must unite in a cluster of positive energy which will aide Morrigan in carrying her burden; her destiny must be fulfilled."

Morrigan was uncomfortable when she felt all gazes on her, and she looked towards Airmid, who kept a stiff ceremonial countenance, but whose face, Morrigan could see, was wet with tears that the wind chilled. She even saw her grandmother's lips quiver, ever so slightly.

For Morrigan herself, the closer to fulfilment the prophecy came, the least scared she felt. In a way, she was thrilled to embark on this awesome adventure.

In that moment of reflection upon the excitement of things to come, Morrigan realized how much she loved life, nature, but most of all she loved people, especially "...The children and the animals."

One question burned into her mind, and she decided she was going to ask Sandda this one. When she told Airmid, the baffled old woman had to ask: "Why Sandda? Haven't I been satisfactory in answering your many questions, child? I am a Druid too, you know that!"

"Yes," Morrigan replied with a smirk. "But Sandda is older and wiser..." and she burst into laughter at the sight of the expression on Airmid's face.

"Well, well, how very clever of you, little one, but let me remind you that I am old enough to deserve respect." She wasn't really upset, she was playing along with her granddaughter, who doubled over with laughter, and soon Airmid joined her.

"You know, grandmother," Morrigan said smiling. " I often forget your age, because most of the time, you are as young as I am."

Airmid reached over and kissed Morrigan's forehead. "Bless your heart child, bless your heart. I have welcomed the shrivelling of my skin and the shortcomings of my body, but I have always wanted to remain young inside," Airmid said, putting a hand over hear heart as she said "inside."

"You better go ask Sandda your question, before he retires," Airmid told Morrigan, and the girl walked over to the old Druid.

"I have a question," she said.

"What is it?" he enquired.

"Tonight I saw the spirits of my parents; will I see them again?" she asked.

"Not until you will join them on the Higher Plane."

Chapter Seventeen

Over the sixteen years since the takeover of Aileach, Urien and Rhiannon had managed to strengthen their position as subjugators and to keep away interfering rulers.

The city of the living-dead looked like a gigantic gray cloud to those who saw it from afar. The sun never seemed to break through the intrinsic bleakness of Aileach's atmosphere, ever since Urien and Rhiannon took possession of it, and of the lives of its people.

In the beginning, the soldiers were put under a spell which numbed their wills and which made them comply to Rhiannon and Urien's demands. However, the spell had a limited span of potency and, in the meantime, the oppressed people became restless.

They wanted to live, not just survive. They wanted a future of freedom and happiness for their children and they began to organize themselves in "underground" groups of fighters against Urien and Rhiannon's reign of terror.

They were aware that the price of freedom would have to be paid in blood, and they were prepared to lay down their lives for what they yearned to achieve.

Urien's soldiers, once out of the spell, were never themselves again. Rhiannon, the alchemist, had been aware all along of the fact that her initial spell could only be cast once during her lifetime and that it had a limited life-span, so she planned ahead for what she had to do once the spell wore off.

During the time of the soldiers' enchantment Rhiannon diligently applied her genius to tampering with their physiology. Being the number of soldiers rather limited, Rhiannon worked on each warrior individually, aided by mercenary Briton Druids who shared her criminal genius and who had extensive medical training as surgeons.

She herself had developed a potion which altered the men's brain chemistry in such a way that a state of deep depression was induced, so deep as to obliterate any feelings except that of despair, and that of the physical perception of pain.

Rhiannon needed the Druids to perform complex neurosurgery which consisted of the manipulation of the brain's memory centres, so that the men would have no prior sense of identity or ties to their families, friends and their former sovereigns.

The success in the manipulation of the soldiers' minds was based on the fact that Rhiannon had developed a drug that temporarily counteracted the depressive symptoms of despair, confusion and anxiety that she had induced in them.

In order to obtain their daily dose of the counteractive drug, via their meals, the men were required to obey and carry out any order that came from Urien and Rhiannon.

Through this process, Rhiannon had managed to make monsters of honourable men, depriving them of their passion for life, their potential to love, and of their memories. Because of their chemical dependency, these men became victimizing victims who remembered no other life but the one they were living.

The Druid Cathbad was notorious in Britain and Ireland for his cruelty. He directed the surgery team, whose members were lavishly compensated by Rhiannon and Urien with some of the gold, precious stones and money which they had stolen from the people of Aileach and from the treasure that once had belonged to Cano, and to the rulers who preceded him.

The team of surgeons worked intensively on the soldiers for over three years, shortly after which the spell wore off and their work began to show its fruits.

All soldiers were to be killers on demand, but they felt no pleasure from their acts of violence. Rather, they felt guilt and shame, and many had committed suicide to escape that life.

What Urien and Rhiannon needed were a few fighters with specialized functions, a strong sadistic drive, and for whom the pleasure they derived from torturing and killing would be its own reward.

These would be maximum-performance death machines, and Urien and Rhiannon's personal bodyguards. These men, like the others, were programmed to respond only to orders given by Urien and Rhiannon, whose voice patterns were made biologically unmistakable to the men's hearing.

When all the dark work was done, Cathbad and his team were proud to introduce to Urien and Rhiannon their special weapons; their worst, best men.

Calatin had been named the 'torture master.' Having been put to the test, he had performed well in accordance to his programming. Cathbad commented with pride that "...Calatin can work on a human's nervous system as masterfully as a bard can play his harp."

Urien and Rhiannon smiled, looking extremely pleased.

Alator had proven to live up to his design; he was the most ruthless fighter, on and off chariot.

Ogyruran, the 'executioner,' handled the bodies of those who were tortured and were condemned to die, and finished them off publicly in creatively brutal ways to terrify the people of Aileach into political passivity.

Belacatudor was the chief of this singular army. He was programmed to be an outstanding tactical genius and a master at the logistics of war-strategy and command.

Llew, the blacksmith, was brilliant at creating complex torture machines and weapons.

Ragnar, the 'diplomat,' smoothly but treacherously handled public relations with an iron fist, and excelled at psychologically manipulating and violating people.

Although these men's skills had been tested within the bounds of Caer Balor on local rebels and prisoners of war from neighbouring cities, they were anxiously expected to prove themselves in real life situations.

The castle's walls were majestic in size and of an overpowering greyness, especially on the outside.

***

Lugh, looking outside of his room's window, appeared pale and withdrawn after celebrating his sixteenth birthday the night before, by drinking himself into a stupor. He stood tall in the dark chambers, witnessing the rise of the early lights of dawn. He had his mother's raven-black wavy hair, which he wore long but well groomed, and tied at the nape during military training.

From his father he had inherited his narrow, jade-green penetrating eyes, and his height. His body, clothed by a black leather tunic, a belt and his sword fastened around his waist and deer-leggings, was hard and bore many scars which documented and early history of rigorous physical training, the result of which was an uncommon dexterity in his use of the sword, and the promptness of his reflexes.

Lugh's strong body and mind hardly compensated for the emotional void he had always felt was swallowing him from the inside out. As he stood there by the window that morning, he fought off a feeling of despair and gloom that often flared up for no apparent reason, other than an intuitive knowledge that he was not meant for the life he had been raised to live. He was no soldier; he knew, and had always hidden the fact that he had been born with the soul of a poet whose verses he did not allow himself to vocalize.

Verses held captive in his mind were beginning to break down the barriers of his self-deception and fought to get out. He thought with dread of the shame and disappointment he would cause his parents to feel if he was to actually do what he had many times envisioned himself doing and saying.

"Here it is," he would tell his parents, setting his sword and battle gear down on the floor before their feet. "I'm not fit to fight, in here," and he would hit the left side of his chest with his clutched fist. "I am no fighter. I can carry out the motions but my spirit is not in it, my spirit wants to be free to dance with thoughts and words and feelings, not to kill. Not to maim; release me."

With the eye of his mind he saw the hurt, the disillusionment and even the rage appear on Urien's and Rhiannon's face, and he felt shame.

He could find no peace: if he acted on that wish, he would lose his parents' respect and maybe their love too.

If he did not begin to act according to his true nature, he would never find fulfillment or self-respect.

"There must be a way out and I shall find it," he promised himself that early winter morning, knowing full well that, first, he had to accomplish his dreaded mission: to find his sister.

As a young boy, Urien and Rhiannon had told him that his twin sister lived to kill them all.

"Your birth parents died at the hand of Dylan, Rhiannon's infamous father, who incriminated us of the murder of your parents. He could never forgive us for having fallen in love with each other and held me responsible for taking his daughter away," Lugh remembered Urien say.

"The night your parents were murdered we were there, guests at a banquet. Your sister Morrigan was ill and was left in the care of Airmid, your paternal grandmother.

"Dylan's sudden burst of violence was most unexpected and happened too fast to be stopped, though we tried. After having stabbed your mother and father to death, he moved towards you, who happened to have been in the arms of a wet nurse, and that's when we decided to grab you and make a run for it, which, thanks to our knowledge of magic, allowed us to escape quickly and to bring you to safety. A short while after that we had to have Dylan murdered, you understand, to protect you, beloved son," he was told.

"However," Urien and Rhiannon had alternately continued, "An evil and most viciously untrue rumour was spread by Dylan before his death, which made us responsible for killing your parents, and for kidnapping you.

"Airmid, your grandmother, ran away from Dooey somewhere my mind cannot see," Rhiannon said, "Believing that she had to keep Morrigan hidden to protect her from us and she vowed, according to reliable witnesses, to dedicate her whole life and her magic to the indoctrination of Morrigan and to make her very powerful, and very strong.

"After that, your sister would be ready to be unleashed against us, maybe even against yourself, whom she might have been brought up to believe to be as corrupt as she has been told that we are.

"The truth is, we saved your life. We have given you shelter and love. We would have done the same for Morrigan and Airmid, had they been at that ill-fated banquet.

"Dylan, you see, was an evil and bitter man, power-hungry, and overwhelmed by the jealousy he felt towards your parents, who, he knew, were far greater magicians that he could ever hope to be," Urien had said.

"He hated me, too," Rhiannon said. "According to my mother, who died when I was a bit younger than you, Dylan did not want any children. He had resented my mother for becoming pregnant, and me for being born and finally, once mother had died, he disowned me and pushed me to run away.

"When I did, he was not upset for having lost me; he was angry he could no longer control me and because, by running away with my lover, I had challenged his authority.

"What a perfect opportunity he had that night, when we showed up unbeknownst to him and upon king Ossian's invitation, to blame his atrocities upon us. The very child he had punished many years before for being born, he was now conveniently using to hide his dark deeds. We learned later that he killed the sovereigns, some potential eye-witnesses, and then proclaimed himself king of Dooey."

Lugh was too young when he was told this story to question it therefore, what he had heard from his parents, to him, was and would be the only truth. He knew that his adoptive parents raised him, protected him and educated him. He would inherit their expanding kingdom some day, as their only heir.

Everything he had ever been told by his parents about him and about themselves was untrue, and Urien and Rhiannon had a good memory, which ensured that the truth would never leak between the lies.

Throughout Lugh's young life Urien and Rhiannon concealed from him their true identities, their true feelings, and their real intent. They claimed they did not know from where Amergin and Kalos had come, only that they had earned trust and esteem as Druids at King Ossian's court.

Lugh had been sheltered from real life by his adoptive parents. Nannies, personal tutors, then military trainers, made sure that Lugh would be occupied and kept away from the people of Aileach and the truth they knew.

Lugh never even saw the people's suffering as his parents' evildoing, but rather as the result of an iron-fist rule.

"Tough measures are necessary to gain the respect of the people and to ensure discipline. Ruling a kingdom without discipline is detrimental to the king, as well as to the subjects," Urien had told him.

The boy found it very hard to lead the regimented life that he did; it felt very much like a prison to him, but he blindly believed in his father's wisdom, and in his parents' love for him.

"They must know, and want, what's good for me," he rationalized every time he was in combat with his father against neighbouring towns; every morning, when he had to get up so very early to train, and at night, when he had to retire early to ensure that his energy level be up the following day, day after day.

"A man's character is forged by pain and constraint, which are the by-products of discipline," Urien always said.

***

"Lugh is old enough now. His latent psychic powers should be able to emerge if triggered. It is time we start trying; the sooner he finds out where his sister is, the better off we shall all be. After she is dead we will educate him in the knowledge of magic, of our creed and our purpose. He will realize the magnitude of his place as future ruler of the restored Fomor dominion," Rhiannon said while brushing her hair at her vanity table, in the castle's only lavishly decorated room; her bedchambers.

That was one of the few rooms in which the original tapestries and crystal sun-catchers adorned the windows. A fur carpet, soft and deep, covered the otherwise cold stone floor. Artfully crafted dark, amber-hued furniture decorated the chambers and created an intimate and warm atmosphere.

Urien, who had been lying in bed, sat up in the middle of it.

"It is time," he said. "I have been waiting all these years for this moment to come; we do not have to patiently wait for much longer. The little twerp has disappointed us for so long, unable to express any tangible signs of his powers.

"Remember," he said as he got up and walked towards Rhiannon. "What Dylan told us about Amergin and Kalos' children's potential, and how we verified the truth of it through our magic? The old bastard was not lying, he was not lying. All we have to do is tap into Lugh's mind and soul, and he will come through for us."

"...Especially if we keep stressing, now more than ever," Rhiannon added with a sneer, "...that his mommy and daddy are in mortal danger, a danger which becomes more intense every day as Morrigan grows and learns, and plans our murders!"

They both laughed at Lugh's predictability, at how sure they were that their manipulation of him would be successful.

"He is such a serious, good little boy our Lugh, and he certainly would not want any harm to come to us. For us, he will do whatever we ask of him," Rhiannon said while looking at Urien, who smiled and nodded in assent. Then he spoke.

"It is essential that he trusts us. He must never doubt us."

"Why should he?" Rhiannon asked as she got up from her vanity-chair, let her robe drop to the floor and got into bed.

"As he will come in contact with his sister, she might reveal things to him that could lead him to question all we have ever told him about himself and about us...like the fact that we are siblings and lovers, among other things. How can we control his reactions to such revelations?" Urien asked Rhiannon, who frowned, displeased, at Urien's musing.

"He trusts us and loves us too much to even conceive of such a thing as doubting us. Besides, once we find out where she is, we shall work on him intensively so that he does not stray, and we shall kill her way quicker than she will have time to instil any reasonable doubts into his mind," Rhiannon said, punching down her pillow and turning her face away from Urien, who leaned over and nibbled at her nape. He whispered, "And what if things do not go according to plans? What if our good boy Lugh doubts us, even betrays us? You remember the agreement; he turns against us, and he dies too. You promised me that the day we got him."

Rhiannon furiously kicked the blankets off herself and Urien, and leaped out of bed.

"I know the agreement, damn you, I remember! But it simply will not happen. We raised Lugh too well for that to become even a remote possibility, do you hear?" She yelled outraged at Urien's insinuations that Lugh might allow his estranged sister to violate the trust he had in his own parents.

Urien, irritated, lunged across the bed and kneeled at the edge of the bed so that his eyes were on the same level with Rhiannon's, looked at her with rage and grabbed her by the shoulders.

"You idiot! Frail, emotional wench that you are, you are letting your feelings cloud your reason! You even reject the possibility that something might go wrong rather than facing it, and preparing for what we would need to do!"

"Let go of me you animal, you selfish, dirty pig...you are telling me you have absolutely no feelings for our son? Uh? Are you that cold...our son?" Rhiannon yelled as she extricated herself from his hurtful grip.

He slapped her across the face and she hit him back harder, taking him aback a little.

"You forget I train alongside Lugh, with the same soldiers you train and with whom you consort. And that is all you do. I, I have raised that boy, I love that boy.

"We looked upon him as bait since the day he entered our lives, and if we can use him to get Morrigan and Airmid out of our way that is fine with me! But remember this: I will never touch a hair on my son's head, not to save my own skin, much less to protect yours, you swine!

"Remember this, also: I hold the key to our magic, not you. Has it ever occurred to you that I could turn it against you?"

"You could not. If you could have torn yourself apart from me you would have done it long ago but you cannot, because of this!" Urien said grabbing at Rhiannon's crotch and one of her breasts.

She pushed him away in disgust.

"Our little game has no power over me when Lugh is concerned," she uttered in a seriousness and clarity of intent that surprised Urien enough to scare him, and he realized he must be careful with Rhiannon.

She was indeed powerful and determined, and he was aware of the fact that, should she truly overcome her sexual dependency on him, after the ritual mating there would be no link left to hold their relationship together.

He would have to rely on ruthlessness and cruelty alone to protect what power he would have left. Her magic would not only not be there to shield him and to further his schemes; it would probably be directed against him.

**

The Spartan decor of Caer Balor's long corridors and dark chambers was interrupted by the presence of owls, one in each corridor and each room, including the dungeons. The birds, very still but very much alive, seemed to oversee everything happening within the cold, stony walls of the castle.

Rhiannon had biologically engineered the owls so that what their eyes saw and ears heard, she saw and heard. She could "switch off" the bio-telepathic connection at will, at times when her intuition told her that she could let her guard down.

The owls had specifically been created to control what Lugh saw and heard. He had no idea of what Rhiannon had done to the soldiers.

He did not know about the statue of Balor in construction in the castle's basement, and about the looted treasures that financed the building of that statue, whose eye would come alive upon the monument's completion, and would signal the imminence of the second coming of the Fomor.

If Lugh were ever to become curious about the dungeons and challenge his parents' depiction of them as "...muggy, dark, insect-swarming chambers to be restructured some day, to use as goods-storage..." then the owl set at the top of the staircase leading to the castle's basement would inform Rhiannon of Lugh's presence there, and she would take care of it.

She herself, or some of her soldiers, would be able to prevent Lugh from going further. Lugh was to be initiated to the mysteries of Fomor theology, but not until he had murdered his sister.

The snowy-white owl in Lugh's stark room was Bryn Gwyn, his oldest and dearest friend, or so Lugh had come to believe, having had Bryn as far back as he could remember.

His other two animal friends, with whom Rhiannon had not tampered, lived outside of the castle: Corax, the black raven, and Tharan, the falcon.

Lugh had cared for the two birds since their birth and trained them to fly from post, to post, to post, and back to his leather-gloved arm. They were a source of great pride and joy to him, the only beings which allowed the nurturing side of his nature to emerge and develop.

Aside from his personal trainers, he was not familiar with the soldiers, and therefore not aware of their abnormalities. Lugh only saw them while fighting or practicing, when they acted as it was expected: martially.

Because the warriors received their dose of anti-depressive drug with their food, Lugh was never allowed to share his meals with them, under his parents' pretext that doing so would not be fitting his status. Although Lugh did not agree with his parents' elitist philosophy, he obeyed them.

The reality of the few soldiers who were punished by being denied their daily dose of the anti-depressive drug, was skilfully concealed from Lugh. He simply was not let to be aware of the true nature of things around him. Urien and Rhiannon had laboured hard to ensure that, and would do so until the time was right for his initiation.

The act of murdering his own sister would lure his soul into the world of darkness in which his adoptive parents lived and waited for his coming. Rhiannon and Urien knew that the killing of Morrigan would be an act of consecration, on Lugh's unaware behalf, of his eternal loyalty and devotion to the Fomor.

Lugh would be engulfed by the blinding vortex of blackness and become an inextricable component of it. He would be amoral, no traces of love left in him to rescue him from himself so that, as a leader, he could carry on the will of the Fomor to oppress the humans who would oppose them. Lugh was to become the person that he would loathe to be.

The boy's only human friends were the servants, people who had been subjugated and blackmailed into servitude, but whose capacity to love and to trust had not been lost with the pain that had come with the duress.

A second generation of servants had been born to the original group in bondage. Among a few of such peers of Lugh was Clodagh, his first love.

She was willowy and small. She had long, dark brown hair parted in the middle. Her complexion was translucent and ivory-pale; her eyes, large and doe-like held, like jewels set in a white-lined, sloe-shaped box, large, sapphire-blue irises which captured the light and held it in her gaze.

Chapter Eighteen

One unusually bright winter morning, Lugh was getting ready to visit Corax and Tharan and sneaked into the servants' quarters to get Clodagh, and let her fly the birds.

He found her outside of her parents' dwelling, peeling some potatoes for their lunch. She heard Lugh's voice and raised her gaze: the sight of him made he heartbeat rise and the blood flush to her cheeks, the awareness of which made her feel even more self-conscious.

"I am happy to see you here," she said smiling.

Lugh sat next to her on the stone bench, and at the sight of that light in her eyes and of her sweet heart-shaped lips, his heart missed a beat. All he wanted to do was kiss those lips, but had not worked up the nerve to do it yet, not until he felt sure that she would want to be kissed by him.

"You are very precious," Lugh said languidly and sincerely, while caressing the perfect oval of her face with the back of his right hand.

She pressed her face against his steady fingers, thus declaring her acceptance of him, of her need for his caresses.

"Let me help you peel the potatoes," Lugh said, taking the knife out of her chapped hands and finished peeling the vegetables. She hesitated a bit, but let him help her; he had done so before and was just being himself, and she loved him for it.

After having set the basket with the peeled potatoes aside, Lugh took Clodagh's reddened hand into his and kissed it.

"Come with me," he said. They stood up, she looked into his green eyes and knew he had a surprise for her, so she followed him without asking where to.

When they arrived to the courtyard where Lugh kept his birds, Clodagh's heart felt full of freedom, just thinking of the birds rising in flight and soaring high above everything, above her prison. She felt she was flying with them.

Lugh fit his glove to Clodagh's right hand and forearm.

"The birds are familiar with you enough now, so they will not mind setting themselves on your arm, and flying for you. Just give them the commands you have heard me give and they will fly," Lugh instructed her.

She was trembling, both nervous and excited, and loved the feeling of being genderless around Lugh; just as he had, many times, helped her with her girl chores, so he would let her into a world that had been traditionally made inaccessible to all servants, and to most women.

Yet she knew that Lugh was not just trying to impress her. He had a nobility of soul which gave her the assurance that he would always be that way. He was kind, and he was just.

His slightest touch was so charged with the passion and trueness of his being, of his maleness, that she quivered and she felt she wanted to take him, and to be taken.

She wanted to be with him forever, but the thought of the impossibility of that happening killed any hope in her heart, and she refrained from letting him know how she felt.

She believed that the actualization of love between them could never happen; Lugh's parents, and his status, would never allow them the freedom to love one another. Yet, she could not bring herself to tell him not to come and visit her any longer.

She felt they were both entitled, at least, to the mutual pleasure of their company and the happiness that they both felt when they were together.

Tharan came flying down and rested on Clodagh's arm, which she strived to keep very steady under the unexpected heaviness of the falcon. The birds looked straight at her and appeared so goofy that it made her laugh.

"He is funny, cute, but so serious-looking at the same time!" She said, every word bursting with excitement which Lugh sensed and found very pleasurable, and showed her his joy by smiling at her.

"Go!" She commanded. The bird hovered, not very high but steady, towards the first post, where Lugh was waiting for it with a chick in his hand.

The falcon gobbled his food almost in one gulp and, at a further command by Clodagh, progressively flew, low, to the other two posts, to which Lugh quickly ran, with the chicks that he was pulling out of a bag.

Then the raven's turn came. Corax liked to soar high and had been trained to fly away and to return to the food, so Clodagh waited for the raven to make its descent on her gloved arm, and had its food waiting in her other hand.

The moment in which Corax took flight, Lugh looked with never before felt tenderness at Clodagh's profile as she was looking up towards the sky, and he knew he would some day take her away from there, and they would both soar high, carried by their freedom and by the power of their love. He loved her; he realized in that moment that he did, and hope made a breach in his palpitating heart.

Unaware that she was being observed so closely, she turned her face towards his and he leaned over and kissed her. Time felt slower, the bleakness dissipated and they simply knew each other's passion.

He slipped his heavy hand to the small her back and pulled her closer to him. The heat generated by his hand on her back made her body tingle with a new pleasure, a pleasure she wished to explore and experience to its full extent.

They tenderly nibbled at each other's lips, red and bursting with the desire to lock in the rapture of a kiss that they knew would make them wish it did not have to end.

Corax flew by them, expecting to find Clodagh's arm there waiting with its food, but seen it was not there, it soared high, once more, and crowed.

The raven's cry broke the ecstasy. The lovers felt dazed, having been so brashly recalled to the state of unexcitement and flatness in which they were used to live, and which they disliked. They were both creatures of freedom and discovery, meant to soar, but earthbound.

Once home, Clodagh's mother looked at her daughter with contempt; she wished the girl would have fallen in love with someone like herself, not a nobleman, least of all the son of their tyrants.

"That one will break your heart," her mother said.

Clodagh was not that naive: she would not have trusted any other 'nobleman' in Lugh's place, but she knew that he would never hurt her, and she did not argue with her mother because she knew she would not understand.

"Time will tell," Clodagh said instead, and walked inside her dwelling to eat her cold potato soup.

***

Once in his room Lugh felt that, since he could not be with Clodagh at the time, he would rather sleep, but once he lay down he found that he could not. Disquieting thoughts made their way into his mind and made it restless.

"What else does she eat everyday, other than potatoes? Is she nourished properly?" He wondered, and doubted that she would be as well taken care of as he was. He realized he had taken so much for granted.

"She probably cannot even nap when she wants to, or needs to, because of the damned chores she has to do. It is not fair," Lugh thought in anger, aware for the first time of the inequality of it all, not just of the conditions of the servants.

"We are all born the same, we should all live the same," he thought while moving to a sitting position at the edge of his bed.

"Maybe my parents do not understand inequality because they have always been privileged. If they knew need, if they saw it like I do, maybe they would grasp this truth, and rule more fairly," he thought, surprised that, for the first time in his life, he was questioning if not the ethics behind his parents' methods, at least the lack of awareness that was behind their political actions.

"They must not know what I know. I must let them see, and give them the awareness I have gained through Clodagh," Lugh thought.

That one possibility had momentarily sedated his spirit and he felt the fire of hope burn in the pit of his stomach, thinking that, "…If we feel hope, we must know, at a deeper level, that change is possible."

Lulled by that sense of eventfulness he lay back and fell asleep, but briefly. A headache woke him abruptly and once he was awake he felt he must speak to Rhiannon to confide in her about his love for Clodagh, and to offer her a chance to gain awareness about her subjects' living conditions.

***

It was evening and dinner was just over. Urien retired to his chambers, while Rhiannon and Lugh stayed in the dining room, sitting by the fire.

"You need to tell me something, do you not?" Rhiannon asked.

"You are always very perceptive, mother. Maybe that is why you understand me so well," Lugh said smiling.

"I am pleased to hear that you feel that way about me. Your trust and appreciation mean everything to me," she said punctuating her words with a gracious smile.

"Mother, I believe I am in love," Lugh said with frankness.

Rhiannon was at a loss for words. Her breathing grew noticeably faster, and her face looked flushed.

"With whom?" She asked hesitantly, forcing a quick flash of a smile.

Lugh noticed her discomfort, so held her hands in his and felt that hers were cold. He looked his mother in the eyes.

"Clodagh, I love Clodagh," he confessed. A flash of disconcert blitzed from her eyes to his.

"A servant?" Rhiannon yelled, her voice growing higher with outrage and disappointment.

"I anticipated your reaction mother, but I was hoping I could rely on your open-mindedness to discuss this matter with you," Lugh said in one breath.

"What else is there to discuss?" Rhiannon replied, visibly annoyed.

"It has occurred to me that, maybe, you and father might feel this way about servants, and whomever you think you may be superior to, not because you lack fairness and compassion, but rather because you have been brought up this way, in luxury, and you never had to question your beliefs. Otherwise, how could the unfairness of it all not perplex you?"

Rhiannon was raging within, but had to contain her anger. She tried hard to look and sound unaffected by Lugh's speculations. She had indeed always believed that she was a being superior to most others, perhaps to all others. Furthermore, the fact that others might have rights too was inconceivable to her.

"Son, I am going to overlook the fact that you assumed too much about my, and your father's, upbringing and accused us of being selfish and ignorant of the world..."

"That is not how I meant to come across," Lugh defended himself.

"...Let me continue," Rhiannon warned with a glee of annoyance in her voice and in her eyes.

"...As I was saying, I am going to disregard the arrogance of your judgment and prove to you that, indeed, I am fair and I am compassionate, and that, although I cannot change the status quo, I will certainly make sure that Clodagh and her mother will be taken care of.

"To show you how deeply I love you Lugh, I will order that Clodagh and her mother no longer live as servants, and that they be moved into the castle.

"I guess, given time, that I could come to see the girl as the daughter I never had, and bestow upon her education, refinement and affection," she concluded emphatically, beaming at the centre of the halo of glory and sanctimony that she had woven around herself.

Lugh was transfixed. He realized that he could not have hoped for immediate social reform, but this was certainly a bold and generous first step towards it on his mother's part.

He walked up to his mother and hugged her, feeling his love for her deeper than ever. Rhiannon hugged Lugh back, closing her eyes, revelling in his gratitude.

"Mother, you never cease to amaze me. Your generosity and broad-mindedness make me proud to be your son," he said kissing Rhiannon's cheek.

She held his delicately chiselled face in her cradled hands, and appreciated the beauty of his eyes, with their innocent yet penetrating aqua gaze.

"I love you too, Lugh," she said with sentiment, sealing her statement with a kiss on his lips.

"Mother," he added, "there is one more thing..."

"Yes?"

"Will Urien agree with your decision?"

Rhiannon smiled broadly, showing no concern at all for the matter.

"Dear Lugh, I have always maintained the illusion that your father rules this kingdom but who, do you think, rules your father?"

Lugh looked at her with relief and admiration, sure that if Rhiannon had promised his Love shelter and advantages, Clodagh would get them.

"I will have some soldiers go fetch your girl and her mother. You may accompany them, if you please, and show them to their new dwelling yourself. Come with me, I will show you the location of their chambers," Rhiannon said while heading for the castle's most reserved and quiet wing, the same where her bedroom was located.

Lugh's heart pounded with excitement, he felt as though he was walking in a dream, and could think of nothing but his Love's name, and of the immense happiness which awaited them.

Chapter Nineteen

The morning came, the sky looked gray and heavy. Rhiannon had gathered her husband, her son, Clodagh and her mother, Iweridd, in their private-audiences chambers, and exhorted everyone to sit comfortably and to enjoy the warmth emanated by the blazing fireside. It looked orange and powerful like the mouth-like fire pit of the gods' blacksmith that the child-Lugh had imagined.

Clodagh and Iweridd sat still and uneasy, shocked at their overnight change of dwelling and of status, and at what possible reasons could lay behind it. Iweridd was afraid for her daughter.

"Powerful people never care to give comfort to people like us, unless there is something they want that only we can give them," she had said.

Rhiannon had ordered that warm milk and honey be served to the guests.

"You must be nervous," she said addressing the two women. "The milk will relax you." She smiled and sat herself down across from Clodagh and Iweridd.

"The reason you are here is due to a simple fact: Lugh is in love with Clodagh and she with him, I understand," Rhiannon said.

Clodagh blushed ardently while Urien found he could not lift his gaze off the girl. He found the freshness of her youth and her apparent vulnerability irresistible.

"I bet she is a virgin," he kept thinking, dying to find out first-hand; he loved the thrill of discovery.

"...And so," Rhiannon continued, "I have decided to make things easier for these young people in love. You see, Lugh knows about this: when Urien and I fell in love, my father tortured us night and day about it, until Urien and I felt that we had no other choice but to run away so that we could be together. The idea to part from each other was unbearable to us.

"I never want Lugh to feel that way. If he is happy, I am happy, but I am not doing this for him alone. You see I want to get to know Clodagh because if I do so, then I might grow to love her too." Rhiannon stared intensely at Clodagh with a successfully self-imposed look of tenderness in her eyes.

After listening to Rhiannon in obsequious silence, Iweridd spoke.

"You are queen of this land, and many others, and while I appreciate your offer to upgrade our existence of lowly servants, I hardly believe we will become gentle folks just by living under this noble roof.

"What do you ask of us in return for the favour you are extending to these young people? What guarantee do I have that Lugh will not discard my daughter like worthless chattel, when his infatuation for her wears off? Is this a whim of yours, young Lugh?" Iweridd dared say, shifting her focus to Lugh, who blushed at her insinuations.

"You see," Iweridd went on, "I am not asking you to marry her; I have no right to, and I know it could never be so. What I am asking you is to release her now. Do not hurt her, she knows nothing of the world, and how cruel life can be. I think she is much too young to discover pain. By the look of things, she will have the rest of her life to know pain intimately."

Clodagh winced all through her mother's appeal, feeling shame for being so mercilessly exposed and made to look more vulnerable and naive than she really was.

Then her embarrassment turned into fear, fear that just when things were beginning to look hopeful for her and for Lugh, Iweridd's pessimism might destroy it all. She stopped blushing and she rose, looking at her mother.

"Whatever happens, I'm prepared to face it. I am ready to accept pain, if pain will come to me for being with Lugh. But I will not turn my back on this most generous chance I have been given to find my happiness with him," she said stunning everyone with her boldness, except for Lugh. He knew that, while he liked the loveliness of her exterior fragility, what he loved were her inner-strength and her wisdom.

Silence fell over everyone for an instant, then Rhiannon spoke.

"Iweridd, you are insolent in so openly accusing me, and my son, of planning a treacherous future for your daughter but, as a mother, I understand your concern and appreciate your honesty. I see you have passed on to your daughter if not your suspicious mind, considerable courage. For that, I forgive you. People in this kingdom have died for less," she stated sternly and convincingly, sending chills even down Urien's back.

"I must agree with my queen," Urien added quite laconically, then Lugh felt he had to answer Iweridd's questions about his interest in Clodagh.

"Iweridd, I speak your name and your daughter's with respect in my heart. Like my mother, I understand your concern for your child, but I feel it is very important to me that you believe me when I say that I love her." Lugh looked at Clodagh and took her hand in his.

"My love for her is not a whim, and it is not limited to the loveliness of her appearance. What I love most about Clodagh is the beauty she holds inside of her, and that I have been fortunate enough to be allowed to see and to share in.

"She would not be here if I knew that she did not want to. Clodagh," he said while looking in her eyes with frankness, "If you feel that you do not want to go through with all this, you do not have to. It will break my heart if you choose to go, but I will respect your will. I will not ever want to take away your freedom and the right to choose what you want."

"I choose to stay," Clodagh said, very sure of her decision.

"As for me," Lugh continued addressing Iweridd, "I can only hope, not guarantee, that we shall be forever happy together, but I can promise you that I will always do whatever is in my power to ensure that Clodagh is happy and safe. I will never harm her; I would rather die than let that happen."

Rhiannon stood proud by Lugh. "You see," she said looking at Iweridd. "My son is a very honourable young man. Clodagh could not have found a more loyal and loving companion."

Iweridd lowered her eyes to the floor. She felt she could trust Lugh a bit more than she could trust his parents, but still, she had her doubts.

After all, these people who had so easily opened the door of their cursed fortress to her daughter, once had shut it on her freedom and that of all others in Aileach. Terrible misery had befallen all, thereafter.

"Time will tell," Iweridd said, and no more.

***

Weeks had passed since Clodagh and Iweridd had moved into Balor's Castle and Clodagh seemed to have adjusted to her new life with more ease than her mother.

Iweridd kept waiting for the worst to happen, as she was convinced it would, sooner or later.

Clodagh and Lugh enjoyed their togetherness and looked at their future with great hope. Lugh trusted his mother and her promises regarding his and Clodagh's happiness. Clodagh felt happy, but was not sure that her happiness would last.

"If things should fall apart, if Lugh's parents were to suddenly change their minds about us and oppose our love, then I will always have my memories of this love, of this happiness," she told her mother in response to her predictions of doom.

Clodagh and Iweridd were clothed regally, were fed the best foods, entertained at the banquets that were held at the castle and themselves were being served, quite awkwardly, by baffled but understanding friends who much missed them as their former selves.

Iweridd kept more to herself and felt restless. She was used to working hard and steadily, and now had to place her energy into weaving, sewing and embroidering, which kept her quite content after all.

Clodagh and Lugh spent much time with one another. Much like Lugh, she was learning quickly about the life of nobility and was not sure she liked it. Their dream was to move away and live out their own destinies, away from the oppressive glamour of Caer Balor and of Aileach.

Rhiannon perfected and honed the art of deception, making herself appear genuinely accepting, approving and happy about the presence of the two servants she had so skilfully integrated into her life.

Urien was quite enjoying the presence of Clodagh and spent most of his waking hours scheming about three issues: the assassination of Morrigan; the completion of the statue of Balor, and the forcing of Clodagh, and Rhiannon was aware of her mate's desires.

She kept waiting for Urien to openly fail her then, after their ritual mating that would bring about the coming of the Fomor, she would be rid of him, and have a younger, more exciting companion with whom to share her future role of empress.

"So," Urien asked Rhiannon in the privacy of their bedchambers, "Are you truly as happy as you make yourself look, about the presence of those plebeians in our castle?"

"Do not mock me. You know full well how I feel about those wenches having to be here, in my castle. Every time, every time I see them around me," Rhiannon said becoming animated and clenching her fists, "I have to stifle my outrage and my will to scream and to kick them out of my sight.

"Little Clodagh, she thinks she is quite brave, does she not? Truth is, I could have slain her myself a long time ago if she did not serve my purposes. Do you think I would put myself through such humiliation and misery if I had nothing to gain from it?"

"Of course not," Urien replied with a giggle. "I was just waiting to watch you spew bile over all this, and to reveal to me the schemes you have upon Clodagh and Iweridd. I know that you are doing this to please Lugh and to upstage me in his eyes...yes, he has always liked mommy better than daddy, has he not? What a splendid opportunity this is for you!" Urien lamented resentfully. "But you see, I am going along with your plans, whatever they are, because I, too, have something to gain from this situation."

"I know, I am aware of your attraction for the little bitch, but I no longer care. I only care about my son's happiness and about achieving utter and complete power over Ireland. However, know that your passion for Clodagh fits perfectly within my schemes. You are free to fuck her, in fact, I want you to," Rhiannon stated calmly while sipping a hot concoction she herself had created, which would ensure a restful sleep every night. She needed it to maintain her beauty, and to energize; she had much to do.

Urien stood speechless by the fireplace, his arms folded over his stomach.

"Does this mean that we both have the freedom to sleep with others? Or is this just a one-time opportunity?" He enquired.

"Is this all you are concerned with? Yes, yes, it does mean that we may both enjoy other lovers, but we must stay together because we need to, if we want to rule this land. I have the magic and the cunning. You certainly have the ruthlessness on your side, and the fact that we share the same blood, but not much else," Rhiannon uttered, enraged and sarcastic.

Urien was used to that kind of talk and was past the stage of feeling resentment or taking offence. He had grown to find it quite amusing and even exciting that Rhiannon would speak to him the way she did. As long as he had a semblance of power and all the sex he could get, Urien was satisfied.

"Why do you want me to take Clodagh?" He asked, looking serious.

"You see, that is how we can get her out of Lugh's heart. When he will discover the affair he will be shattered, disappointed and willing, more than ever, to turn to us."

"What are you saying? Do you hear yourself?" Urien exploded. "You must either have lost all your logic, or you must think that I am grotesquely stupid. If Lugh is made to find out about the affair, he will turn to you and hate me for good! Why should I help you do that?" He asked bewildered.

"Dear, simple Urien," Rhiannon smirked, holding his hand to mockingly feign sympathy. "You underestimate me. When I plan something, I carefully weigh all options, look at all sides of a situation, try to predict contingencies, at the best of my reasoning abilities which, as you know, are high."

Urien lifted one eyebrow.

"The way I have figured it out," she continued, "Lugh will believe that Clodagh wants you, that she loves you, and that she only used him to get to you. Do you follow?"

"Perfectly," Urien said looking intrigued. "I just want to know how I am going to get Clodagh to cooperate: she loves Lugh, body and soul, and it is plain to see that she is revolted by me and by what I have done to lowly worms such as her mother.

"So, have you given any thought to that? Sure, I knew that to have her I must force her, but what will keep her from telling Lugh?"

"Blackmail," Rhiannon uttered. "You are so stupid; how could you not have seen it? What we must do is, first of all, to get Lugh involved in something that will take him away from Clodagh, on a certain day, and for a certain part of that day. I shall take care of Iweridd, I shall think of something.

"In the meantime, you get into Clodagh's room. I will warn the soldiers not to intervene once they hear her screams. You will rape her and, when she threatens to tell Lugh, or even if she does not say anything at all, you must tell her that if she wants to keep her mother from dying a slow and painful death, she must keep her mouth shut about the rape; she can tell no one."

Urien appeared more fascinated than ever. She continued.

"Then, you will tell her that you must meet again, over and over; you make her your sex-slave like you did with me, and after you have fucked her a few times and made her more familiar with the situation, we will set up a trap for our wholesome, unsuspecting Lugh to discover the earth-shattering truth. What do you think now?"

"Uh, I must say I am impressed. Tell me more," Urien teased.

"You will tell Clodagh that she must tell Lugh to come see her in her room at a certain time. Then, she must go along with the entire plan. Keep threatening her mother's safety, and her own. Kick her around a bit if she holds back. You are resourceful when it comes to sadism: follow your instincts.

"Anyhow, you start raping her near the time that Lugh is supposed to meet with her. When he will open the door he will see the two of you. You will try to act shameful and regretful. She must appear as though she is enjoying herself, and she must tell Lugh that it is finally time that he found out the truth about her feelings for you. It is of the outmost importance that Clodagh be convincing. I leave that responsibility up to you.

"After that, you will be humble and ask for your son's forgiveness: remember, we are going through all this so that he will not hate you, and he will not start doubting us. You will tell him that she came on to you, that she bewitched you with her sexuality and that, after all, you are only human. Promise to make amends to him and tell him that I do not know about the situation and that I do not need to know, to protect my feelings.

"If you appeal to his sense of compassion he might take pity on you and feel bonded to you, somehow inclined to forgive you. After that, you may dispose of Clodagh and Iweridd as you wish. You may keep the girl as your lover by continuing to threaten her mother's life if she does not comply, or you may get rid of them both. Kill them, I do not care, as long as they are kept out of my sight."

Urien walked up to Rhiannon and kissed her forehead.

"Such deviousness in this precious little head of yours," he said, and they fell into one of their ardent embraces, both excited by the perversity of their schemes. Afterward, a thought occurred to Urien.

"What if the little bitch's love for Lugh should surpass the love for her mother? What if she told Lugh the whole truth, and ask him to help her and Iweridd run away with him?"

"I do not think that that is a possibility; you may have no qualms about killing your mother. But Clodagh is the kind of person that could never let that happen and be able to live with herself. She is outspoken, but she is wise enough not to push your limits, not when her mother's life is at stake. Peasants have unusually deep family bonds. Misery bonds some people, while it breaks other apart. You will see, the girl will comply with your demands and if Lugh hears her tell him that she has no love for him, and never did, he will release her and, hopefully, will gradually fall out of love with her.

"This kind of trauma should also act as a trigger for his capacity to telepathically reach Morrigan. Anger will be the catalyst, anger which will be channelled into finding and killing his sister. I will take care of that."

Chapter Twenty

Spring had graced the island of Iona, making the sky blue, dressing up the trees, especially the majestic oak, with tender green, crimson-tipped leaves. The hawthorn was in blossom and the herds were freed from their winter confines to be released into the greening pastures.

Rivers and springs flowed again, free from the grip of the ice and the birds filled the light air with their melodies. The people of Iona were getting ready to celebrate the awakening of Danu.

Morrigan had matured into a stunningly bright and beautiful woman. She was a most rare combination of delicacy and strength. Her thin frame carried itself with the elegance of agility, and exquisitely chiselled features graced her oval face.

She had hazel eyes which darted mystery and a certain wisdom which the full lips contrasted, giving her an exotic and sultry quality. Long, wavy dark hair dazzled auburn in the sun and framed her face, adding to its beauty. She had inherited her mother's full, long eyebrows which had always been a shade darker than the hair, and which delicately curved and slimmed outward, above her eyes.

Clothed in a mid-length red tunic and black leather leggings, adorned by a three, clear-quartz gem necklace, she moved within the forest very skilfully and comfortably. It was her home: not once in her life had she lost herself in it, or had been frightened away by its animals, and its mysteries.

She was gathering berries and enjoying the return of spring to the woods. The wind's voice was softer then. The trees, the grove and water, now awakened by the sun from the icy stasis of winter, spoke to her again.

Many times she heard her name being called as if from a remote site, carried by the gusts of warm wind which bathed her in bliss. The voices she heard calling her name were those of benevolent spirits from the world beyond, the doors of which were opened again by the coming of Beltane.

She loved to stand still in the strong, warm wind and absorb it all with every pore of her skin, and drink it into every cell of her body.

She knew she must ready herself for the latter part of her physical and metaphysical training, and communing with nature was an essential part of the preparatory process.

Airmid looked stronger and fitter as she became older: that was the beneficial side effect of being Morrigan's teacher. She was very much involved in the same activities that she taught her granddaughter.

Morrigan's body had become curvy and firm, and she had grown taller over the winter. She loved to run along the beach and to hike the slopes of hills and rocks. She had a restlessness that made the duty of her physical training a necessary vehicle in which she could channel her energy.

The sea water was not warm enough for her to swim in it yet, but she could not deny herself the pleasure of being in contact with water and, although shivering at first, she would immerse her legs into the spring's water up to her knees.

Life was good, but not blissful. There was no man-love in her life, and she lived expecting to be at the receiving end of her brother's call.

Sensual desires, that had always been quite strong in Morrigan, were now surfacing more powerfully than ever, seeking expression and fulfilment. They pervaded her dreams and her thoughts. She was ready, but she had no mate, nor would she settle for just any man.

She had a recurrent dream in which events repeated themselves in a pattern, and in which she had only a glimpse of a man whose face she never saw.

The night would come, and the dream appeared vivid, illuminating the darkness of her sleeping mind. She saw herself clothed only by a sheath, a transparent, violet sheath through which her voluptuous form revealed itself in all its sensuousness and the ripeness of her youth. Each curve bursting with sexual awareness and the need to be caressed, to be stroked by the hand of an ardent lover.

She saw herself walking through a steamy chamber in which many braziers burned with high flames. Then she came to a round pool of water, a bath, sunken in the marble floors of the room, surrounded by pillars and by curtains as sheer and as impalpable as the wings of butterflies.

As she approached the tub, she wrapped her arms around one of the columns hot from the steam, and the sheath dropped off her body and slid into the pool, as she watched it being slowly engulfed by the water. She found herself compelled to shift her genitals and breasts forward to rub them against the pillar, and felt cheated and frustrated, unable to carry out appropriately the desires of her flesh.

At the point where her libido found itself suspended between burning desire and the fear that the flesh will never be satiated, she felt her nature being inundated by a warm fluid which felt thicker than the menstrual blood she was accustomed to. She felt and saw the hands of a man cover her breasts, palpating her erect nipples, getting closer to her body until she felt his, hard and warm, pressing against the back of hers. A maddening need to be penetrated gripped her as if it were the only thing in the world that mattered; her body overruled her mind.

She felt his breath suffuse the skin at the base of her neck with warmth, as soft lips kissed it incessantly all the way to her nape, breathing in the scent of her fiery hair which he held aside, draped over her shoulder.

He spread his large hands in fan-like fashion over the small of her back, and entered her passionately, thrusting through the sultry gates of her opening, breaking through the virginity she could no longer bear.

At that point she felt the deepest satisfaction she thought physically possible. Her breath grew faster and faster with the intense excitement of the lovemaking. She wanted to face her lover but he would not let her, resisting the movements of her body wanting to turn, by gently gripping her waist with his hands as he penetrated her with more intensity and the urgency of a nearing climax.

She came, instinctively arching her back as she felt him flooding her. She yelled her pleasure out wildly and shamelessly in her dream, but enjoyed the pulsating sensation between her legs quietly, once the orgasm woke her.

She told Airmid about the dream and about experiencing such intense physical pleasure, and how much happier she would feel if she could only meet the man she was waiting for, and make her lovemaking real.

"I just wish that in the dream he would at least let me see him," Morrigan confessed to her grandmother, who smiled.

"Maybe the dream is a prelude to what is to come; you might see his face in real life one of these days..." Airmid teased lovingly.

"Love, do not despair. It will happen when you least expect it; he will seem to appear out of thin air. I am happy to hear about your blossoming into womanhood. It is nice, is it not, to let the body guide you for a change? I have always believed that each time we make love and let our body show our mind its own rapture, our souls sparkle with more life." Airmid looked a bit lost in her thoughts.

"Grandmother, have you no need for a lover?"

"Quite frankly, once your grandfather died my passion was buried with him. I just felt no desire and now I am fulfilled by my work. But I do not feel cheated out of anything: I had my bliss, and if Danu wills it, I might again. I do not know. But you, beautiful and young...it is your birthright to experience love, and you shall."

Chapter Twenty-one

Sandda, the old Druid, was ill. While Beltane had come, restoring Danu's life-force and heralding spring's progression into summer, death was insinuating itself into Sandda's dwelling.

Winter had been harsh on his body and kept him bedridden. His lungs had filled with too much phlegm and were plagued by the spasms of frequent coughing, while arthritis added the finishing touches to the bones it had distorted over time, into a masterpiece of grotesque deformities. His fingers had been the most affected by it and were also the most visible parts of the human sculpture he had become. His fingernails had grown longer and had yellowed. Sandda felt death coming with each cell of his decaying body and looked forward to it.

The pain and the discomfort he felt competed with his inability to function in making him feel worthless.

"Why am I not dead yet? What is the purpose of keeping me alive, if I cannot be of service to my people, or to myself?" Sandda had often asked himself and his son, Finn, who took care of him most of the time.

"You are not a burden, neither are you worthless: do you realize that the mere sight of you brings me joy and inspiration daily, and gives me the chance to give you back a small fraction of all the love and the care that you have generously bestowed on me, from the moment I was born till now?" Finn replied.

Sandda drifted into sleep often, which provided him with temporary relief from the pain that plagued him almost constantly while he was awake.

Airmid was spending more and more time aiding Finn in nursing Sandda, if not back to health, into a state of comfort. Herbs, berries and certain kinds of mushrooms were all experimentally processed and distilled, made into potions and ointments that tricked Sandda's body into perceiving the pain not as sharply as it could otherwise have. When even those treatments proved weak and failed, Airmid resorted to administering to him highly sedative medication which caused Sandda to hallucinate.

Finn, having chosen not to pursue the study of the magic arts, did not believe that his father's utterances, while under the effect of the sedative medicines, might be anything else other than nonsense. Often Sandda slipped in and out of consciousness, uttering undecipherable phrases. On one of those days Airmid happened to sit by Sandda's bedside. He seemed to be asleep, but suddenly, she felt him grip her hand with the strength of a young man, and he startled her into paying attention to his ravings. His gaze was fixed upon Airmid's face; his pupils dilated.

"She...she who wears crimson, slays the little...the little children. Morrigan must be warned!" Sandda fatigued to say.

Airmid looked puzzled and felt it unsettling to hear Morrigan's name being spoken within that context by the dying Sandda. She felt that she had to make sense of Sandda's ravings; perhaps, they were more than just the words of delirium.

Airmid went to sleep without mentioning a word about Sandda's utterances to Morrigan.

In one corner of Airmid's room lay the new ceremonial robe of Druid which Sandda had ordered her to sew for herself, so she would be ready to take his place. The thought saddened and scared Airmid. She could not even make out the meaning of an old man's ravings, how was she supposed to be the seer and the wise woman for the people of Iona? She fell asleep feeling her chest heavy with anxiety, but what she experienced would forever change her.

On the cloudy mists of Sandda's muddled thoughts, Airmid felt transported far away from Iona. She felt his presence but could neither see or hear him, yet he was there, guiding her towards the dark Caer Balor.

She soon realized that she was not dreaming. It was her astral body which was travelling, and it was that body which perceived Sandda's presence so near.

She slipped easily through the castle's thick walls into its lugubrious basement, lit only by one powerful torch-chandelier hanging above a smooth stone altar.

What Airmid saw, she could not believe. A small child lay on the altar, stretched, pinned down and gagged. Her eyes were opened wide by terror as she looked at Rhiannon's face hanging expressionless above her own. Rhiannon wore crimson.

Airmid, intuitively aware of the woman's identity, scrunched away in a corner of the dungeons and noticed the cold, the smell of dried blood and of death. She wanted to help that child, but she couldn't, not in her astral body, and she certainly would not watch her be brutally killed. Airmid realized she could not hide in that corner, she had to think quickly of something to do.

Rhiannon was circling the altar chanting a spell invoking the power of the gods of the abysses, holding a very thin, long dagger in her left hand, looking deeply into the child's eyes as she walked circles around her and, when she felt that the child had been terrified enough to be wanting to scream, she ripped the gag off her mouth and cherished the desperate sound in the shrill yell of the child's voice.

Rhiannon's nostrils and upper lip quivered with enjoyment, which she intensified by cutting the skin of the little girl's collar bone, causing the little one to scream louder, to call out for the parents she never had, to come and save her from the red demon.

Airmid, just then, felt a surge of energy that jolted her from a state of helpless desperation and pity for the child, to the self-assurance that she was not going to let that murder happen. She moved close to Rhiannon, the aqua-blue of whose irises had extended to the entire eye, dilated, to push aside the white. Rhiannon sensed the presence of somebody she could not see, and she threatened it by waving her knife in the space around her.

Airmid knew what to do, as if she were following instructions. She punched Rhiannon hard in the face and she actually felt the physicality of the impact and watched its consequences. Rhiannon fell on her back completely disoriented, and too angry to notice the pain.

"Show yourself to me now. Let us fight fairly, shall we?" She provoked, while Airmid was busy untying the child, as Rhiannon picked herself and her knife up, and kept waving the dagger uselessly around the room in the hope to uncover her invisible enemy.

Airmid wished to become visible to the child only, and she soon noticed that she did.

"Shhh..." she indicated to the little girl by pressing her index finger to her own lips, and the child was quiet. Airmid rejoiced at the sight of hope she saw flashing in the child's eyes. Then, abruptly, Airmid having lost concentration, she saw Rhiannon lunge toward the child whom she saw had been untied, and she stabbed her brutally through the heart and she immediately placed her mouth over that of the dying child to breathe away her life-force as it was flying out of her little body.

Airmid, still not visible to Rhiannon, felt paralysed and transfixed: she had not been able to save the poor child from that horrible death. She could not believe what she had just seen and began to cry, to mourn the loss of the precious child.

Rhiannon lifted her mouth away from that of the child, now looking cold and perfectly still, and she realized that she could hear the invisible Being's cry.

"Ah! So I've hit you where it hurts, have I not?" She said cruelly, then began to walk slowly towards the source of the lament. Airmid kicked Rhiannon in the stomach hard, causing her to fold over.

"Who are you?" Rhiannon was furious.

"Why do you do it?" Airmid wanted to know.

"Who are you?" Rhiannon asked again, her voice getting deeper and louder.

"Why do you do it?" Airmid repeated yelling and kicked Rhiannon again, breaking down her defences.

"I do it to keep myself looking young and beautiful!" Rhiannon yelled out angrily to the presence whose identity she could not guess, having ruled out that it was Morrigan: she felt it was not her.

"If you are the spirit that guarded this child's life from the parallel world, well, you have certainly not done a good job, which goes to confirm my theory about the superiority of the gods of the Fomor above those of Danu," Rhiannon dared.

"Maybe I come from a dimension unknown to you," Airmid found the strength to whisper just before she felt herself being drawn back into her physical body and found herself awake, and horrified.

Before she woke Morrigan to tell her about the experience she had, she felt she had to run to Sandda. She ran faster than she ever had before, carried by the wind which she had raised with the power of her will.

Upon entering the Druid's home, she saw he was expecting her. She sat beside him and held his hand. He looked in her eyes intensely, then spoke.

"I was there, I saw. I brought you there so that you could witness at least one of Rhiannon's atrocities."

Airmid's heart leaped. "I could not feel your presence in the dungeons."

"No matter," Sandda said, sounding more and more intelligible. "I was there, but you were so involved with what was happening that you did not notice me. Do not worry, the spirit of the child has crossed over to the world of the Sidhe. Rhiannon has only possessed her life-force, her vital energy," Sandda explained, answering the question which was burning inside Airmid's racing mind.

"Why could we not stop it? Why did you not help me?" Airmid asked out of pain and frustration.

Sandda tried to lift his head up, but could not. Airmid propped his pillow so that he could be more comfortable in an almost sitting position. He held her hand tight.

"The child chose to be the object of the sacrifice. She had pledged her soul, before her physical birth, so that you could witness Rhiannon's evil and warn Morrigan about it. The prophecy must be fulfilled; this is just one little step towards its accomplishment," Sandda said, lucid but exhausted. "...What you saw, also served another purpose. You have seen evil in its purest form. You have been witness to the ultimate horror; the death of a helpless creature for the perverted enjoyment and benefit of another.

"Are you angry? Have you felt the limits of your humanity, and of your compassion, in realizing that you could not help the child?"

Airmid realized she had.

"You have been initiated to the life of a Druid. You must always do your best to help, but when you cannot, do not crumble under the weight of guilt that does not belong in your heart. Remember the limits of your humanness, and the sometimes hidden purposes of Danu, behind everything we are, and everything that happens to us."

Airmid understood, but she had many questions she knew she could never ask. Sandda's voice was becoming feeble.

"Use the anger and the outrage that you have gained at Caer Balor with wisdom," Sandda warned as he pulled her close to him.

Airmid bent towards Sandda to meet his efforts half way, and he looked into her eyes for the last time.

"I shall give you the weapon of my knowledge to be used at your discretion when you will feel that the anger you have inside must be expressed," he whispered, and sealed his words with what Airmid thought was a kiss. When their lips touched, they both instinctively opened their mouths and it was then that Airmid realized that she was being entered by Sandda's life-force, some of his knowledge and some of his memories. The kiss dissolved and Sandda was dead.

Airmid held his head gently in her hand as she rested it back onto the pillow. She let out a muffled cry of sorrow, for the loss of Sandda to the world. Then a cry of joy, for Sandda had begun his journey towards a higher plane of existence.

Hours went by. Finn and his wife had awakened and, once inside Sandda's house, had found Airmid stretched across his body in the abandonment of grief, and they joined her.

Chapter Twenty-two

Sandda's death was announced throughout Iona. By evening, people from every corner of the island gathered into a funeral procession for Sandda. Morrigan knew nothing more than the others did. Airmid looked different, she noted, more aloof and self-assured.

"She looks like a Druid should," she thought.

Airmid had clothed herself with her new white ceremonial robe, which covered her entire body except for the head, the hands and the feet. She looked wise and peaceful.

The darkness of night came. Sandda's body was ready for burial. Torches were lit and carried by everyone in the procession.

Sandda's body, clothed only by a simple black, gold-rimmed tunic, was carried on a wicker stretcher by two men and two women, out of the Druid's home and into the quietly grieving crowd. Airmid followed, solemn, sensing the love and acceptance of her emanating from the people she was committing herself to serve, unconditionally, until her death would come.

Airmid and Sandda's family members were leading the funeral procession. Morrigan blended with the people, her hair glistening red in the light of the torches and against the velvety blackness of the night.

The funeral gathering marched orderly towards a sacred mound where all Druids on Iona had been traditionally buried. The mound, located high on a hill, was a large, wide dome the inside of which had been carved right out of the hillside. A chamber was visible from the outside through a narrow horizontal opening which was the chamber's only source of light.

The chamber itself was much too small to accommodate more than the deceased Druid's family members and the new high priest. Sandda's body was laid to rest.

Outside, Bards were playing sad and moving melodies. The sounds of the chords of the harps vibrated powerfully within each person's soul and brought many to tears. They so expressed that Sandda would be missed among them, all the while comforting themselves in the belief that he was going to a better, sacred place.

Sandda's corpse was simply lifted from the wicker stretcher and laid on the cold earth floor of the burial chambers. Once Airmid and the few others who had buried Sandda exited the mound, a thick oak door was shut in the face of the inner darkness. The procession quietly made its way towards the centre of the village where the celebrations of the festival of Beltane were to be officially opened by Airmid.

The fired burned, powerful and purifying, like it had at Samhain. The atmosphere was the same: ethereal, dream-like. Airmid stood at the core of a large human circle with the fire burning behind her, and she spoke.

"I want you to know that I have felt your acceptance of me, and that I intend to honor it by pledging my commitment to serve you for as long as Danu will keep me breathing, and I do so willingly and joyfully. Like Sandda used to say, keep in mind that I love you, but remember that I'm not infallible.

"As you know, at dawn the first rays of the sun will project through the mound's window into the chamber where Sandda is buried, and will wake his spirit to take It to the world beyond the World Beyond.

"At dawn, we will also hold the council meeting where I will answer all the questions and suggestions you might have in relation to my new responsibilities, as well as to the many facets of our community's life. Celebrate Beltane, enjoy the beauty of this season, its foods, the music, the dancing and, once again, communing with the spirits."

Airmid took license from the people after her brief speech and sought out Morrigan, needing to talk to her. Morrigan was close by, apprehensive about the fact that, as of that night, her grandmother was to dwell in Sandda's house and she was to live alone in the woods, preparing for what she must do.

"Morrigan," Airmid said, finding the girl deep in thought and calling her back to reality by placing her hand on her shoulder. "We need to talk."

They both began walking towards Sandda's house, now Airmid's.

"It feels odd to take possession of somebody else's dwelling. I will miss my own, and your constant presence," Airmid confessed with sadness clearly audible in her voice.

Morrigan's face was already streamed with tears which she tried to hide. Airmid stopped Morrigan's hand motion to wipe her eyes discreetly, while turning her head casually to the other side.

"In case I have not told you this before, there are two things you must never fear: don't be afraid to cry, and don't be afraid to laugh," Airmid said.

Morrigan blushed. It was true; regardless of her open upbringing, somehow she had always believed that she had to hide her sorrow and her joy. No longer. The realization was powerful enough to let Morrigan give herself permission to abandon herself to her emotions, much like she did in her dreams.

She hugged Airmid, overcome by the need to be held, which Airmid joyfully satisfied by pulling the girl close to her, and Morrigan cried tears she had silenced for a long time. She cried passionately and shamelessly, savouring the richness of the freedom to express herself fully.

"That's better. Now you are yourself; you are following your true nature," Airmid said as she cradled the girl's face in her hands.

"I feel scared..." Morrigan admitted. "I don't think I like this. I have never been completely alone before."

"Neither have I!" Airmid replied with a supportive hint of humour in the tone of her voice. "But we'll adapt; that's one of the skills that life requires us all to develop.

"Tonight will be one of the hardest nights of your life, and mine. I am sure, though, that neither fear or loneliness will kill us. Tomorrow we'll see each other at the council meeting and after that, whenever you feel you need to see me, or I you."

Morrigan nodded she understood, completely trusting, like a child.

"Love," Airmid continued, helping the girl dry away her tears. "I must tell you something, come in the house with me. While Sandda was ill, he seemed to be raving, mumbling about visions he had about a woman wearing a red gown, who was 'killing the little children...' and then he would insist that I warn you about her, Morrigan. It is important that you know what this woman does."

"He was speaking of Rhiannon," Morrigan said right then, taking Airmid by surprise.

"Was it a guess, or did you know? And if so, how did you know? You never heard Sandda's...."

She was interrupted by Morrigan's sudden jolts of insight. The girl was holding on to Airmid's arm when the old woman had begun telling her about Sandda's visions, and Morrigan saw what Airmid knew. She was able to psychically read her by touching her. The experience was not easy; receiving the visions was like receiving a jolt of electrical current throughout her body, and her head began to ache.

The ugliness of what Morrigan kept seeing made her breathe frantically and wince, even cry out at the horror of what she saw.

Airmid was worried; this was Morrigan's first real waking vision and she did not have a previous frame of reference against which to measure the intensity of the experience. She tried to literally peel Morrigan's fingers off her arm, but found that the grip was not only very secure, but terribly cold. She realized that Morrigan could not stop the process, she had to follow it through.

When Morrigan saw the knife so violently and unexpectedly pierce the child's chest, she screamed with the child and felt what it was like to die, as Airmid had. After that, Airmid felt the grip on her arm loosen and Morrigan collapsed on the floor of Sandda's dwelling. Airmid dropped to her knees and put her ear against the left side of Morrigan's chest. Her heart was beating fast, her breathing was resuming a regular pattern of rhythm. She knew her girl would be fine. She rose, looked through Sandda's medicinal jars and found some salts of sulphur.

"A whiff of these, and she'll come to."

Airmid held the opened jar under Morrigan's nostrils until she began to show signs of consciousness. As the girl began to turn her head slowly, from side to side and to breathe in deeply, Airmid slapped Morrigan's cheeks briskly until she was fully conscious, and she held the girl's head to her breast for a while, rocking her gently.

Later, Airmid told Morrigan about Sandda's last moments of life and what he had revealed to her about the experience she had.

"You see," Airmid said, "Sandda could not die until Rhiannon's sacrifice was fulfilled, and until he made sure that I had witnessed it. Now you have, for better or for worse. Sandda hinted that this information about Rhiannon might help you, when the time to face her comes.

"He's given me a power inaccessible to you, until I feel, and you feel, that you are ready. I know now I could shatter a person's bones with the power of my will, if I had to. I hope I never have to."

Morrigan lifted her eyes up towards Airmid's and felt grateful that she would not be allowed to pick up that knowledge by just touching Airmid. She did not want it, not yet.

Morrigan walked alone to her home in the woods, as part of her efforts towards developing inner-strength. The full moon looked like a jewelled eye of the sky, following her with each step she took, climbing up the side of the hill that led to the forest, dark and thick with vegetation. Once there, she saw the moonlight illuminate the woods subtly, making them appear festive and open.

The trees whispered: "Come lay underneath us, our roots will be your pillow. Sleep. The sky is a deep-blue mantle tonight, and while you sleep, we'll weave your dreaming and reveal to you a secret."

Morrigan heard the wind hiss softly, also encouraging her to sleep outside, to commune with nature and she felt, after getting past the first feelings of reluctance, that the voices were indeed those of the Trees' Spirits, and that of the Wind.

She entered her cabin, lit a candle and looked around. Without Airmid the house looked different. Before attending the council at sunrise, she promised her grandmother that she would bring her few belongings and some of her own herbal preparations. She was to keep the rest; Airmid had everything she needed at Sandda's house.

Morrigan took two blankets with her. One with which she would cover the tree's roots, so that they could serve as pillows, the other to cover herself.

The willow that had so clearly invited her to sleep at its feet was not too far from the cabin, a fact which Morrigan found somehow reassuring.

When she arrived to the willow, she set herself up to sleep, but found that she could not. The loneliness she felt was crushing. Soon after that, she realized that the trees and the wind, and the other spirits of the woods had invited her to sleep among them so that she would not be alone.

"You will protect and comfort me, won't you?" She asked the tree, caressing its powerful trunk. The tree did not speak to her mind, as it usually did, but she noticed that its roots began to sprout gentle and long offshoot which curved softly under and around Morrigan's body, forming a cradle which rocked her lightly through the night.

During her sleep, the erotic dream recurred more powerfully than ever. Sensations and emotions seemed heightened; she could even smell the burning incense.

"Sandalwood..." she found herself uttering in the dream. In the waking state, Morrigan would not have known the word 'sandalwood,' or its scent.

The trees were gifting her with new and very realistic sensations. The atmosphere in the dream possessed a quality of enchantment. There, Morrigan forgot that anything and anybody else existed outside of that sensual little world and, aside from herself, her soon-to-appear faceless lover. She felt the steam, warmer and moister, caress the skin all over her body as she slowly walked towards the pillar by the sunken pool.

He came; she felt his body pressed against hers and soon the lovemaking began. She sighed deeply, sampling the delicious pleasure of his thrusting, cherishing it, wanting it never to end. She smelled the sultry, sweet and acrid scent of their mating and revelled in the essence, ecstatic.

The moment came in which she began to turn her body around so that she could see him. Her gyrating waist found no opposition in his hands, and they saw each other.

"...Haakon..." she whispered as if in recognition.

"Morrigan," he said softly, acknowledging the impact that her beauty had had on him by the way he was looking at her. His eyes spoke to her mind. "I know you," they said. "I love everything you are."

They felt no other instinct as strong as the urge to kiss with complete abandon. They had been hungry for each other for so long.

That kiss seemed an auspicious beginning towards the satisfaction of their craving to touch, to become one.

Morrigan woke abruptly. Her body was still in a state of pre-climactic excitement. In the dream, after she turned and saw her lover, the lovemaking had stopped, but the falling in love had begun and had ended with her waking up.

"I have seen him," she said to herself. That was all that she found herself repeating, her mind still locked on the revelation of the image of his face.

Somehow she interpreted the feeling of intense reality of the dream as an omen that her lover was real, and that they would soon meet.

Chapter Twenty-three

The sun was still far from rising and Morrigan looked around her expecting to see somebody; she felt as though hidden eyes were watching her every move. She physically perceived the touch of that gaze on her back, and that plunged her in a state of dread. Whoever might be out there, she knew that he, or she, was not friendly.

She rose and walked around watchfully while her heart beat too fast, she noticed. Following a rustling sound she heard coming from the nearby grove, she proceeded cautiously towards it.

"Don't be afraid to fight," Airmid had taught her.

Whatever or whoever was hiding behind the bushes quickly moved and she instinctively knew that he, or she, was standing behind her. Afraid to turn, she felt shock in the realization that the stranger, who was moving closer to her, emanated vibrations belonging to a man, and one she recognized. As soon as the name 'Nyssien' appeared in her mind, she turned around very fast and stood back three or four steps from him.

Nyssien stood still, adding a feeling of unreality and anxiety to Morrigan's perception of what was taking place. She saw that he was staring at her with lust and violence in his eyes. He had grown taller and larger than she, and she tried to assess quickly what her chances to fight with him, and come out unscathed or alive, were.

Her first impulse after that thought was to run, but she could not and would not. Nyssien broke their mutual silence by bursting into laughter, which irritated Morrigan in the extreme.

"You better listen well, Nyssien Ilbreach. I don't like you, and I know that you don't like me, but I would never hurt you for the sheer pleasure of it. In fact, I do not want to hurt you. But if you touch me, I'm warning you, I will go to any extent to protect myself, even if that means killing you. I'll do it." Morrigan convinced herself, as she heard her own words, that she could be able to defeat him after all.

Nyssien, who found himself paying sudden attention to Morrigan's words, had stopped laughing.

"I don't want to kill you," he said. "I just want to pay you back for humiliating me in front of my family that day. Remember that day? What I intend to do to you won't hurt a bit; you may even enjoy it."

Morrigan had fallen asleep in her day clothes. Ordinarily she slept unclothed, which felt more natural to her. Her athame, the ceremonial knife with which she used to cut plants and to cast circles, was still hanging from her leather belt, resting against the outer side of her right thigh. She pulled it out and, instead of backing off to threaten Nyssien with it from afar, she stepped forward very close to him and put the knife at his throat.

"All I have to do is cut your throat; you lay a finger on me, you die," she warned.

Nyssien, who had barely moved his head back from the knife-point, suddenly pushed her away and lunged forward, aiming at grabbing her by the waist and pinning her to the ground.

He had been watching her for a while; he saw her body and her face bloom into a tantalizing femaleness and character that he felt he wanted to possess and devastate. Lust and hatred combined in his heart so powerfully, that his mind had worked obsessively on achieving its purposes.

His brain had conjured up a scenario in which everything would go smoothly. He would rape her, defying and violating her greatness, and would thus become the possessor of her power. Then he would flee Iona, aware of the fact that there a woman's word against that of an assailant was never doubted, and the penalties for rape were severe.

As soon as Nyssien's head impacted Morrigan's chest, she struggled to keep the knife pointed at his neck, he fell on top of her and the dagger bounced out of her hand. He was breathing fast, savouring the thrill of the conquest that he was about to make. She was struggling under him with her whole body twisting and pressing up towards his, in the attempt to kick him and push him off of her. She couldn't breathe easily, but as she kept up her struggle while Nyssien was groping her, she remembered what it was like to breathe under water.

She fixed her gaze on Nyssien's eyes and, at the same time, the recall of the feeling that she experienced while submerged happened again, and she restored her capacity to breathe fully.

"Don't look at me, bitch!" Nyssien shouted while shutting his eyes. He could not cover hers, because his hands held her pinned to the ground. He felt her becoming completely still; even her heartbeat seemed to have settled and to have sensibly slowed. It all began to feel charged, like the calm before the storm. He realized that things were not going as smoothly as he had anticipated. He had foreseen witchery on her part, but was convinced that his brawn would ultimately triumph over her craft.

He felt her eyes stare at him through her now closed eyelids and he shouted in anger and frustration: he saw her eyes, but she saw his mind. She was roaming in it like a predator, unlike the soft and tender female that she appeared to be.

He saw her as a beast he had never seen before, roar at him, and he jolted and recoiled in panic. The huge, black cat he saw courting his death, had burning eyes which stared incessantly. Just when he felt that he might get off of Morrigan and run away, he was possessed by a rage that broke through even his terror and he rose to his knees, and began slapping and shaking Morrigan, but she was stiff and cold.

"I haven't touched you, bitch, why do you act dead? Why?" He shouted frantically, shaking her torso, but she would not move, not breathe or blink, and showed no signs of a heartbeat.

Morrigan was fully conscious but had purposely shifted into a state of trance, suspending every vital function of her body yet living, watching everything happen behind the screen of her consciousness. Her will was what sustained her altered state.

Nyssien, scared as Morrigan had anticipated he would be, sprang up to his feet, but rather than fleeing he began kicking Morrigan's still body around, in a fit of rage and madness through which he was going to make her pay for scaring him so. He was not convinced that she was dead after all, but was dubious enough to be afraid.

She could control the pain of his kicking, but when he finally grabbed her athame, tore her clothes open at the chest exposing her breasts and proceeded to cut the skin between them, pressing deeper as he went down further, she had no choice. He was simultaneously reaching between her thighs, grabbing her, his sweat dripping on her chest.

Her life-force was powerful and she knew she would never surrender to death: not by a man, not like that. The sacredness of her individuality had to remain inviolate. She would never be anyone's victim. She reacted to his violence with the intensity of elemental destructiveness. She cried out loudly, sounding more like the big cat roaring than a woman screaming, which distracted and threw off Nyssien's senses.

At the moment when his focus had been shattered, Morrigan rose up to him while he was punching her in the stomach and trying to hit her in the face, and took a back stance, giving herself just enough space and the momentum to kick him in the face. The sole of her right foot smashed into his nose, breaking it. Like an animal made furious by pain, he threw the whole weight of his body against hers and she was, once again, knocked off her feet.

But while he struggled for a few seconds with his pain and to restore his concentration, she found her balance. She was on her feet again, unbelievably to Nyssien's eyes. He swung his fist towards her face but she caught and stopped his wrist with her hands.

"Witch, damned witch! You think this scares me, but you won't get out of these woods alive!" Nyssien shouted, not yet dissuaded by the demonstration of her power, to let go.

He picked the dagger up again. She held her body still and centred, her limbs positioned to fight in such a manner that, from afar, she would have looked as though involved in the slow motion execution of a martial dance.

As Nyssien lunged forward towards her with the knife, determined to deliver the death blow, she did feel the blade graze her left upper-arm and she thrust her whole arm, the palm of the hand kept open, at the base of his already broken nose, causing him to lose consciousness and to drop to the ground.

She thought that she had killed him, but upon checking his vital signs was relieved to discover that Nyssien had just passed out. The important thing was that she had stopped him from hurting her then and there; she would deal with him in the future, should he provoke or threaten the integrity of her personhood again.

The horizon began to show the first signs of light. She realized that she and Nyssien had fought in the semi-darkness and marvelled at the fact that she had not even taken notice of the dark around them during the fighting.

She ran towards the village to get help. She wanted to take care of Nyssien's broken nose but she did not want to be alone with him when he regained consciousness.

Morrigan bunched up her ripped tunic to her chest, trying to stop the cutting wound from bleeding. Unbelievably, she saw Airmid, Finn and Nyssien's father appear through the trees.

"...I was just thinking about you, about coming to the village to get help..." Morrigan uttered while greeting her grandmother with a hug.

"I saw everything that went on here; I saw it in my head as it was happening. My heart began to pound for no apparent reason, then I saw you struggling with Nyssien and I felt scared. I saw your parents being murdered, I felt them dying without being able to help them. I could have intervened this time, but I would not. You must live out your destiny, and you must learn the skill of survival. So far, you have done exceedingly well," Airmid said, caressing Morrigan's dirty cheeks while she stared, proudly, into her granddaughter's eyes.

Morrigan felt she had been lucky, more so than skilled, and she wondered how she would fare should history repeat itself.

Airmid gave Morrigan a bandage pre-moistened in disinfecting and healing thyme-tea, to plaster on her cutting wounds. The old healer then kneeled by Nyssien to examine him. She checked his heartbeat, his breathing and then his broken, bleeding nose which she began to medicate. He was unconscious still, but would soon come to.

Finn and Brian lifted the boy holding him by his limbs, and laid him on a stretcher they had brought with them. Brian, although worried about Nyssien's health, felt deeply ashamed for his son's actions and could not bring himself to look at Morrigan in the eyes.

"I'm sorry," he said addressing Morrigan, while keeping his head bowed.

Morrigan did not have to imagine how Brian felt; she herself could feel his embarrassment.

"Do not feel responsible for what your son has done; you and Fionnualla have done your very best to understand him. You have taught him right from wrong. He has chosen to do wrong," Morrigan said staring with empathy at Brian's bowed head.

"You are kind," he said, and he began to turn the stretcher around and started his way back to the village.

"I will soon follow," Airmid told the men.

Chapter Twenty-four

The fires of Bael were burning in the village, which was surrounded by meadows covered with colourful flowers. The herds were roaming and feeding freely all around. The smell of fire and burnt leaves, of the animals and of the sea, blended into what most islanders recognized as 'the aroma of Beltane.'

Merchants were setting up their shops for the fair, each hoping to sell or exchange crafts and artefacts. Brightly coloured cloths, jewellery, ornaments, pots, tools, toys and all sorts of objects created a beautiful and cheerful environment that made Morrigan's heart leap with joy and pleasure.

Lost in the enjoyment of the morning breeze, she looked around and saw some of the cattle being walked between the fires to be purified of their long winter stay in the barns, and to prevent any possible infections from proliferating.

There was an electricity in the air; the revitalizing force of spring pervaded everyone and everything. Although the celebrations of the glory of Belenos, the Shining One, the life-sustaining sphere in the sky, had gotten off to a late start because of Sandda's death, everyone was ready to indulge, with abandon, in ecstatic celebrations.

Morrigan saw many young couples necking and later heading for the woods, where they honoured the coming of spring, and its fertility, by making love.

Saddened, she walked to the seashore and locked her gaze onto the undulating motion of the waves. She squatted to bathe her chest and arm wounds with the caustic salt water. As she removed the blood-soaked bandages, she felt disturbed by the sight of her own blood and, in that instant, she felt the coolness of an unexpected wave shatter against her knees, and the mind began the verse weaving:

"The fire and the blade.
The blood that gushes from the wound,
Washed away by the sea...
The flame extinguished by the water,
The blade ravished by the waves.
My heart beats with the water,
Pounds with the water shattered by the wind.
I'm calling you now:
When are you coming?"

She stood by the seashore, her feet bathed by the waves of cold water, and to her it looked like her message was been taken to him, thought by thought, heartbeat by heartbeat, riding on the crest of each wave that came and left, indefinitely.

***

The Council was gathered. People sat in a double circle, the first ring of which was made up by the elders of Iona. Airmid stood in its middle, looking tired but tranquil. A powerful bonfire flamed behind her and puffed up smoke when she threw in it handfuls of verbena, primrose and clover, to create a purifying incense.

"The Council begins," Airmid uttered tapping the earth with her staff three times. She was going to act as Brehon, the law-officer, and dissolve the handfastings that had joined couples in trial marriages during the last Lughnassadh, the celebration of the summer solstice.

"If there are among you any couples who wish to dissolve their union, come forward and you shall be free to part," Airmid said.

A sturdy-looking, beautiful young girl with strawberry-blond hair, clad in a green tunic, stepped forward, followed shortly after by her mate, a tall, black-haired youth who looked too shy to stand the scrutiny of the crowd. The girl spoke.

"Wise One, we have found our union to be a barren one in more than one way; children have not come, and harmony between our characters has failed to happen. We are unhappy with one another. We ask you, in your wisdom, to grant us a divorce."

Airmid listened quietly.

"What do you have to say?" She asked the young man, who coughed nervously and paced slightly forward.

"Ainee is right: we are not suited to each other, and since we both wanted children, we think we owe it to ourselves to try an union with a different mate, to see if it will be more fruitful."

Airmid moved closer to the couple.

"So be it," she said. "You two may go your separate ways. Each of you shall take away no more and no less than whatever possessions each brought into the marriage.

"Possessions acquired jointly during the union are to be sold, and the profit equally shared between the two of you. May the spirit of the goddess grant you the strength to withstand the pain of separation, the will to remain friendly, and the grace to bless you with happier unions. You are released." She kissed both members of the dissolved couple on the cheeks for good luck.

The boy and the girl hugged and walked away from each other in opposite directions, to re-enter the circle.

"Need any other couple come forward?" Airmid asked. Silence followed, so the meeting progressed into discussions concerning the work to be done by the farmers, some fishermen, and all those who had not been able to do their work during the winter.

They would help one another, cooperate and share the fruits of their labour with each other and with the community, in exchange for the material support they had received during the winter months from the labour of artisans, bakers, blacksmiths and many other groups of workers.

Barter was the major means of exchange, while money seemed to be an option on the island of Iona.

People worked together, enjoyed the good times together, and together they endured the bitterness of rough times.

Class distinction was non-existent, their community having been built on the belief that all human beings are born equal, and on the trust in the potential of the human soul to love and to respect all life.

Morrigan attended the meeting physically; her ears heard, her eyes saw, but her mind was on the beach still, her heart still pounding with the motion of the waves.

Chapter Twenty-five

In the days following the council meeting, people honoured the festivities by visiting with one another, enjoying the bargains and the wonders of the fair, the children especially so, and singing and dancing the spiral dance which would ensure a good harvest in the season to come. In the meantime, they truly honoured the month of the fecund oak with their cheerfulness and feasting.

Morrigan felt lonelier than ever and visited Airmid often to talk about her training, rather than about her loneliness and her unfulfilled desires.

She had used her solitude for introspection, to analyze the alien images that had populated her thoughts and her dreams; "...The baths; the big cat; the sandalwood" she thought. She knew that she had begun to access some of her mother's memories spontaneously.

She had a feeling that a transformation was taking place within herself. She asked Airmid many questions in search of answers that could help her understand. Airmid listened to Morrigan's perplexities.

"I knew it would happen!" She exclaimed, pleased that Morrigan's inner transformation was indeed happening.

"Now, you have to put some effort into deliberately travelling to your foetal stages of existence. That will prepare you for the next step: experiencing the moment before and after creation, and being one with it."

"When will that happen?"

"It will be an experience instrumental to the enacting of the ritual that you and your brother will have to carry out in order to call the ancient warrior-gods of Danu into our dimension."

"How do I 'travel back with my cells?'"

"You have to shift into the *other* state of consciousness, tune into the Universal Memory and let the experience happen. You will need to be alone in a quiet site, possibly near water. It is your element, as you know, and it will help you relax and guide you intuitively throughout the process. Don't forget to do your ritual when the moon is new." Morrigan smiled faintly.

"What is ailing you?" Airmid asked, noticing that the girl was absent-minded.

"Uh?"

"What is on your mind?" Airmid repeated.

"I am so lonely, especially now at Beltane."

Airmid understood Morrigan's feelings perfectly. She pulled her close and stroked her hair.

"Isn't it strange that, when it comes to ourselves, our vision is either unclear or absent? I wish that with my third eye I could spy your mate coming and reassure you that you must not despair, that you will not be alone this Beltane, but I can't."

"I saw him in my dream, the dream I told you about before, only this time I saw his face. He is handsome and soulful; I have read love in his eyes. But is he real?"

Airmid looked at Morrigan speechlessly, but pleasantly surprised.

"You saw him?"

Morrigan nodded.

"Well, I can assure you that this is a definite sign that your lover does exist, and that you are bound to meet in the flesh sooner or later!" Airmid explained enthusiastically.

Still, Morrigan did not seem relieved.

"If he is real, if we are bound to meet, will I not lose myself by making love with him?"

"Oh, that is what is truly worrying you!" Airmid realized. "Where did this anxiety come from? What about the bliss you experienced in your dream? What made you afraid of loving and of being loved?"

Morrigan looked at Airmid with tears welling up in her eyes and anger in her heart towards Nyssien. Airmid could see it plainly on Morrigan's face, and she could feel it.

"It is hard to accept the fact that I could have been violated intimately when I fought Nyssien, and now I am not sure I could give myself completely; to trust a man with the very essence of my being."

"When your lover's soul is bared to you, you will be in no danger to lose your personhood in loving him."

Chapter Twenty-six

Morrigan waited for the coming of the new moon with the excitement and the thrill of knowing that she would be travelling into a secret. She remembered the day in which, with Airmid, she felt herself leaving her physical body, and from above watched it get smaller. She saw the many faces of the creatress that day. She was about to experience the prenatal and she wondered how it would feel to be there, in her mother's womb, to hear the beating of her heart.

She realized that she would recall the image of her brother there, and that thought further brightened the prospect of what she must do.

On the night of the new moon Morrigan, having shed her ritual black robe, sat naked by the stream in the woods where she had learned to breathe the water and discovered that she lived, still.

She slid in the stream and sat at its bottom, the water grazing her erect nipples. It was cold but she began to look inward to isolate the outside world.

"Only the inner-world matters at this moment. Nothing else exists, except the sound and the power of the travelling water," she thought.

She inhaled deeply and slid completely under water. The familiar lights of the multicoloured candles that she had arranged by the side of the brook, she saw dancing on the surface of the water above. All else was blackness. The moonlight was not nearly intense enough to illuminate the shape of the trees, or anything else.

The cry of the screech-owl echoed throughout the otherwise silent woods, sounding muted and haunting from beneath the water, filtered through its rushing noise.

Morrigan's mind ran with the water; she was beginning the inner-projection. Just as her spirit had travelled outside of her body before, it now raced unbelievably fast inward, within the depths of the place where all is known and guarded secret from the conscious. She found it to be a place of deep silence and darkness. After the first instants of adjustment to the fluid entering her lungs, Morrigan looked around herself and she realized she was in her mother's womb.

She looked at her hands and saw that they did not look like her own. They were small and not fully formed. Her skin, her flesh, a jelly-like substance, startled her while the sound of her little heart drummed away faster than she would have ever imagined it could.

Then her hearing discerned the sound of another heart, and yet another. She slowly turned her alien body to the side where she felt another body bump into hers and compete for space with hers. She found herself staring in the unfinished eyes of her brother, unborn like her, floating like her, in the womb of the mother they would never come to know.

A strong force had pulled Morrigan out of the inner-projection and into the dimension of ordinary reality. Once again she coughed up the water and resumed breathing air. Once out of the stream she wrapped herself in a blanket she had prepared and put the candles' flames out, except for one, and headed back to her cabin.

She dried her body, lit a fire in the hearth and climbed into bed leaving only one large candle burning in the window by her bed.

Chapter Twenty-seven

The morning after, Morrigan went to see Airmid to discuss the experience with her. She expressed a certain disappointment in the brevity of her inner-projection.

"You are missing the point," Airmid said. "It is the fact that you were able to project back to your foetal stage that matters, not what you thought you might learn in that state. The next time, you should be ready to re-live the moment of creation and to be one with Danu."

"I understand that getting there was the aim, but seeing my brother and not being able to connect with him left me dissatisfied."

"You and Lugh will connect soon enough. Now, just go, go to the fair and enjoy Beltane, because after the festival your next task will be to astrally project yourself to me, first, then, to project yourself to me again, in body and spirit," Airmid said.

"What does that feel like? Tell me, you have experienced both forms of projection."

"Go, go, go!" Airmid yelled teasingly. "You are so impatient! My little sponge; you want to absorb all knowledge and you will, in due time."

Morrigan laughed at how correctly Airmid had described her curiosity, her ever-present drive to know.

"I am going out there and I will have fun. Feel better?" Morrigan teased.

"Much!" Airmid smiled and kissed her granddaughter.

Morrigan strolled light-hearted through the colours, the smells and the sounds of the fair. It was there, that their eyes met and held each other's gaze.

"It is my dream's lover!" Morrigan's mind kept repeating in astonishment, while she found it hard not to scream for joy and surprise, upon realizing that across from her, only a vendor's table between them, stood the man she had loved, over and over, in her mind.

Her knees felt weak and her heart beat out of control; her breathing was erratic, and her face bright red. They could not turn away from each other. Their eyes began to weave a web of emotions and desires in which they both knew they were meant to be tangled. The compulsion he felt to walk towards her gave him the nerve to do it, and she felt immobilized.

He was tall and lean. His remarkable frame was defined by elegant, smooth muscles, rather than the common bulges she had seen on many men, and which she found vulgar and unappealing.

His face was a masterpiece of finely chiselled features; he had prominent cheekbones and rather slanted, narrow eyes the blue of which sparkled vividly in the light of the sun.

It was his provocative mouth that filled her with desire. His lips were full and the upper-lip teasingly dipped in its middle, looking like the spread of an eagle's wings. They looked pale and pink by contrast with the amber tone of his complexion.

His hair literally fell, very straight and extremely blond, to brush his shoulders and uneven, wild bangs covered most of his forehead.

Morrigan found his nose to be his most endearing feature. It appeared to be small, rather straight in the bridge and slightly up-turned at the tip. His profile looked sharp and severe like that of a warrior, while the front of his face had the guile-less expression of a child's.

When he was close he took her hand, looked in its palm and said: "I found the sun." They both recognized one another from their common dream. There was nothing left to do but kiss. They embraced, she felt his body against hers, and it was real.

"It is really happening," she thought while enjoying the strength of his arms around her.

He looked so unlike anyone she had ever seen. His clothes were different also; he wore an oversized green shirt over narrow pants made of thin deer-hide. He wore leather straps around his wrists, and a similar ornament around his neck. Everything about him was new and fascinating.

His lips felt soft and moist to Morrigan's and, close up, his iris darted aquamarine in the sunshine. She felt truly happy for the first time. She felt she knew that man and that she and he belonged to each other, and with each other.

"You are very, very beautiful," he said while caressing her hair. "Now that we have found one another, we'll never be apart again," he whispered, which made Morrigan tremble and cry with emotion. They held hands and, along with the many other young couples on Iona, they entered the woods to celebrate their love.

Airmid had been watching them from afar. She had seen the encounter happen in her dreams just the night before, and cried at the happiness that she knew Morrigan would find on that most blessed day. She, too, knew this was to be Morrigan's life's true and only love.

Morrigan lead the way to her cabin, her heart pounding with the excitement of anticipation and the hope that reality would live up to the dream in intensity.

"What brought you here?" Morrigan stopped and asked Haakon.

"You called me, and I came," he replied. She kissed him tenderly, looked at his slim and strong hands and felt aroused by the way his thumb curled back at the tip. They resumed their walk, and finally reached Morrigan's abode.

"This is my very own place," she announced proudly, while letting him in. The door shut the rest of the world out and they were both breathing fast with desire.

He put his hands around her waist and kissed her, provocatively and tenderly teasing her tongue with his, as he began to gently pull Morrigan's tunic off.

The sight of her nude body was a marvel to him and he found no appropriate words to express his awe, so he kissed her skin all over. He began with the breasts, round and firm, with pink nipples which issued an invitation to be kissed and to be played with. He noticed the fresh scars between her breasts and on her arm and kissed them tenderly as he asked how she got them.

"It's a long story," she said. "But I'll tell it to you sometime."

As Haakon tongued her nipples, she moaned with pleasure and felt the touch of his fingers between her legs. She lay languidly on her nearby bed, watching him undress with hungry eyes. All of her felt moist: her mouth, her eyes, welling up with tears of desire, and the innermost core of her femaleness. She watched his body being bared bit by bit, with fascination and the urge to be penetrated.

She spread her hands on his hairless chest and placed her ear against his heart, which was beating with passion as he caressed her face and mane, noticing it smelled like flowers. As she lay back on the bed, she caressed her inner-thighs with increasing excitement.

He climbed on top of her with the grace and slowness of a feline, his sexual lips parted. She felt the warmth of his face and breath close to her face and revelled in it.

He entered her slowly and she winced at a sensation of tearing and heat which also generated pleasure. Soon, the opposition he had found had been broken through and he found himself thrusting slowly at first, but increasingly faster with each deep kiss, each caress, each stroke of her buttocks and by her touch.

Morrigan felt the bliss of the dream become part of the reality of her first lovemaking experience. She kissed, tongued, nibbled at his body and savoured with him every possible way of enjoying sexuality.

At the point when she felt very close to climax she wanted to lie on her stomach and asked to be penetrated from behind, like she had been in their dream.

Haakon kissed Morrigan's thighs and buttocks as she was turning to lie on her stomach. He slipped the palms of his hands under her chest and gently cupped her breasts into them, teasing the nipples with his fingers, and entered her thrusting harder than before.

She moved her hips and crotch to meet the rhythm of his thrusts and she, too, began to move faster and faster. Just time for one, last deep kiss and they both sighed and moaned shamelessly at the experiencing of their synchronic orgasms. Morrigan found the fact that Haakon had gotten her wet more exciting than ever, which caused the erratic pulsation of her nature to linger.

While the intercourse had ended, the lovemaking continued. They lay close in each other's arms under the blankets, kissing tenderly and enjoying the intimacy of being lovers. They knew that they could do what they had just finished doing every time they liked; they knew it would be soon, and that it would happen often.

Morrigan realized that she had spontaneously revealed to Haakon all the mysteries of her femininity and she did not feel, as she had feared she would, that she had been robbed of her personhood.

"I love you," Haakon whispered in her ear, making it tickle.

"I love you," she said between the giggles that the sensation of his breath in her ear had caused. "I have waited for you a very long time, and now you are here. I almost cannot believe it."

"I want to learn everything about you. How you think, how you feel, who you are, because I want to love all the things that you are, Morrigan," he said while looking deeply in her brown eyes.

"I want to learn everything about you too," she said and kissed him softly. "Where do you come from, and how did you end up here?"

"It's quite a story," he began. "And you may find it hard to believe it, but it's all true, true to the point that gives me reason to believe that you and I were meant to meet and to love one another."

"Tell me the story," she said smiling with much love in her heart and her eyes.

"I was born in a not too far away land which is known as Norge, the Way of the North. My father, Gunar, is a Norseman. He was a trader when, in the very north of his country, he met my mother, a Suomi woman named Umma.

"She is a Vittka; a seer and oracle by virtue of a tradition that had been passed on to her by her mother, who herself inherited it from her mother, and back to remote generations of Vittkas."

Morrigan could not help but interrupt. "I myself am a Druid, and so were my parents, and so is my grandmother, Airmid, who raised me. She is High Priestess of Iona." Haakon's eyes smiled. "I knew that you had to be special."

"A few moons after my birth, my mother began to have a dream which often repeated itself. My parents had heard many tales from navigators, of a beautiful Emerald Island where the climate was mild and the land rich. In her dreams, my mother kept seeing this beautiful, austere woman clothed by light, who called herself Danu and motioned mother to come to her, to travel to the Emerald Island.

"My father, open to my mother's intuition and trusting of her gift, had to listen to the telling of her dream a few times before he, too, was convinced that the dream was a sign from the gods that they were meant to come here to find a better life.

"I was five years of age when we came to Ireland. We lived almost everywhere, in search of a place that would feel right, the place that the woman in my mother's dreams would have meant for us to settle in.

We lived in Dooey, by the sea, where my dad had found good business and established himself as a curragh builder. I was sixteen when I began sharing a dream with my mother. A beautiful young woman with auburn hair stood by the sea, calling me. While mother's dreams of her slowly faded, mine continued, and I began to dream of making love to her...to you, and I knew then I must find you." She smiled and kissed his lips.

"I told my parents that I must go to Iona; I intuitively knew my destination. Soon we were told this was a rather deserted island with not much of interest on it, but my parents were happy to follow me here. We never really had roots anywhere." Morrigan put her arms around his neck and they kissed.

The following day, Haakon's parents, Haakon and Morrigan were to gather at Airmid's home for a modest evening meal, and to get to know one another. Airmid was eager to introduce them as welcome new members to the small community.

When Haakon and Morrigan arrived at Airmid's home after having enjoyed another day at the fair, the sight of cheerful children and long walks by the sea, they found that Gunar and Umma were there already, sitting with Airmid around a low, round table by the hearth.

Upon seeing that Haakon's parents were already there Morrigan felt nervous and so did Haakon, who was going to meet Airmid for the first time.

Morrigan smelled the familiar vegetable stew that Airmid had prepared and that helped her feel more relaxed. She looked at Haakon's parents and she understood why Haakon looked as breathtaking as he did.

Umma was the most beautiful, most captivating woman she had ever seen. She was small in stature and, now in her mid-forties, robust but in a graceful manner. Her face was an olive-hued, smooth surface where perfectly rounded and high cheekbones established a definite air of mystery and ancientness about her. Haakon looked much like her. She saw that Haakon had inherited from his mother not only those alluring cheekbones, which made her think of mother and son as having both the spirit of warriors and of sensuous lovers, but also the captivating almond-shaped eyes.

Umma's eyes were dark and looked like discreetly scintillating onyx stones, full of mysticism and full of wisdom. Her mouth was shaped like Haakon's, but fuller. Her hair, black and wave-less, was worn long and looked very shiny, like silk. It was cut straight across her forehead, and straight across her back.

She wore a very simple deep-blue long tunic gathered at the waist by a thick leather belt. The jewels she wore were simple in their beauty, but bedazzling. They were ritual gems that she had inherited from her maternal Vittka ancestors, and she wore them with a pride devoid of vanity.

When Umma saw Morrigan, she rose from her sitting spot and she moved towards the girl in obsequious silence and a knowing gaze. When she was close to her, Umma touched the contours of her face, to which Morrigan reacted by smiling and touching Umma's moving hand.

"My little dream girl...wondrous to see you in waking," Umma said in her broken Gaelic. She had never fully mastered the language of a country which, she felt, was beautiful but incomparable to her much loved, and much missed, motherland.

"I feel so honoured to have met you and Gunar..." Morrigan uttered, looking with warmth into Umma's and Gunar's eyes.

Gunar, tall, slender and rather fit for a man in his early fifties, stood up and smiled with friendliness, his complexion looking pink by contrast with his son's and wife's amber skin. He was very blond, as blood as Haakon. His lips, ruby-hued and thin, broadened into a big smile and then a greeting.

"You are even more beautiful than my wife and my son told me you were. You are also a very special woman: I understand the gods have given you many gifts."

Morrigan was overcome with the warmth of the vibrations that she received from Haakon's parents. "These are good people," she thought. Goodness was the quality she most appreciated in a person. "Beauty fades and cunning dims, but a good heart is everlasting," Airmid used to say.

"Welcome to Iona," Morrigan said sincerely, followed by Airmid, who had been stirring her stew in the fire-pit, and who rose to hug Umma, Gunar and Morrigan's young lover.

Haakon blushed at Airmid's demonstration of affection, but appreciated it. He felt immediately welcome.

"Thank you for being so hospitable and so kind to us," Haakon said, feeling very much at home. He took a place around the table while Morrigan looked at Airmid with beaming eyes full of happiness and excitement.

Airmid loved seeing her girl looking like that, and she found it amusing to observe how chatty and exuberant Morrigan became when she felt joyous, and she had never seen her as alive as that.

"I understand you two truly honoured Belenos this Beltane!" Airmid murmured to Haakon and Morrigan with her characteristically forward but well-meaning sense of humour.

Morrigan laughed and nodded affirmatively.

"That we have done...and plan to keep doing," she replied in kind, while Haakon blushed so violently he wished he could become invisible.

Gunar laughed heartily, appreciating Airmid's open humour, while Umma was not quite sure of what she heard, so her husband translated it for her and she began laughing as well.

"It makes me wish I was young again!" She said.

"It makes me wish for a lover!" Airmid added, and everyone roared, even Haakon.

"We very much approve of your love," Gunar said.

"We know," Morrigan said, knowing she was speaking for Haakon also. "We consider ourselves very fortunate."

They all ate Airmid's flavourful stew and talked well into the night, of how Umma came to dream of Danu and then of Morrigan. She talked of her heritage of Vittka, and of Gunar's work as ship-maker.

Often Umma spoke in Suomi, the language she had learned before Norse, and Haakon and Gunar took turns translating.

Morrigan looked with astonishment and admiration at how Haakon shifted from one language to the other, and to the other. He was certainly very bright and full of surprises.

"Will you teach me to speak like you do?" Morrigan asked Haakon tenderly.

"I will be happy to," he replied and kissed the inside of her wrist.

Morrigan found Haakon even more provocative when she heard him speaking languages that were foreign to her. She wanted him right then, but the realization that she must wait until later to love him, crushed her.

She took his hand and squeezed it with as much erotic intensity as she was capable of under the circumstances, and gazed in his eyes. He gazed back with as much passion and desire, looking forward to being alone with her. They both ate very little and dreamt of making love.

"Gunar," Airmid said. "Tell us about your trade."

Gunar cleared his throat. "Well, I build curraghs, your traditional boats, but I also build smaller ones in the manner of the Suomi shipwrights. I fasten them together with deer sinew, not nails, and with withes of willow, rather than with keels. Each boat can carry up to twelve people. I learned this craft in my days as trader with the Suomi people, and that's how I met my wife."

"I am so pleased to hear that you build boats; the man who had the job of master shipwright on our island has grown very old, and we will soon need a new master-builder. Would you like the job?" Airmid offered.

"I am honoured to accept work, and very grateful to you for offering it to me. It has been always hard for us to re-establish ourselves after each move," Gunar said, as Umma also expressed her gratitude.

"Umma, tell us about your heritage," Morrigan asked. Umma's eyes smiled.

"She loves nothing better," Gunar said, delighted in his wife's joy.

Umma made it clear that it was very difficult for her to talk at lengths about this subject in any language other than Suomi, and asked Haakon to translate for her.

"You need to practice the ancient speak," she added before beginning, looking at her son with pride.

Umma's skin and hair glowed in the subtle light of the many candles flickering all around the room. She sat with her legs folded one under the other and looked still and pensive for a moment, that posture being both a meditative stance, and a sign of respect towards the art and ancestry that she was about to bring to life through her words.

Morrigan was as excited as she usually felt when on the brink of a mystical revelation, and could not keep her eyes off Umma's jewellery, a necklace and pendant-earrings set made up of icy blue crystals which evoked an aura of magic around Umma's person.

Umma began to speak in the ancestral language of her people, talking in a well modulated voice which resounded warm and rich around the room, and Haakon began translating while Morrigan watched and listened, spellbound.

"In the far, far north, my people carved a living out of ice and later, when the Norse traders travelled that far, we extended our hospitality to them and the benefit of our magic.

"The Thul, or Vittka, was a wise woman who had been trained to recite incantations from a very young age, and had both the responsibility and the honor to pass on The Art to her daughters, if she had any, or to train some other gifted little girl if she did not have a daughter of her own.

"I remember..." Umma said, her voice broken by emotion, her eyes glistening with nostalgic tears. "My grandmother. She was a small woman, like myself, but looked majestic and powerful once she entered her role of soothsayer.

"She wore a blue cloak bedecked with gemstones all the way down to the hems. Around her neck, she wore these crystals; at her earlobes, these very earrings hung." She touched her pendants.

"A black hood of lambskin covered her head and her silvery hair. In one of her hands she held a staff which had a knob on it mounted with brass, and many sparkling stones were set at the base of the knob.

"I remember as it were not so long ago, being a little girl. My grandmother would look at me, holding my hand, and would say: 'You watch me, and you learn,' sounding so solemn and making me feel so very important, and mindful. I would not allow myself to miss a single instant of her doing.

"I was fascinated by the pouch which hung from her touchwood belt. The large skin pouch contained her runes, her magical charms. She walked slowly in her hairy calfskin shoes and I loved the lilting sound that the tiny, round tin-knobs at the ends of her shoelaces made as she walked.

"She was greeted very respectfully by the people who had summoned her to come and look at their homestead. Once there, she rose on a platform that had been set up just for her, while I gathered around her along with the other women in a circle. She looked still and eerie, not like the grandmother who held me and sang to me, and then she closed her eyes and uttered chants and prophecies of good fortune to befall the homestead.

"Later, she answered questions and then we moved on to another farm, after having been fed a warm meal that had also been prepared especially for us."

"Who, or what, did your grandmother invoke in her incantations?" Morrigan asked.

"She ordered the evil spirits to vanish and summoned the good ones to appear and to dwell in that house."

"Do Vittkas have waking visions?" Airmid wanted to know.

"We do, but I'm afraid that our magic is not as sophisticated as yours."

"I don't believe so; yours seems to be less metaphysical and more practical. It will be of great help to this community if we could combine our magic," Airmid proposed.

Umma felt moved. She switched to Gaelic. "No one, since we came to your beautiful land, has ever showed an interest in my Craft. I have been helping my husband and my son with the curragh-making. It is such a joy to be able to be a Vittka again."

Umma looked at Morrigan and spoke.

"After the birth of Haakon we waited for more children, but they did not come. The daughter I awaited, never came. The son to be Haakon's brother was stillborn. Forever I asked Freyja, goddess of marriage and of the little children, why was my son stillborn? Why are you not sending us a daughter?

"Now, and ever since I saw you in the dreaming, I know you will be my daughter," Umma emphasized by placing her hand on her heart. "These crystals are yours one day."

Morrigan found herself unable to stop her tears from flowing freely, for everyone to see. She could not escape her feelings and was learning not to hide them. She rose from her spot, walked to Umma and embraced her.

Airmid was moved and happy, but she did not interrupt Morrigan and Umma's moment. She knew that Umma, being younger than herself, might outlive her, and she could take her place as Morrigan's mother and High Priestess of Iona.

***

The day after their dinner at Airmid's home, Umma, Gunar and Haakon were introduced to, and welcome by, the community. Haakon's parents were to dwell near Airmid. Haakon would live with Morrigan, as it is befitting a relationship between lovers.

Morrigan and Haakon spent every day together, loving each other, enjoying nature, talking, swimming and dancing. During one of the festival's evening dances, Morrigan noticed that Nyssien, still convalescent, was among the crowd of onlookers. She tried to ignore him, tried to dismiss the look she saw in his eyes again, one of vengeance and bitterness.

"Let's stop dancing, please," Morrigan asked Haakon, who obliged her, and they walked out of the human ring encircling the other dancers. The lovers walked to the seashore, their very favourite place second only to the cabin where they knew each other's flesh.

"Why do you look sad?" Haakon asked.

She could not lie, never could, and since she had been asked, did not conceal the truth from Haakon.

"There was a young man in the crowd who was looking at us with hate. I know him, he's violent and vile. He was always loath of my powers and not too long ago he came to the woods and tried to rape me. He is the one who cut between my breasts. I broke his nose, and now he wants revenge over me, but I don't want to have to deal with him again, nor do I want you to become involved in this matter. I don't want any harm to come to you and if I must, I will kill him rather than let him come near you."

"You broke his nose?" Haakon repeated with a chuckle.

"In two parts of its bridge, Airmid tells me. She had to heal him."

Haakon stopped walking, put his hands on her shoulders and kissed the wound between her breasts.

"I love you. You are as beautiful as you are courageous. I know that you can take care of yourself, but remember, I can take care of myself too. Should he attack me, it would in no way be your fault. Should he come near you, I will kill him," Haakon said. She sought shelter in his arms, looking very small next to him.

"I love you," she whispered looking up at him, and his lips met hers half way. His blond silk threads caressed the contours of her face, while her hair waved in the wind and they both breathed in the smell of the sea, which they cherished, and resumed their stroll by the blue water.

"I was born in a village by the sea and, like you, I have always lived by the sea. It is very much a part of my soul, of who I am and I can see that it is very much a part of you," Haakon said perceptively.

"It is true, the sea is all I know, and this island. I cannot conceive of living away from either. Tell me we'll always live here," she said with a smile.

"I would not want to live anywhere else," he reassured her.

Chapter Twenty-eight

The evening began to descend on Iona. The bright colours of the island seemed to fade. The voices of the feasting people became progressively fainter as the night advanced.

Haakon and Morrigan walked quite far from the village and reached the site in which Morrigan had seen the spirits of her parents at Samhain, among the tall menhir on the hill by the sea.

They entered the circle of stones illuminated by the moonlight, and watched the light dance and break on the surface of the deep blue waters. They kissed and pledged their love to one another among whispers, in-between breaths full of longing and desire, in the rapture of the embrace. They teased each other's lips before they let them come together, and later fell asleep in each other's arms.

The morning found them huddled still, trying to keep warm. They began their walk up to the cabin. Haakon wanted to know more about Nyssien, afraid that he might attack Morrigan again.

"Was Nyssien punished for what he did?" He asked.

"It is the law here on Iona that once a man has attacked a woman he has to be exiled. Because Nyssien is still convalescing he has been given time to get his things in order, but he must leave as soon as Airmid and the Council will find him healthy enough to sustain the journey out of Iona. He can never come back," Morrigan explained. "But don't worry; I don't think that he would attempt to hurt me again." She smiled to reassure Haakon.

"Whatever happens, know that I'll keep you safe; you won't have to carry the burden of defending yourself all alone. Not as long as I live and breathe," Haakon declared.

"I know I can count on you; after all, I know I am not invincible," Morrigan confessed brimming with appreciation for Haakon's protectiveness of her and for his declaration of loyalty.

Once at the cabin they warmed up by eating some porridge, and they talked.

"Do you know how lucky you are to have grown up with your parents? I wish more than anything to have known mine, and my twin brother," Morrigan commented.

"There is so much I don't know about you. You heard all about my family last night and I am now realizing how hard it must have been for you to grow up without your parents and your brother. I wasn't even aware that you had any siblings and, as it turns out, you have a twin brother! Tell me, did he die also, or does he live somewhere else?"

They spent their morning and afternoon talking. She told him everything: the circumstances of her parents' death; the kidnapping of

Lugh and most of all, about the mission that she and Lugh had been assigned to fulfill, all the while feeling anxious at the thought that all that information might scare Haakon away.

"I will be with you always," Haakon intuitively reassured her after he had listened to her life story. "I will fight for you and with you. We'll find Lugh, and I know that once he has met you and heard you out, he will believe in you, you'll see." He kissed her hands softly. She cried.

"You give me such hope, such comfort, but I cannot help feeling badly if I think that now, because of me, you are involved also. I truly believe that it would make me feel better if you stayed here when the time comes for me to go to my brother."

"Never. I cannot let you go alone and wait here without knowing whether you will ever come back. Do you really expect me to stay behind?"

"I know that I will not be able to stop you from coming with me, and that's what is scaring me. I feel responsible." Haakon stroked her cheeks.

"Why do you suppose Danu appeared in my mother's dreams after I was born? Why do you think she led us here? I believe that you and I were not only meant to love each other, but also to fight alongside one another. I feel honoured to be part of such a noble plan. I also was born with a gift," Haakon revealed.

Morrigan looked in his eyes trying to see, trying to understand. She had sensed that he was special, but attributed that to the fact that she was so in love with him.

"Come with me," he said grabbing Morrigan by the hand, leading her outside. They ran all the way down to the village, to the sea.

"Wait by the shore and watch me," he told Morrigan, who looked very puzzled and very curious as she watched him run and climb the massive rocks overlooking the sea. She saw him position himself to dive but, in the moment just before his body was supposed to impact the water, she saw her beloved turn into an eagle which soared low, almost grazing the surface of the sea, and which came to rest next to her, where she watched it change back into Haakon.

She was speechless, flabbergasted, and all she was able to do was to look at him with an intensity which scared him.

"My love, it's just me, Haakon. This is who I am, a human being. The gods saw it fit to invest me with this power by which I can transmute into an eagle. There must be a reason for it and I don't know it yet. When I was a child, I just thought it was funny, and I wondered how I could do it. Now I wonder why I can do it."

Morrigan, who had regained her capacity to think and speak, looked at him with tenderness, caressed his face and said: "I am sure you have been given this gift for a reason. We'll find it out together." She curled up to his body.

"My parents gave me a nickname when they found out what I could do."

"What is it?" She asked, looking into his magnificent blue eyes with infinite love and fascination.

"Erilaz."

"What does it mean?"

"Erilaz is the quality of magic incarnated into human beings. It is the point where the reality that we know and the reality of the realms of the spirit meet. I hope you understand what I mean."

"I do, I do. At times, I hear the voice of the wind speaking to me. I hear the voices of the trees, of the leaves, of nature, as distinctly as I hear any human. They communicate actual words and thoughts to me. At first I believed I had too much imagination, but as I grew older and my purpose in life became clear, I realized that I had been allowed to overstep the boundary between the world of humans, and the world of the spirits and I no longer feared the voices." Haakon listened, his eyes full of wonder.

"We both have been given powerful *Ond*, life-force. Among my father's people the possession of this force, in such an intensity as you and I do, is said to assure good fortune and success to its possessor," Haakon commented.

"We call that Nwyvre. We all carry part of this universal life force within us, some with more strength than others. See? We do understand each other so well!" Morrigan said enthusiastically. They kissed passionately and lay on the sand to listen to each other's heartbeat.

Chapter Twenty-nine

Haakon and Morrigan stopped by Airmid's house to visit with her, and found his parents there also. Haakon told them what Morrigan had revealed to him about herself; her estranged brother, her mission in life, and the likely possibility that he would become involved in fighting her battle. They were neither apprehensive or surprised.

"I always knew you had been given a special task by the creatress," Umma said. "I always hoped I would not lose you to it."

"All we can do, you, Gunar and myself, is just that: hope that we'll not lose these children to the destiny they must fulfill," Airmid said.

Haakon and Morrigan joined the feasting crowd once again. Morrigan, drawn in by the rhythmic and potent music of the drums and of the bagpipes began to dance.

Haakon enjoyed watching her move with such grace and lightness. She twirled and almost glided, as her feet and arms moved instinctively and skilfully to the sound of the all-enveloping music.

Suddenly Haakon felt someone's breath on the back of his neck and heard a voice. He turned and he knew he was staring at Nyssien. A look of harshness and greyness appeared on Haakon's face. Morrigan kept dancing, unaware of what was happening.

"Let me warn you," Nyssien hissed with a smirk. "She may love like a woman, but she fights like a man."

"How sad it must be for you to have known her fury, but never her love," Haakon retorted. Nyssien left abruptly, infuriated, hating Haakon too, and Morrigan more than ever.

When the music stopped, Morrigan, out of breath, sat by Haakon, who told her what had just happened and he swore again to her that should Nyssien come near her, he would kill him without hesitation.

"He's just barking. He is so weak, so pathetic. I wouldn't worry about him," she said, but Haakon remained disturbed and pensive for the rest of the evening, whose colours, sounds and smells became a blur to him.

The following day Haakon seemed to have regained his peace of mind. They decided not to go down to the village at all. Haakon was going to teach Morrigan how to spear fish in the very brook where she had died and reborn; where she had touched the bottom of the secret well of genetic memory.

Morrigan watched Haakon spear the fish very skilfully, and relished the sexual rush she received from seeing his naked torso splash so dynamically in and out of the water. The wet leather strips which made up his bracelet and necklace, set against his young, amber complexion, made him look very virile.

135

He was a creature of contrasts and she loved that. She loved his very blond, very straight hair; she loved the ultramarine blue of his eyes and the tawny shade of his skin which did not seem to belong with the rest of his colouring and yet, was so becoming to him and so appealing.

He loved her for the same reason; she was a mysterious and extraordinary woman. He was also attracted to her exotic looks.

"My mother was part Latin and part Greek," she had once told him, but he had no frame of reference. He had never seen a person from the Mediterranean lands, and assumed that all women there must be as enchanting as Morrigan, although he was convinced that no other woman could be as exquisite.

Once out of the water he walked up to her and pulled her close to him.

"I never saw more beautiful eyes. I love your brown eyes; they become transparent in the light. I love your dark hair, and how it glistens, red in the sun," he said burying his face in her mane, inhaling its intoxicating lavender and clary sage scent.

As they walked back to the cabin to cook the fish that Haakon had speared, Morrigan became vigilant and restless.

"What is the matter?" Haakon asked.

Morrigan scanned the surroundings. "I have the feeling that we are being watched. Things feel the way they did the night that Nyssien was here."

Haakon looked around too, walked to shake the leaves of nearby bushes, checked behind the trees, furious at the thought that Nyssien might dare stalk Morrigan again. But no one seemed to be around.

"I am confused; when I sense a presence usually someone turns out to be there," Morrigan said.

"Remember, it's Beltane: the doors to the Otherworld are open. Maybe it's the presence of the spirits that you sense, or animals," Haakon suggested. Morrigan did not disagree, but she knew she would have known the difference between a human being and a discarnate entity.

By the time they had arrived at the cabin Morrigan felt she was in a state of quiet panic, as if the fear of being stalked had become more real with every step they had taken towards the house, and she finally felt enlightened.

"Get ready to fight," she said to Haakon, arresting him from proceeding towards the cabin's door. As they backed away from the house, someone leaped down from a tree and landed in front of them.

The boy was not a stranger to Morrigan. He was among those of her peers who had joined Nyssien in teasing and taunting her in a past not too far away. Haakon noticed, reading Morrigan's expression on her face, that she knew the stranger and did not like him.

"Who is he?" Haakon asked Morrigan.

"He is one of the people I told you about, one of those who always despised me," she replied sounding cold, while looking dangerously into Nyssien's friend's eyes.

"What do you want?" She asked the young man. He stepped towards her and Haakon grabbed him by the throat. Morrigan advanced closer towards the boy and motioned Haakon to let him go.

"I asked you what you're doing here," she repeated.

"I am here to deliver a warning on Nyssien's behalf: he will have your body, and devastate your lover's. He's not through with you, and he is serious about vindicating his honour," the messenger said stepping back and beginning to make his way to the village.

"He cannot vindicate his honour, because he has none," Haakon said as the young man turned away.

"I'll kill them both, I swear!" Haakon yelled.

"Haakon," Morrigan said. "I believe that Nyssien is more imbalanced than he is evil. It should not be hard for us to protect ourselves, he is not a master strategist, far from it.

"I hope you are right," he whispered in her ear, and he pulled her close to him and held her. They both found pleasure in a soft wind which carried messages of comfort to their hearts.

Chapter Thirty

A few moons went by before Morrigan and Haakon went back to the village and spoke with Airmid and with Haakon's parents about the threats they had received from Nyssien through his messenger.

"I'm not surprised," Airmid stated. "I suppose if Nyssien is well enough to plan an assault on the two of you, and if he's stupid enough to be so blatant about it, then it's time that he left Iona." Everyone seemed relieved in contemplating the possibility of banishing Nyssien from the island earlier than expected.

"I will pay a visit to him promptly." Airmid seized her cape and headed for the Ilbreach's home. As she expected, Nyssien denied everything, but his parents believed he was guilty.

"What is wrong with you? Wasn't having to leave Iona punishment enough for you, that you had to make it so very imminent?" His mother yelled amidst the tears. "I thought that maybe being hurt by Morrigan had tamed your desire to overpower her. I was so wrong!"

"You have disgraced us before. Touch the girl again, and I will take your life myself!" Brian shouted at Nyssien while his face was only a few inches from his son's.

"It was Duncan's own idea to threaten them. I had nothing to do with it," Nyssien said.

"Why would he do that?" Airmid asked.

"Because he hates her too," Nyssien answered, and his mother slapped his face hard.

"I will give you the benefit of the doubt. I shall speak with Duncan now, but you're coming with me," Airmid said while taking him by the arm. He extricated himself from her grip, outraged that she would drag him into a matter with which he claimed he had nothing to do.

"I'll find out with or without you," Airmid said as she walked away.

At Duncan's home, his parents felt anxious about the Druid's unexpected visit. Airmid explained the matter to them and questioned Duncan about it.

"Nyssien asked me to take his threat to Morrigan and Haakon because he's not well enough to climb up to the woods," Duncan explained.

"Nyssien said that the threat was your idea, that he had nothing to do with it," Airmid said. Duncan's face blanched when he realized that Nyssien had used him and betrayed him.

"Nyssien is lying. He told me that he hates Morrigan and Haakon and that, had he had the strength, he would have gone up to the woods himself to make them suffer very painful deaths. He needed me to go up there, he said, because he wanted them to start fearing him; to make them feel the power that he has to take their lives at any given moment."

Everything was clear to Airmid. Nyssien was going to attempt the murders of Haakon and Morrigan and planned to blame them on Duncan, but Duncan had no reason to kill them.

"Why did you consent to take his threats to Morrigan and her lover?" Airmid asked.

"Because Nyssien paid me. He gave me some of the gold pieces that he has been stealing over the years from his parents, and from other people in the village. He was going to use the rest of the gold to take us both away from Iona, he said, to start a new life on the mainland. I told him that I would be his messenger, but not the accomplice in the murders that he was planning," Duncan confessed.

Airmid felt enraged. Duncan had acted greedily and irresponsibly, but what angered her the most was the complete lack of remorse in Duncan for having engaged in the dark conspiracy with Nyssien.

Airmid looked at Duncan's parents, who stood quietly watching and listening to Duncan's involvement with Nyssien. "What your son has done does not seem to me any less damaging than what Nyssien has intention to carry out. I have realized that, disappointingly, there are more evil hearts on the island that I wanted to believe. My eyes have been opened. Duncan and Nyssien are to pack their belongings and leave Iona by tomorrow's dawn, and they are never to come back."

Duncan's face became flushed with amazement and fear, while his father began to cry and his mother sat with her hands covering her eyes.

Duncan's parents cried and begged Airmid for clemency, claiming that their son had not known what he was doing, and to let him stay.

"I wished it could be so," she said. "But Nyssien and Duncan have chosen to be deaf to their conscience and they seem to have no reverence for human life," Airmid said as she tried to hold back her tears and dashed out of Duncan's dwelling, knowing that part of her had died in there, the part which could not stomach being stern and heartless. She knew it had to be so, so that infamy would not proliferate on the island as she had seen it expand and strengthen on the mainland.

She went to Nyssien's home and made her wishes clear to him and to his family then left, on her way to calling an emergency council meeting where she would inform the community of her decision. If approved by the majority, her decision would be implemented. First, she talked to Morrigan, Haakon and his parents about what she had learned, and what she had planned.

Airmid suggested that Morrigan and Haakon spend the night at her place.

"We can take care of ourselves, especially now that we know that Nyssien wants us dead. We'll be safe at the cabin," Haakon said.

"I agree; we are able to look out for ourselves, and for each other," Morrigan echoed.

Airmid reacted. "It is the arrogance of youth and inexperience which speaks through you. It is foolish to challenge danger when you can avert it, and unwise to boast to be invincible. We are all human after all; witches or not, we are all mortal. And one more thing: what I told you to do was a suggestion. Now, it is an order. You two will attend the council meeting which I have called and then you will retire to my house for the night," she concluded, gaining the immediate approval of Haakon's parents.

Haakon blushed with shame and Morrigan, although her pride was hurt, saw the logic in Airmid's decision and admired the authority that, for the very first time, Airmid had not hidden from her. She was proud to see her grandmother think, talk and act like a full-fledged Druid.

"I am sorry if we hurt your feelings Airmid; we did not mean to, we just wanted to prove to you that we can take care of ourselves, when the truth is, we ourselves do not know whether we'd be successful or not. Forgive me if I disappointed you," Morrigan said, while Haakon was too embarrassed to talk.

Airmid smiled at them both. "I knew you would see it my way."

Late that night, while the island was asleep, Airmid sat awake and vigilant by the hearth. Even in her own house she felt that Morrigan and Haakon might not be safe from the evil and the madness of Nyssien. Small noises made her jumpy. She looked outside the window and peeked out the door many times, discovering no one lurking about. Then, she fell asleep.

Nyssien had kept his own vigil outside of Airmid's home too, waiting for her to give up and succumb to sleep. He suspected, but had not been sure, that Morrigan and Haakon would spend the night at Airmid's, so he sent Duncan to the cabin while he kept his post outside Airmid's house. By then, Duncan had observed enough to be convinced that Morrigan and Haakon were not there.

"You're falling asleep, old crone," Nyssien whispered, while he stood in complete stillness within the darkness of a moonless night. "I liked you better when you were spineless, but now, now you have challenged my greatness and you shall pay for it!"

Slowly Nyssien made his way from the back of the house around it, to the window of one of the two bedchambers. All he needed to do was to break in. Afterwards, he'd find and kill the lovers then, it would be Airmid's turn.

A curragh that he and Duncan had prepared to escape awaited them by the shore. He had told Duncan he would light a torch as a signal that they were ready to leave. In case Duncan found Haakon and Morrigan sleeping at the cabin, he was to kill them and then meet Nyssien by the curragh.

Duncan had been so outraged by Airmid's decision to exile him, that he found it poetic justice to be able to murder her loved ones and then leave. Nyssien never told him that he intended to kill Airmid also; Duncan wanted her to be alive so that he, even if from afar, could enjoy the thought of her ceaseless sorrow.

Nyssien found both the bedrooms windows sealed with wooden shutters. Somehow he had thought that it would have been easy to force them open, but in reality he found the task as hard as trying to get through the front door. He decided to gamble and to enter through the window which had not been nailed shut, the one next to which Airmid was sitting.

He peeked through the window and having seen that Airmid was still asleep, as quietly as he could he began to make his entry into the Druid's house. Once in, his steps became extremely light. He glanced at Airmid.

"Fast asleep," he murmured, pleased with himself for being inconspicuous and in control.

Swiftly, he proceeded towards the bedchambers, protecting the flame of the small candle he was carrying in his cupped hands. He happened to enter Airmid's first.

Although he realized that Morrigan and Haakon were not there, the sight of a crystal sphere set on a bedside table distracted him, and he began to estimate how much gold he might receive in exchange for it on the mainland. He advanced closer to the object and saw his image reflected in it, in the dim candle-light.

As his image was reflected on the surface of the sphere, so it refracted into Airmid's mind, waking her. She opened her eyes suddenly, feeling her blood rush through her system, aware of the intruder.

She walked slowly and quietly to her room and having recognized Nyssien from the back, she headed for the other room anxiously, but in utter silence.

The door of the guest bedchambers was ajar; Nyssien approached it looking at the sleeping lovers with a smile of disdain and victory on his face, while he extracted the dagger from its sheath and felt ready to plunge it into Haakon's heart first, then into Morrigan's. But not before he had made sure that she had seen her lover die. He would keep his hand on her mouth to muffle her cries and then he, excited by the rush of power he'd feel, would penetrate her, then stab her through the heart and, he believed, triumph over her.

Airmid stood very still and very tall behind the guest bedroom door when, as Nyssien lifted his knife to plunge it into Haakon's body, Airmid, summoning ancestral powers of cosmic energy emitted a thought which caused all the bones inside of Nyssien's body to shatter, subjecting him to a level of pain he had never even imagined could exist.

Nyssien's wild cries woke Morrigan and Haakon abruptly. They looked erratically in the surrounding darkness, getting ready to fight.

"Don't be afraid, it's me," Airmid said. "I had to kill Nyssien, otherwise he would have killed you."

Nyssien lay lifeless and harmless on the floor, his body reduced to a heap of contorted flesh. His face seemed buried in the cold stone pavement.

Upon hearing Airmid's voice Morrigan and Haakon crawled out of bed and followed her out of the room, unable to not stumble on Nyssien's corpse.

In the hearth room, where Airmid had lit some candles, Morrigan and Haakon looked at her, bewildered, not yet sure that Nyssien had actually died at the hand of Airmid whom, shaken and confused, stood by the fire.

"We must inform his parents and call yet another council meeting. I am not proud of what I've done, but I am convinced that it was necessary. He had been pursuing his own death for a long time. It was bound to happen.

"I feel sadness for his death. I wish I had not had to do it." Airmid broke down crying and collapsed in the chair by the window. Morrigan promptly covered her grandmother with a blanket and lit a more robust fire.

Haakon asked Morrigan to follow him to their bedchambers with a candle. He dragged Nyssien's body into the light of the fireside in the main room, where they all stared at it, half hoping they were dreaming, half grasping their first breath of freedom since the troubles with Nyssien had begun.

"Say something!" Airmid implored. "...I'm a murderer now!" She cried burying her face in her hands.

"I love you," Morrigan said looking at Airmid with tenderness and tears in her eyes. "I love you because you have always looked out for me; if you had not intervened you know he would have killed us. I do believe that his end was coming, like you said. Part of me grieves for him, as I still wonder whether Nyssien chose to be evil or was simply deranged."

Haakon warmed some milk for Airmid; she was shivering uncontrollably.

"We'll never know," Airmid said amidst the tears. "I just wish I had not been his executioner. How am I going to tell his parents?"

"Let Haakon and I talk to them before the council is gathered. Maybe by then you'll be able to face them."

"Thank you Morrigan, but I have to speak to them myself. I will do anything I can to help them and I realize that they are entitled to hate me. To us, Nyssien was a threat; to them, it was their boy, and I took him away from them."

Morrigan feared for Airmid's emotional well being; her peace of mind had been shattered when she realized that she had taken a life. Could she live with that, or would she torture herself till the end of her days? Morrigan turned to Airmid.

"You had no choice. If you had not intervened Haakon and I would be dead. Would you feel less guilty had that been the case?"

Airmid answered with a newly found, faint smile. "Of course not. You know that life would be unbearable to me had that happened."

***

Days had gone by since Nyssien's death and burial. The island was in mourning for three moons, grieving not for the absence of Nyssien the scoundrel, but for that of Nyssien the human being as he had been born: beautiful, valuable, full of potential.

Duncan confessed to having been the accomplice in Nyssien's murderous plans and was exiled from Iona. Nyssien's parents, although they fully understood the circumstances of their son's death as people, could not accept the reality of it as his parents, and decided to join Luibra, their other son, on the mainland. There they would try to start fresh and make a better life for their son and for themselves.

"I never thought that the little girl I nursed as my own, would turn out to be the cause of my son's death." Fionnualla whispered as she hugged Morrigan good-bye.

"I am so sorry," Morrigan cried, and releases Fionnualla from the embrace.

Chapter Thirty-one

The spring air was light and effervescent, flowers and plants were covered with dew in the early hours of the morning and Iona buzzed with activity.

Crops were been sowed; fishermen and women went out to sea, while shopkeepers and herders were busier than ever.

"This is the happiest time of my life," Morrigan told Haakon. "Do you think we'll always be this happy?"

Haakon kissed the tip of her nose. "As long as we are together we'll be happy and, unless the gods wish it differently, I believe we'll be together forever." He pulled her close to him, as they were both sitting on the beach with their backs against a rock.

"I feel this impulse, this inner-surge of psychic energy surfacing from the depths of my soul. I think I am ready to project myself outside my body. I know I am ready, I feel it, but I am also scared in a way that I never have been before you came into my life," Morrigan said. "I fear that, should something go wrong during projection, I might be lost in space and I won't be able to return to you, and I know I couldn't bear that."

"What could go wrong? From what I hear from my mother..." Morrigan interrupted him."...Your mother has experienced leaving the body?"

"Yes, of course; it is as much a part of being a Vittka as it is of being a Druid. You have nothing to fear; my mother and Airmid can tell you that.

"When you're out there, there is a link between you and your body, like an umbilical cord, because you are a baby born into the dimension of bodylessness, but still, not totally autonomous. That cord is there not just to ensure that you return but to remind you that you must return, that you still have a lot of living and learning to do as an incarnate entity. Should the creatress need you dead to the physical world, you would be," Haakon said.

"Such wisdom," Morrigan whispered lovingly, while caressing Haakon's lips with her fingers.

"Meeting you, loving you and being loved by you, has brought me the greatest happiness I have ever known and I never want to lose it," she said with sadness woven in the tone of her voice.

"I feel that somehow, before we were born, we might have chosen our paths, but I also believe that Danu will reward us for our actions by allowing us to survive, to keep loving one another. We deserve that much. We deserve to live our lives for ourselves once our duty is done. We might want to have children some day," he said.

Morrigan's eyes glossed over; she had thought about those things too, wondering if they would ever come true. She rested her head on his shoulder and began to cry quietly.

"Right now I feel selfish," she said. "I want to forget about what must be done and I just want to love you. I want to live a happy, quiet life with you."

"Trust me, we will," Haakon comforted her.

She looked up at him, into his tender blue eyes.

"I hope so."

That night, the compelling feeling of readiness for astral flight that Morrigan had been having surfaced more powerfully than ever, while she lay in her bed next to the sleeping Haakon.

As she tried to deny the feeling of anxiety and anguish, by hoping for sleep that she knew would not come, a sensation of dread vibrated cold inside of her, and she felt that she had touched the bottom of hopelessness. She found herself in the middle of a spiritual labour that had started and which was going to cause her soul to be born out of her quivering physical body, into what she perceived as 'the dark nothingness of space,' and she could not stop it.

"It must happen," she thought while lying on her back, her hand shaking over her racing heart.

"Haakon, wake up...Haakon..." she whispered as she touched his arm with her other hand and shook him lightly but steadily.

To her surprise, Haakon woke. One glance at her, and he realized what was happening. He was on his knees next to her, and held both her hands.

"I'll be here with you, you'll see me from above. I'll keep holding your hands while you're out of your body, and I will be here when you come back into it.

"Breathe slowly and deeply, like Airmid taught you. Ease into the sensation," he said, his voice providing her with a warmth which sedated her.

"...It's happening" she said, her voice faint and fading, "...it's hap..." she had not had time to complete her sentence when she felt herself gushing out of her body, as she imagined she must have been born out of her mother's.

Bodiless, Morrigan found herself floating in space; it was dark and infinite but, "...It isn't 'nothingness,'" she observed.

"This space feels full of life. The dark has a concealed vibrancy, an inner-light. It isn't scary here, and it doesn't feel that lonely," she thought.

"Airmid..." she remembered; she had to appear to her to show her that this task, too, had been accomplished, and as she thought of Airmid she found her ethereal self in her grandmother's bedroom.

"I knew you were coming" the old Druid said, smiling at the projection of Morrigan's astral body which was wafting before her eyes.

Morrigan felt herself giggle mentally, and telepathically asked Airmid: "What do you think?"

Airmid laughed. "I think you are wonderful, child," she replied, as Morrigan thought herself back into her physical body, where she "woke" into her lover's arms.

"I missed you. I love you, I love you, I love you! You did it, and you came back to me!" Haakon said with excitement while he kissed every bit of Morrigan's face.

"I love you too," she said smiling.

"Tell me about the time when you were a little boy in Norway: what do you remember about it?" Morrigan asked while they cuddled.

"I don't recall much about our lives there, except the almost constant sight of snow. I remember the biting cold of the long, dark winters and how I longed for the sight of the spring sun. I remember pining for 'the sun seasons.'

"I loved it all, though; I still do. I love the sight of the boundless sea, the fjords, the beauty and the scent of the woods, the way the sun shimmers on the ice and the snow as its season approaches," Haakon said nostalgically.

"Will we go there some day?" Morrigan asked. "Will you guide me there through the woods, and swim with me in the sea of your land? The place sounds magical to me, maybe because you are one of its children and I love you so."

"We'll travel to my motherland some day, I promise you," Haakon said between kisses. "But I don't think I could live anywhere but here, in this beautiful, enthralling island of yours where I finally found my sun. I love you, I really and truly love you."

"I feel as though I have known you forever; I cannot imagine life without you. Did we really just meet not long ago? My life before you came seems unreal. It is as if I had been with you, fell asleep and dreamt myself alone and lonely, but I finally woke and there you were," she cried quietly.

"I'm here, I'm here now, and we'll never be apart, I promise you," he reassured her, and wiped her tears with the back of his hand.

"I believe in you, and I believe in our love," Morrigan said smiling through the tears.

Chapter Thirty-two

"The time is propitious. I have studied the heavens for quite a while and this is the right time for you to make your move successfully towards Clodagh," Rhiannon announced to Urien in the privacy of their bedchambers, immediately catching his undivided attention, while she was still buried in a heap of celestial maps.

He was so excited he was practically salivating. "Do you mean now, tonight? When?" He precipitated to ask.

"Try to contain your excitement in my presence; it sickens me," she said with a twist of her lips.

"I mean starting tomorrow, when the sun is setting, you are more likely to get her to cooperate with your threats. A certain planets' alignment indicates that she will be at her most vulnerable tomorrow after sundown.

"I have work to do. I must arrange a diversion for Lugh and one for Iweridd at that time. After the first time, it will be up to you and Clodagh to get together when it is safe, until the stars will indicate the appropriate time to reveal to Lugh what a whore his little love really is.

"I'm hoping that, by then, she will have come to actually enjoy the lovemaking with you, to the point that she will be very convincing when telling Lugh about her betrayal. Ah! By the way, I have subtly explained to Iweridd that should she, or her daughter, mention anything to Lugh about who we really are and how we came to be in power, I will personally eviscerate Clodagh. She swore utter obedience to my wishes, as I expected. She even felt compelled to reassure me of the fact that neither herself or her daughter, had ever dared speak of us to Lugh," Rhiannon gloated.

Urien's heart, brimming with gutter-level lust, kept missing a beat as he rolled down the corridors of the castle, carrying within a juvenile feeling of anticipation, and a predatory instinct the intensity of which he had not felt for many years.

One moon had gone by and sunset approached. Rhiannon had arranged things so that Lugh would be returning from a hunting trip. Although he disliked the hunt, he had gone with Iweridd under the pretext that, because Clodagh's seventeenth birthday was close, it would be a nice gesture if they caught some game to be prepared especially for her birthday-celebration banquet. Urien was to stay at the castle and entertain Clodagh, while Rhiannon faked a headache so that she could retire to her bedchambers.

Clodagh sat in her room looking out the window, expecting to see Lugh and Iweridd come back, she had been told, from running some errands for Rhiannon.

She felt very lonely, even sad. She was used to spending most of her days in Lugh's company. She decided to lie on her back and rest. She closed her eyes and she recalled what had happened between she and Lugh just a few days earlier, when they had become truly lovers.

She kept seeing in her mind the image of Lugh when, in the thick of the woods, he took her into his arms and they began kissing with growing intensity and mounting passion. She knew she was ready; Lugh had never pushed her. He had been waiting for her to want to make love, and so it happened.

Her heartbeat grew faster and she felt warmth suffuse her entire being at the memory of the two of them collapsing onto the soft, grass-covered ground, all sounds and sights blocked out except for each other's.

She lay underneath him, her breasts heaving, their lips being gently bitten by one another, her knees raised off the ground and his hand searching between her warm thighs, then quivering while undoing her blouse to finally see, touch and kiss her breasts.

"I want to see your body, I want to feel your skin," she remembered herself utter in the heat of what felt like a delirium of love, and so he bared his beautiful body to her, to which the presence of many scars, large and small, brought a higher value as she watched every inch of it shake with desire.

She remembered tearing her own clothes off; they felt suddenly constraining and superfluous, their presence between their bodies only an unnatural barrier.

She saw his handsome face slowly getting closer to hers and watched his full red lips part, understanding their thirst, which she instinctively knew was the same as her own.

As their mouths touched so did their bodies. They took each other with a tender fury and felt like they were being molten into one another, body and soul, until they both cried with pleasure and shed tears of passion.

As Clodagh realized that she was crying, she heard a knock on the door.

"Come in..." she said while she quickly sat up at the edge of her bed, wiped off her tears and smoothed down her hair.

"Good evening" Urien said, letting himself in and shutting the door behind him, certainly taking her by surprise.

"What is the matter Urien?" Clodagh asked while getting on her feet, trying to hide her rising anxiety.

"Oh!" Urien said advancing smugly towards her. "Nothing is the matter, my dear, just...visiting."

She shivered inside; everything about his behaviour, physical and verbal, was very disturbing.

"Lugh and mother should be coming home soon," she said firmly, partially to shift the focus from 'them' to something else, and partially to warn him, to let him know he was not welcome to her room, much less to close the door behind him.

"I doubt that they'll get here before it gets dark. I just have this feeling that we were fated to entertain each other tonight," Urien said, becoming increasingly flagrant and excited.

Clodagh felt a cold draft of dread blow mercilessly throughout her. She trembled and, although she tried to hide it, Urien was able to pick up on her fear and to feed off of it.

He moved very near to her and caressed her face, which turned crimson out of disgust and out of fright.

"...After all, I am your king and I can do with you whatever I wish," he warned.

She scuttled from under the rough touch of his hand and became animated.

"You are the king but you do not own people, least of all me...don't you care about Lugh? Don't you know that touching me would not only hurt me, but your son also? You will lose his love, his trust and his respect," she intimidated.

He applauded, behaving in much the same arrogant way he did with Rhiannon, feeling uncomfortable and inadequate in the presence of a confident woman.

"Very well spoken!" He hissed, sending a deep wave of revulsion through Clodagh. "...And such logic! Question is, you don't really believe that I want my son to find out about this, do you? You see," he continued, bringing his hands together, as if in prayer and touching his lips with the tips of his fingers. "Lugh may think of you as one of us, in a noble, dignified sort of way, and I have nothing against supporting that illusion of his, as long as it keeps him happy.

"Me, well, I see you for what you are: a peasant piece of ass, and I shall take you and enjoy you in any way I want, anytime I please. Is that clear?" He yelled out his latter words, breaking his suave facade and revealing to her the violent side she knew he would have.

Rather than feeling intimidated, Clodagh gained the strength to defend herself from the outrage she had felt upon hearing his offensive words.

"You'll never have me!" She screamed. "I may be a piece of ass to you, but I am a valuable human being to myself, to Lugh and to my mother. You so much as try to touch me, I'll scream so loud I'll wake

Rhiannon and attract everybody's attention in the castle. Most importantly, I will tell Lugh about it, I swear I will, and I'll help him kill you if we have to...." She yelled at the top of her lungs, surprised that the guards had not come in to check up on her, as she walked towards the door, opened it and showed him out.

Urien slammed the heavy door shut, locked it, grabbed her by the shoulders and shook her.

"Don't you dare talk to me like that! Don't you dare showing me out of my own house!" He yelled as he slapped her hard across the face, to which she cried out loudly. He began tearing the clothes off of her and put his hand over her mouth. "I will have you, and you cannot tell Lugh or anybody, and do you know why?" She shook her head. "...Because if you do, I will personally murder your wretched mother! I would enjoy taking that piece of trash out of my house by the hair, and killing her in brutal and painful ways...."

Clodagh bit his hand and screamed for the last time and then was mute. Realizing she had no choice, she grimly and quietly succumbed to his violence, swearing to herself that some day the truth would be known and Lugh would understand, because he'd believe in her, and not in the words of his lecherous father.

***

Clodagh did not see Lugh that evening, or her mother. She gave word that she was not feeling well and would go to sleep early. Lugh heard the news from Rhiannon, who had felt pleased upon hearing from Urien that he had been successful in his pursuit.

As much as he wanted to see Clodagh, Lugh respected her request and went to bed happy, thinking that he would see her the next day.

Urien's assault had left Clodagh devastated. Soon after raping her, Urien had gone with an expression of utter power and satisfaction on his face and she felt a shame and a guilt that she could not justify.

He had threatened her mother's life, how could she refuse to comply? He took not only her body but a chunk of her soul and stomped on them, yet, inexplicably to her, she had this bizarre feeling of being dirty.

"Lugh, oh Lugh! I didn't want him to touch me." She murmured those words over and over in a state of shock, soon after she had been left to lie on the floor where the infamous one had violated her in the worst way she could have been violated, and she wanted her wholeness back. She pined for the impossible chance to go back in time, to when he had entered her room, and to run away from him unscathed, on her way to meeting her mother and Lugh, and with them leave Aileach behind.

She knew very well that things could not have gone so smoothly had she tried to escape him. More than likely, Urien's hounds would have caught both she and her mother and killed them anyway. Yet, death sounded like a preferable alternative to the way she felt during the rape and after, and forever after that.

After she had asked a servant to tell Lugh that she had retired early for the night, she cried herself to sleep once she had collapsed face down on her bed. She threw the blankets over her head to hide herself, in shame, from the world and felt as though she had betrayed Lugh.

When tears would no longer come out of her reddened eyes, she felt a deep hatred and a tempestuous rage against Urien. Suddenly, she realized what had really happened: Urien had not made love to her; he had violated her. There was no sexual or emotional bond between them, only duress, and only the certainty deep in her soul, that she would never let him hurt her again if it cost her her life.

"I have to tell Lugh. He will believe me, I know he will, and he will help me to find a safe and far away shelter for mother. Then, we'll plan our own escape."

She fell asleep with that thought of hope. She knew that what had happened could not have been avoided, but she had the option to prevent further violence by confiding in Lugh.

The morning light woke Clodagh and the rape was the first memory and concern on her mind. If her body had not been hurting she could have believed she had just had a nightmare, but it felt all too real. She felt her stomach contract as she quickly ran to the empty water-basin and she vomited in it, feeling her throat burn and constrict to the point that she thought she'd suffocate, and was surprised when she realized that she would live to tell her secret.

A knock on the door came and startled her.

"Who is it?" She yelled, prepared to fight Urien if he had dared to come back for more.

"It's me." She recognized Lugh's voice and she quickly washed her mouth, drinking from the water decanter, and spitting after each ablution until she felt presentable enough to open the door.

Lugh embraced her joyfully immediately after she had let him in and she anchored herself to him by safely clenching her hands behind his neck, and began to cry uncontrollably.

"What is the matter?" Lugh asked worried and surprised, gently trying to break the hug so that he could look her in the eyes.

She could not vocalize at first, then, she whispered to him to please shut the door. Lugh's heart was beating wildly, fearing that something was dreadfully wrong with Clodagh. He had never seen her like that.

She finally let her arms slide off his nape and, as soon as he looked into her eyes, which she immediately cast down, he knew she had been hurt and a feeling of intense panic seized him, especially when he saw the bruises on one side of her face, which were the result of Urien's slap.

"Who hurt you? What did they do to you? Was it one of the soldiers? One of the servants?" He was crazed.

Clodagh was able to collect herself. "Urien raped me last night, and he said that if I did not comply, or I would tell you or anyone about it, he would kill my mother brutally, and I know he can do it. I know he can do it..." she revealed, and it all powerfully overwhelmed Lugh.

"What? Did you say..." he swallowed hard while trembling, looking confused and disconcerted. "...Did you say my fa... Urien raped you, and threatened to kill your mother?"

"You believe me, don't you?" she uttered, her voice in a crescendo of defensiveness. "Why would I lie to you?"

"Oh, no, no love," Lugh sobbed as he sat on her bed, took her by the waist and sat her next to him. "I do believe everything you are saying, but I'm far too shocked right now to face the fact that my father has done this to you.

"What came over him? I always thought he was an honourable man and now, now all my beliefs about him are collapsing. This feels like the end of the world to me. I wasn't here with you, I wasn't here..." Lugh sobbed, looking pale and shivering, and buried his head on her lap.

She held him and lowered her head to touch his.

"I feel dirty Lugh, I feel like I've betrayed myself, you and my mother. But it doesn't make sense, because I did not want this to happen. I never experienced anything more devastating than this."

Lugh put his hand around her nape. "I love you so much. I blame myself for not being here, but how could have I known? I hate Urien, I hate him for hurting you like this. He is a coward! I don't know how yet, but he will pay. We must send Iweridd away first. My mother is the only one who can help us accomplish this: we must tell her without letting Urien know that now I know. Not until your mother is safe."

"I love you Lugh, I knew you would believe me and that you would understand that my mother needs your help. I want you to promise me that once Urien is made aware of the fact that you know what happened, you will not try to fight him. I feel that he would not hesitate to kill you," Clodagh pleaded.

"...He would not hesitate to kill you...." Those words rang more unreal to Lugh than anything he heard up until that point. Urien was capable of anything, and could no longer be trusted; his father, would no longer be loved.

The sound of Clodagh's voice freed Lugh from his thoughts.

"Do you think we can trust Rhiannon? I fear she will not believe me, and that she'll hate me."

"No, no, she won't hate you, because she will believe you. My parents think that I don't know, but I am aware of the fact that they have been distrusting and disliking each other for quite a while, whatever the reasons behind it. I just feel there is conflict between them. My mother will be inclined to believe you because she does not trust Urien. There is no love left between them, if it ever was love that bound them in the first place," Lugh reasoned.

Chapter Thirty-three

"The disgusting bastard! I should have known he'd try something like this; he has done it before! But to hurt you... my sweet Clodagh!" Rhiannon yelled dramatically upon hearing the news from the girl and from Lugh.

"And you, my boy... he hurt my baby!" She said while caressing Lugh's face, convincing him and the girl that she empathized with them, and that she would help them.

"He must not know that Lugh and I know; not until we send Clodagh's mother to a safe place. Once she's gone, I will confront Urien in the presence of you both and I promise, he'll pay!" Rhiannon emphatically pledged.

Clodagh was rather surprised to see Rhiannon so understanding and so cooperative. She had the eerie feeling that the news of her rape had not really shocked Rhiannon, as though she had expected it to happen.

"You said it he did it before. Why did you allow Urien to get away with raping the first time? Why was he not punished for his crime?" Lugh accusatorially asked his mother.

"Because he denied it all, and although I knew he was lying I could not prove that he raped anyone. When I confronted the maids whom he victimized they denied it too, out of fear to be punished by the king. I had to send them away so he could no longer abuse them, but I warned him that, should he violate another woman, our marriage would be truly over.

"You do realize however, that, to all appearances and as sovereigns of this land, we must remain together. We'll simply live in different wings of the castle and he shall lose his privileges as my husband, and some as king. A man who shows such violence and lack of scruples is certainly not fit to rule and to make decisions that call on capacity for good judgment," Rhiannon stated as she sent a servant off to fetch Iweridd.

"You two have to leave now, please. Once I have spoken with your mother, you and Lugh may come and join us and we'll devise a plan. In the meantime, Clodagh, dear, go see my personal physician, Ailim. Tell him what was done to you, not by whom, and he will help you take care of yourself."

"Thank you madam, you are extremely kind and understanding; very generous," Clodagh said kissing Rhiannon's jewelled hands.

Rhiannon batted her lids once, rapidly, and nodded in sign of courteous acceptance of the girl's gratitude.

Lugh kissed his mother's hand and she hugged him. "I love you Lugh" she said, and kissed his forehead.

Iweridd felt very anxious when she was brought to Rhiannon's presence in such secrecy.

"Sit down," Rhiannon ordered Iweridd who obeyed, frightened to death that the meeting might be about Clodagh.

"I don't quite know how to put this; Clodagh was raped by Urien last night."

Iweridd's heart beat faster and faster as she sprang to her feet.

"Sit, Iweridd. I called you here to let you know that I have come to care for Clodagh and, of course, because my son's happiness is at stake, I have promised them both my help, since Clodagh was brave enough to tell Lugh about the assault, and wise enough to appeal to me to protect your life, and her own.

"Urien does not know that anybody is aware of what he did to your daughter. He promised that he would kill you if she told, so I must make up an excuse to send you away to a safe place before confronting him.

"He is an emotional and whimsical man, I am sure that he would carry out his threats just to get even with Clodagh for defying him. She is very worried about you and I feel obliged to put her mind at ease by helping you get away."

Iweridd, who had been crying quietly, stood up and looked at Rhiannon in the eyes, to which Rhiannon reacted by shifting her gaze elsewhere.

"Fair Rhiannon," Iweridd said with a hint of sarcasm woven in the tone of her voice. "You are sending me away to protect my life and Clodagh's peace of mind, you say. I know I have no choice, I shall have to go as far away from Clodagh as you choose to send me. I can only hope that I can trust you when you say that you have Clodagh's well being at heart. If I hear that something else has happened to her while I'm gone, I'll return and I will tell Lugh everything I know about you and about Urien. So, I'll take your solemn oath that you will protect my daughter for as long as she'll live in your castle, in exchange for my silence."

"I promise you that, Iweridd," Rhiannon replied coolly.

Lugh and Clodagh were called in. Iweridd and her daughter hugged and cried together.

"What vulgarity in the display of their emotions," Rhiannon thought while watching mother and daughter sob into each other's arms.

They all sat and talked at lengths about what to do. Urien wouldn't be back until later, returning from a training expedition in the countryside.

It was decided that Iweridd be escorted by a servant to a nearby town's village, a day away from Aileach, by chariot. Once there, she was supposed to sojourn indeterminately, to "visit" an ill relative.

Clodagh and Iweridd said their good-byes that night, because Iweridd was supposed to leave very quietly at dawn.

"Fare well, Clodagh, my daughter," Iweridd said trembling. "Take care of yourself. Trust Rhiannon: she will protect you while I'm gone," she said while hugging her heartbroken daughter.

"I'll see you soon, mother. Take good care of yourself. I love you," Clodagh said, and they kissed goodbye.

Lugh hugged Iweridd as well and she responded in kind. "Take care of my Clodagh," she said, and Lugh swore that he would guard Clodagh with his life.

Rhiannon felt nauseated at witnessing such sentimentality.

Just before dawn, Iweridd and the accompanying servant were ready to go. They took a carriage that had been loaded with provisions and clothes for Iweridd to last her for at least a week. She believed she would be staying with a peasant family and that she would be regularly supplied with food, clothing, and whatever she'd need by Rhiannon, for the duration of her "exile".

Just before they left, while Iweridd sat in the carriage and the horses were restless, Rhiannon called the servant to her.

"You will stab her three times through the heart when you reach the outskirts of Aileach. Once a moon has passed, you will return and will say that you were robbed on your way out of town, and that the robbers murdered Iweridd.

"I want you to cut and bruise yourself, roll in the dirt; it's your responsibility to make it all look believable, very believable. Of course, I want you to bring me her body back as proof that you did what you must. Only then, you will receive the jewels that I have promised you. Now go!" Rhiannon shouted. She knew she could count on Kai; he had not disappointed her before.

When Urien was informed of Iweridd's sudden departure, somehow he felt free of mentally abusing Clodagh with more gusto, just knowing that her mother was not nearby, yet relying on the security that she would come back, so he could keep threatening Clodagh. He was following Rhiannon's plan and enjoying himself all the while.

In the meantime, Rhiannon, Clodagh and Lugh devised a plan to catch Urien in flagrante trying to force Clodagh to have sex with him. They all counted on the fact that Urien would certainly try to get to Clodagh's room that evening after supper, if she retired early, leaving Rhiannon and Lugh behind to talk by the fireplace, as they usually did.

They would follow him discreetly and listen outside Clodagh's door; her first scream was a signal that he had started groping her. Lugh and Rhiannon, taking a bit of time to look as if they had run from the nearby dining room, would burst into the bedchambers and confront Urien.

Although Lugh and Clodagh tried to have a normal day, they were both very nervous.

"Everything will be all right. Your mother is safe; we have Rhiannon on our side and tonight Urien will realize that his threats will no longer bind you to his will. You never have to be violated again, not today, not ever. I'll never leave you alone again," Lugh told Clodagh.

All through the day, and especially at breakfast, Lugh found it very hard to be in Urien's presence because his feelings of outrage and hatred for what he knew Urien had done to Clodagh, and which he had promised he would keep a secret, were overwhelming him.

He could no longer bear it and began talking to Urien in verse, expressing his poetic images aloud for the first time, to show his father he was no longer afraid of being his true Self. He wanted Urien to know that he despised him, his values, or better yet the lack of them, and his damned military life. He was a poet, and he would use his poetry to defy him.

"Lugh, pass me the milk jug and the knife," Urien asked.

Lugh looked at Urien with insolence and disrespect.

"Certainly!" Lugh answered flippantly, passing to Urien that which he had requested, then drifting into verse.

"Here is the knife," Lugh said while sticking the table with it, shocking everyone. "The blade cuts the bread which nourishes the flesh...the blade cuts the flesh which nourishes the earth..."

Urien did not respond as Lugh had anticipated. He found the way Lugh expressed himself to be ludicrous and inappropriate, not to mention incomprehensible.

"Why did you say that? Why in rhyme? Rhiannon, is there something wrong with him?" Urien scoffed.

Rhiannon flashed a faint and blank smile at Urien.

"Excuse us for a moment; Lugh and I need to talk," she announced graciously as she stood up and asked Lugh to please follow her into the next room so that they could confer.

Lugh obeyed, still looking at Urien with insistence and anger as he got up from his seat and followed his mother out of the dining room.

"What are you doing? Just learn to exercise some of that discipline they have been teaching you in training all your life!" She blasted as soon as they were alone.

"This is what it's all about: he has taken seventeen years of my life and done with them what he wished. What about me? For years I obeyed him out of love, trust and respect, suppressing my feelings, stifling my poetry, and for what? He is a lecherous little man who has neither self-restraint or the most rudimentary concepts of selfless love and respect for human life!" Lugh shouted.

"My point exactly!" Rhiannon said while shaking him lightly by the arm and looking upward, sharply into his eyes.

"That is why we need to be patient, controlled, and wait until the time is right to punish him. Now, do you think you can hold back your anger for the time being, and act as though you knew nothing about Urien's deed?"

"Yes, mother, I think I can; I trust you, I know you want to punish him as much as I do." Lugh cast his eyes to the floor in embarrassment.

"I have acted foolishly, forgive me."

"You are forgiven my sweet, sweet Lugh," she whispered caressing the apples of his cheeks, reflecting on how beautiful his green eyes were, how earnest, how fresh, as she longed to possess him.

Breakfast continued and ended without further disruptions, while Rhiannon spent the rest of the day scheming, still perfecting the entrapment plan she had devised for Urien, and which she could hardly wait to put into action.

Chapter Thirty-four

Lugh and Clodagh flew Tharan and Corax, walked through the woods and held one another tenderly, hopeful that the plan would deliver them from Urien's evil.

Urien spent the day with Gwen, the mistress he thought he had been able to keep secret all along from the ubiquitous Rhiannon, and he prided himself in that achievement.

"How can you be so sure that she doesn't know?" Gwen had often asked.

"Because if she knew, you would be dead by now," he always replied, which brought no comfort to Gwen. But she was in love and in lust with the king and he, he wanted an heir all his own to keep secret until Rhiannon would help him come into power and then, he would no longer need her. He would discard her like a broken spear. He would murder her, and Lugh, if he had to. Then, he could live his new life in total control and power and he would raise a son to succeed him, another person to dominate and mould mercilessly into what he thought was greatness.

Gwen, a servant, for the twisted love of him let Urien drown the daughter they had had, many years back, and agreed to let him do the same if and when she would produce another girl-child.

After that first pregnancy, each time Gwen had become pregnant Urien's hopes for a male heir were ended by the reality of miscarriage, which kept repeating itself, weakening Gwen to the point that Urien was thinking of replacing her with a younger, healthier woman whom he could impregnate.

Rhiannon had known about Gwen from the start. Gwen had been the first woman, but not the only one, with whom Urien had been unfaithful to her and, for that, Rhiannon had never forgiven him. It was then that her love for him turned into hatred; her lust for him, into revulsion.

Over the years she patiently refrained from showing, even hinting, that she knew. What she had in mind for Urien and Gwen was an agony of sorrow which she would watch deliciously unfold into tragedy.

She let Gwen's first pregnancy go by; she thought it had been an accident. When she learned that Urien had killed his baby girl, she understood what he was after, and so she had caused Gwen to painfully miscarry ever since.

She used a spell to accomplish what she needed; a formula that worked by the powers of jealousy and hatred. She herself had became pregnant once, shortly after she and Urien had begun their incestuous affair, and what was born from their mating was a being so heinous looking that even the Fomor would not accept it amongst their own, so the creature was eliminated.

Ever since then Rhiannon's heart had turned black, and so had her growing knowledge of magic, for if the Daanan gods had punished her for being her brother's lover by denying her motherhood, she would serve the dark lords of the deep instead. She ruthlessly dedicated her life to the achievement of unlimited power and gratification through the absolute worship of the Fomor gods, and through the knowledge of their bleak wisdom.

The night in which Rhiannon learned that a perfect-looking daughter had been born to Urien, and that her life had been taken by him shortly after her birth, Rhiannon, full of bitterness, hid in the basement of her castle and invoked the power of the abysses.

She hated Urien for having been allowed to father a perfect child, while she had been condemned to birth a monster.

"May Gwen's womb be filled with death, now and forever, Just as mine was filled with ugliness..." she chanted appealing to the justice of Balor while she rocked herself back and forth in a fever of self-loathing and self-pitying, promising herself that she would avenge herself.

From that time on, she would hate growing things; all plants and pets, except for the vigilant owls, were banned from the interior of Caer Balor.

"I despise things that grow; little puppies and kittens are for the amusement of children. I hate the sight of plants and beautiful flowers because I've seen that, after all, they are but fancy weeds," she explained to Urien when he had asked why she had banned all pets and plants from the castle. He was oblivious to the deeper meaning of her words, to the fact that she knew about his other mate, his other life.

Urien had never loved Lugh. He did not even like the boy who, to him, was merely a pawn, the medium through which Morrigan and Airmid might be found and assassinated.

To Rhiannon Lugh became everything from the moment that she held him in her arms. After discovering Urien's affair, and later, Gwen's pregnancy, Rhiannon looked upon Lugh not as a son, but as the lover she was going to rear and groom for herself. She eagerly awaited the day in which Urien would be killed, and she would be free to share and enjoy her power with Lugh.

Chapter Thirty-Five

Dinnertime came and when it was over, Clodagh took leave of the table and Urien promptly announced that he was going to retire for the night, just as Rhiannon had anticipated. Lugh looked pale and tense.

"You were right mother. He did exactly what you said he would," Lugh stated bitterly.

"My poor Lugh," she replied condescendingly as she kissed his cheeks.

"How long before we follow him?" Lugh asked impatiently.

"Right now," Rhiannon replied glancing at the small hourglass she had discreetly set on the table when Urien left the room. "Follow me slowly and quietly; the tiniest little noise might make him suspicious and he'll glance outside Clodagh's room. That poor, sweet girl!"

They walked through the halls leading to Clodagh's chambers with amazing lightness of step and breathing, and came to total stillness once outside her room.

Urien threatened Clodagh the same way he had done the first time, as she was trying to push him off of her. Lugh heard her say: "Get off of me! I'm going to scream this time!" And he stiffened his fists in rage with the impetuosity to bust into the room.

Rhiannon motioned him to be patient. "As soon as she screams..." she whispered. Clodagh did scream, much to Urien's surprise.

Lugh almost went in, but Rhiannon let a few minutes go by, then she herself kicked the door open and stood motionless, as Lugh and she both saw Urien lay on top of Clodagh, who kneed him in the groin and pushed him off of her.

Urien, who was silently dealing with the pain of Clodagh's action, looked more bewildered than hurt as he glared at Rhiannon, knowing that he had been betrayed.

"You disgust me!" Lugh yelled while menacingly advancing towards Urien. "I know what you did to her. I could not believe it at first, then everything was clear to me: you never loved me, or anyone! All that training was supposed to keep me chained down to your wishes, not to benefit me. Know I no longer have any love or respect for you!" Lugh yelled, and Clodagh walked into his arms.

Urien tried to defend himself by blaming the entire situation on Clodagh. "...She wanted me, she wanted that first time; I did not rape her, she wanted it!"

Lugh kicked Urien in the stomach hard and fast. He picked him up off the floor and punched him in the face with the same kind of passion with which he loved Clodagh. When Urien, bloody and spitting out red saliva and fragments of a molar, collapsed out of Lugh's hold, his son let him fall.

"Liar!" Rhiannon yelled at the semi-conscious Urien. "Don't you know you can't lie to me? You know I'm much too smart for that!"

Urien, having regained the strength to at least stand up, thought he would be fit to strike back, psychologically. She had framed him, betrayed him, and he did not know why yet. All he could do at that point was to let Lugh know that Rhiannon had engineered the rape and the entire matter.

He talked and talked, he told all about the nature of his relationship to Rhiannon, but Lugh did not believe a word he uttered. Clodagh knew it was true, but had promised her mother never to tell Lugh, so she kept silent. They turned away and walked out of the room. Lugh stopped under the arch of the door.

"You are pathetic. My mother is the only parent I'll ever have. She has never lied to me." Urien laughed hysterically.

"...She loves me, and Clodagh, and she has proven that in many, many ways. How could you think we would ponder your slanderous, cowardly words, even if for an instant?" Lugh said.

Rhiannon took a breath of victory and of intense satisfaction.

"Sleep well you two; the ordeal is over, at least for now," she said convincingly. Before departing, Clodagh and Lugh, full of gratitude and affection, hugged her.

Rhiannon closed the door behind her, savouring the distraught look on Urien's face as he sat in a chair looking vulnerable to her eyes for the first time.

"Did you go mute?" She sneered.

"Why did you do it?" Urien asked, dumbfounded.

"Do what?" She teased.

"You know what I'm talking about!" He yelled as he sprang to his feet, tearing a piece of the bed sheets to soak up the blood off his face.

"Don't pretend you don't know what I am talking about!"

She advanced towards him, looked him straight in the eyes and murmured, "Because I hate and despise you. And don't ever raise your voice to me again."

Urien yelled obscenities at her and failing that, he tried a softer approach.

"You betrayed me, why on earth did you do it? I knew we have not seen eye to eye for a long time, but I thought there was still something between us...."

That last sentence infuriated her.

"Liar! Liar! liar!" She screamed and lunged forward to hit him repeatedly on the chest.

"Everything you say is a lie. All you ever cared about was to satisfy your basest needs and wants," she uttered, succumbing to tears which Urien thought he could take advantage of, as he stroked her hair to comfort her.

She ripped herself away from his caresses, cursing the day he was born.

"What have I done to deserve this?" He asked again.

"You idiotic swine! Did you really think I didn't know about Gwen? About you two, trying to have a son to replace my Lugh? Don't you think I know you want to replace me with the slut that you have been fucking for years? I've known since Lugh was just a baby, and I have quietly hated you all this time.

"I bet you didn't know I've been screwing every man in and out of Caer Balor ever since, and found that the worst lover among them is more satisfactory than you!"

Urien was at a loss for words. Everything he had done and prided himself to have achieved and kept secret from her, she knew. The very thing he thought she would have never done, being unfaithful to him, had happened under his nose and he had never even suspected it.

He felt rage and fear for this woman compete inside his heart. She was indeed as powerful and as cunning as she said she was, even more so than he used to believe she'd be, and he stood in awe of her.

All that was left to do was for him to beg her forgiveness, abandon Gwen and hope that Rhiannon would take him back. He had felt her power and fell in love with it. Her anger, her jealousy and her vengefulness turned him on at a level deeper than the physical.

Most of all he realized that if they stayed enemies until the time that their ritual mating came, they would race each other, right afterward, to see who'd murder the other first and he knew that she would prevail.

While she had turned her back on him and approached the door, he fell to his knees and wrapped his arms around her legs.

"I beg your forgiveness Rhiannon, I have no words to defend myself!"

"Let me go. Don't hope to convince me. You are a liar, a pathetic excuse for a man and irreversibly unattractive to me. Go charm your slovenly plebeian; don't touch me again!" He obeyed her and let her walk away, his heart aflutter.

He had but one hope left and one desire: that, in time, she could come to forgive him, and that she would fall in love with him as hopelessly as he had just fallen in love with her.

He realized that he was willing to leave Gwen for Rhiannon, and to accept Lugh as the legitimate heir to their future empire.

"If this is what it takes to win her back, it is worth it; it's worth a whole life of faithfulness to her and of tolerance of Lugh, whose trust and respect I must garner back."

On her part, Rhiannon had anticipated Urien's reaction. She had learned over the years that her initial tenderness and love for Urien, who had seduced her, had not won his heart, but that utter deviousness and power, on her part, would.

Now that she knew she had his heart, she was going to tear it out of his chest, because she could not forgive him for having turned her into the monster that she knew she had become.

She had fallen utterly out of love with him and she was determined to watch him grovel. Perhaps, at some point in time, she was going to let him believe that she had forgiven him, if such a lie could benefit her in some way.

Once someone had disappointed or betrayed her, Rhiannon radically severed herself emotionally from that person and had no rest until he, or she, had more than paid for scorning her.

Lugh was the one she loved; he was the one with whom she wanted to share the rest of her life and power. He was the reason why she slew children to keep herself looking young and beautiful.

Chapter Thirty-six

The morning had come. Lugh and Clodagh had woken to the devastating news of Iweridd's death. Rhiannon had told them about the accident and they ran outside to see for themselves, and ever since Clodagh had set her eyes on her mother's dead body and saw her chest carved open, she had collapsed on the corpse and entered a state of mental and emotional absence that made her appear as if paralysed.

Over the following weeks she lay in bed, her eyes staring blankly into the void. She was unable to move, much less to speak or to recognize anyone, not even Lugh, who tried to feed her, and who spent most of his days sitting by her side talking to her.

Rhiannon had been very supportive, all along promising Lugh that she was going to use her magic to distil a medicinal potion that would bring Clodagh back, and she kept her promise.

Urien, who was acting very humbly around Lugh and Rhiannon, made the mistake of going to Lugh to ask for his forgiveness.

Lugh had responded violently to Urien, making it very clear to him that it was because of his actions towards Clodagh that Iweridd had to be sent away, and that he would never be forgiven for her death.

"You are dead to me!" were Lugh's last words to him, after which Urien was confined to a far away wing of the castle, unable to access Lugh's, Clodagh's or Rhiannon's quarters without asking for Rhiannon's permission. He decided to oblige her wishes, hopeful that his obedience would win her heart.

Chapter Thirty-seven

Many moons had gone by. Rhiannon's life serum was ready and she herself administered it to Clodagh who, for the first time since she had entered the catatonic state, closed her eyes and actually slept.

Lugh, sleepless, waited for the morning to come and to welcome Clodagh back into the world of the sentient. He sat by her bed through the night, dozing off and waking up at short intervals until the lights of dawn appeared and he leaned over Clodagh to hear her breathe and to kiss her.

She opened her eyes and smiled at the sight of Lugh; his heart leaped inside his chest.

"You know who I am!"

"Of course I know who you are..." she said, attempting to sit up to hug him.

"You look like you have not slept at all...is something wrong?" She asked, oblivious to what had happened.

Lugh did not answer; he did not know what to say, but it didn't matter just then. She was back, and he would give his own life to preserve hers.

Later, Lugh spoke to Rhiannon.

"Mother," he said with tears glistening at the corners of his eyes. "Once again I am in your debt; you blessed our love, and offered us your protection and your affection. Now, you have given Clodagh back to me. What can I ever do to show you my gratitude and my love?"

"Just keep loving me. Keep loving me and trusting in me," she said simply, with an almost earnest smile.

"How is she doing?" She asked. "Is she hungry?"

"Oh, she's fine, I think she's hungry, thirsty and she mentioned something about wanting to go for a walk in the woods..." Lugh said, sounding pleased and amused.

"Good," said Rhiannon. "I have prepared her a special meal. She'll need to be on a special diet for the next little while; I'll take care of her personally. I want her to gain her strength back fully, so that when her memory of Iweridd and of her death comes back, she will be able to cope with it without slipping back into oblivion."

"Thank you," Lugh kissed her. "Mother, why do you suppose all these horrible things are happening?"

"Lugh, I was not going to bring this up just yet," Rhiannon said feigning an air of concern and eerie seriousness. "But I feel that the power of Airmid and of Morrigan is behind the misfortune that has befallen this house.

"Your sister's power is growing every day. She must know where we are, and must have put a spell on Clodagh, on us all, just to keep us guessing and to demoralize us. Once she'll feel that we are weak enough against her ever growing power and evil, then she'll come and she'll kill us.

"She is just playing with us now. This is just a demonstration of what she can do, and a way to probe my power to see how strong, or how weak, it measures against hers. I am warning you: I am barely struggling with this force but, as much as I hate to admit it, my magic is no match for hers.

"If you do not locate her and charm her into coming here, amongst strangers in a strange land, her power will only grow and in the end, she'll murder us. She began with Iweridd, now Clodagh is ill, then the rest of us," Rhiannon concluded hypnotically.

Lugh looked as scared as he felt and secretly trembled at the thought that anyone would have the power to harm the only two people he loved.

***

Frustrated and utterly bored, Urien decided to ask Rhiannon for a private audience and sent a servant to summon her. Rhiannon accepted; after all, she so loved to see him in subservience, that it was worth her trip to his branch of the castle.

"What do you want?" She asked brashly once she had reached his room.

He walked up to her and kissed the back of her right hand, and she wiped it against her gown.

"I do not appreciate the feeling of slime against my skin," she said with an amused smirk. He humoured her by laughing as to a clever joke.

"Rhiannon," he whispered close to her nape. "What do I have to do to win you back?"

"Ah, that!" She joked. "I want you to tear Gwen's little heart, liver and kidneys out, make soup out of them, and I want to see you eat it!" She replied in her very bleak humour.

On her way out of Urien's chambers she stopped by the door, turned around.

"I couldn't care less about your lover...lovers," she said. "I simply don't love you any longer; I just want you out of my way until the mating must happen. After that, may the best one of us win," she stated very clearly, and left.

Chapter Thirty-eight

The following day Gwen's body was found slashed open and, upon inspection by Rhiannon and her physician, it was noted that some of the internal organs in Gwen's chest and abdominal cavities were missing. Rhiannon stormed into Urien's room, where she found him dining on soup.

"I knew you'd come," he said scooping Gwen's heart out of the cauldron which hung in the fireplace.

"See? Anything for you, anything!" he said almost flippantly.

"And I am supposed to be impressed by this? You knew I didn't care about you and Gwen. You have gained nothing. If anything, you have managed to make me sicker than ever, and you have challenged me...mocked me!" She yelled while pointing her index finger at him as she advanced towards him.

"No!" He snapped. "This was not meant to mock you. I didn't kill Gwen to impress you, or to make you sick. I killed her to prove to you that there is nothing I won't do for you. Your wish is my command, lady!" He retorted becoming increasingly irritated as she rushed out of his room.

Once out of his sight, she ran outside the castle and vomited in the surrounding bushes. He had gotten to her, somehow. He had at least managed to commit an act of such gruesomeness that it had made even her ill. She knew beyond the shadow of a doubt that she had some control over Urien. And she knew that, by contrast with Urien, she loved Lugh's purity and youth more than ever; Lugh would never be capable of murder, much less of an act of such brutality...of cannibalism.

Clodagh's health was quickly restored under Lugh and Rhiannon's care, but Rhiannon still insisted that, although she could return to her usual diet, Clodagh should still drink, twice daily, a special fortifying tea which would keep her healthy.

The memories of her mother's death had not surfaced to Clodagh's conscious mind yet, and Rhiannon told Lugh that, if everything worked out, the tea should permanently suppress them.

"Mother," Lugh had said. "If that happens, Clodagh will not have any memories of her mother at all. It will be as if Iweridd had never existed; that can't be right."

Rhiannon, slightly irritated by Lugh's comment, kept her demeanour unaltered and replied, "Would you rather risk her happiness, perhaps her health, again?"

"No, mother, of course not. If you think that this is what is best for Clodagh, then so be it. I am but an ignorant boy," Lugh replied respectfully and full of trust in his mother's judgment.

"Mother," Lugh observed extemporaneously. "You are a very beautiful woman. You look almost as young as Clodagh; how do you manage that?"

Upon hearing those magnificent, unexpected words, Rhiannon felt a happiness the intensity of which she had never known before. "He noticed!" He finally noticed!" She thought in the interval between the moment in which Lugh had complimented her, and the moment in which she responded.

"You flatter me," was all that she could say.

I know you are my mother, you raised me, but I have always seen you as a...cousin perhaps, because of the way you look. Mother, are these thoughts and feelings improper?" Lugh asked candidly.

"Oh, oh no, no...they are unusual, but not improper," she replied, a bit taken aback for having discovered that Lugh had perceived her more as a woman, than a mother.

"Oh, Lugh," she sighed in her heart. "You don't know the happiness you've brought into my life!"

Her longing gaze followed him out of her room as her heart burst with desire for him. She was obsessed with his body. Everything about it had a strong erotic quality to her, and she felt that she wouldn't be able to refrain from making explicit sexual advances to him for much longer.

She had to wait for the time to be right, but she doubted that her passion would allow her to respect timing. There was something about Lugh that was overwhelmingly provocative, and she had to struggle with herself to control her behaviour when she was alone with him.

On Lugh's part, nothing was further from his mind than the thought of finding his mother sexually attractive. His compliments to her were genuine, but purely coming from him as her son.

***

Lugh and Clodagh spent relatively carefree days together, walking through the woods, talking and making love. Lugh was constantly haunted by the guilt of knowing that Iweridd had lived and died, while Clodagh did not even remember she had a mother. That knowledge he had of Iweridd, enveloped their encounters in the eerie and unnatural atmosphere of a spell, a spell he had not cast, but the existence of which he was justifying and concealing from his beloved.

One night Lugh and Clodagh made love in his chambers. Usually, they loved one another in the woods. They had begun necking while cuddling on his bed and they had gone too far to turn back, so Lugh walked to the door and locked it.

Clodagh was heaving as she undressed, and by the time Lugh was back on the bed he had shed his clothes also, his phallus erect and flushed, seeking her sex, and easily finding it, as she lay back and parted her thighs waiting to be entered with all the passion that she knew he was capable of loving her.

They were both hyper-excited that night, knowing that they were making love so close to Rhiannon's bedroom and that they might be heard. A certain defiance clutched them both and each made love to the other with a vengeance, as if they did want Rhiannon to hear them. Perhaps even Urien, in the far away wing of the castle, so that he might become aware of what their lovemaking was like, and know he would never experience it with Clodagh.

She seemed to moan louder and sigh, reclaiming the enjoyment of the sexuality that Urien had violated, realizing that it belonged to her and that she chose to share it with the man she loved.

Lugh thrust deeper into her, bit her nipples gently as she swayed and ground her hips in the fur pallet, and was so excited that she had to bite the edge of the blanket to keep herself from crying out.

He was sweating and breathing heavily, saying her name, over and over, sweeping her face and her lips with his tongue, biting her lips and she bit back, in-between their kisses.

She climaxed under her lover's frenzied thrusting and the sweat of his strong body. He kissed her deeply as she moaned with the pleasure he gave her and just then his excitement peaked, and he felt closer to her than he ever had. As he spilled inside of her he swore to himself that, as long as that woman lived, he would make love to no other.

Rhiannon had not been able to hear the lovers through the castle's thick walls, but she saw and heard what went on in Lugh's room through Bryn's eyes and ears.

When she began to see, the shock of actually watching Lugh making love to another was such that she collapsed on her bed and laid herself down, as she took all of the images and sounds in from the owl.

When the shock had begun to vanish Rhiannon felt her insides torn by two primal feelings: excitement, at seeing Lugh making love, and anger, for not being the woman heaving with pleasure under the weight of his body and the rhythm of his thrusts.

She concentrated on watching Lugh only, mentally replacing Clodagh with herself, until the feeling of raging jealousy slipped away and she felt only pleasure. Somehow the intensity of her focus on him and on the mental picture she had constructed, made her feel as though Lugh were making love to her.

She disrobed slowly and with more urgency as she sank deeper into the images that Bryn was relaying to her brain. Once undressed, she caressed herself to the point of orgasm, calling Lugh's name under her breath.

Rhiannon sighed deeply, satisfied and hopeful that, one day, that fantasy would become reality. She already felt more connected to Lugh, sexually. She thought that actually making love to him would be achieving bliss.

"You are not my little boy...you never were... you were destined to be my husband, Lugh. I know that you'll come to understand that, you'll come to desire me," she whispered before falling asleep.

Chapter Thirty-nine

The next day Rhiannon had to make a conscious effort not to betray her knowledge of Lugh and Clodagh's lovemaking every time she looked at them. She was all smiles and charm, especially towards Lugh, as if to point out to him that it was time that he truly noticed the woman in her, and possibly entertain thoughts of what that could lead to.

"I'll give you improper thoughts..." she silently mused, sarcastically, "...those are the only kind of thoughts mommy wants you to have for her!"

When Clodagh and Lugh were not looking, she stared at the back of Clodagh's head wishing that she could bash it in. She hated her more than she hated Urien, because she was the beloved of the man she had wanted more than any other and could not have.

When Lugh and Clodagh went for their walk, Rhiannon ensconced herself in the dungeons, distilling more of the tea that she brewed exclusively for Clodagh.

Many moons had passed and Clodagh was suddenly growing sicker every day. Her hair began to fall in clumps; she looked pale and felt so weak that she had to be confined to her bed. Rhiannon's arsenic-laced brew had begun to take its toll on Clodagh's health and Lugh was in a deep state of despair, spending every waking moment at Clodagh's bedside.

"Morrigan is behind this," Rhiannon kept telling Lugh. "...I told you at the beginning of the darkening of our fortune, and I'm telling you now: if you love Clodagh and if you love me, then you must try very hard to contact Morrigan before it is too late!"

Those words, "before it is too late", were branded into Lugh's brain. He could think of nothing else but to get in touch with Morrigan and let her pay for all the sorrow he believed she had brought into their lives.

"I find it hard to concentrate," Lugh complained to Rhiannon, describing the stressed-out state of mind in which he was, and which made it hard for him to focus on accessing Morrigan's subconscious.

"Keep trying; you'll get better at it as you practice, and the more you practice, the more focused you become. I am very proud of you for trying at all. It must be hard for you; I know that you don't like hurting anyone," Rhiannon said.

"I am not sure about that anymore. Every time I look at Clodagh, I wish it were Morrigan languishing there in her place," Lugh said.

"I understand," Rhiannon whispered stroking his cheek with the back of her hand, and kissing his lips softly with a new intensity which took Lugh aback.

"But remember to appear calm and unthreatening to her. She must believe that you are a victim here, and that you need her to come and free you of the evil that she is convinced Urien and I represent. Of course, she'd be right on Urien's account..." she sneered with sarcastic bitterness in her voice.

"I love you mother." Lugh embraced her as tears streamed his face and wet Rhiannon's hair, an experience that she would relish for the rest of the day.

"I don't know what I would do if I were to lose you too," Lugh said.

"You won't lose me," she said, touched by his feelings for her.

"You are doing all you can to keep me and Clodagh safe. Everything will be alright, you'll see," said Lugh, his eyes stung by the tears which kept welling up in them.

Lugh tried to make contact with Morrigan for days, unsuccessfully. He watched Clodagh slip away feeling that he was responsible for her well being, and he was failing her.

***

Urien joined his best warriors in facing the beginning of a popular uprising over which he felt he would have little control. He realized that he had ignored the people for far too long, having left the job of terrorizing and oppressing them mostly to his men. Now he had no choice; he had to become involved if he wanted to survive until the time of the ritual mating with Rhiannon came.

The statue of Balor was next to completion, and Urien interpreted that as a sign that he must work faster to ingratiate himself to Rhiannon.

She had allowed him to move back into her wing of the castle, but not her bedroom, and in private she was warmer to Urien than she let herself be in the presence of Lugh.

She was very well aware of the fact that the time for the mating was drawing close and that, as much as she hated the thought of it, she needed Urien to accomplish what she thought was her life's mission: the achievement of absolute power and a sort of mystical sublimation that would transfigure her humanness into godhood.

Chapter Forty

Clodagh's condition deteriorated steadily, leaving Lugh feeling frustrated and guilty for not being able to reach his sister and beg her to reverse the process.

Lugh looked pale and tense and did not speak to Rhiannon as much as he used to. He could not even fall asleep; the rare times in which he did, he slept very little and woke to the depressing and unstoppable reality of Clodagh's illness.

Rhiannon was bound by the laws of magic of the Fomorian underworld to the condition that, as long as she performed the sacrifice of children to remain young, she could not cast a love spell on Lugh. It was either one or the other. Yet, the challenge of trying to make Lugh fall in love with her, rather than bewitching him into it, was a potent aphrodisiac for her.

"You look pale and gaunt. Just because Clodagh is ill it doesn't mean that you should starve yourself to death, or that you should deprive yourself of sleep." Rhiannon caressed his face, sounding very maternal in the attempt to let Lugh become accustomed to the idea that he had to emotionally detach himself from the dying Clodagh, and that he could fall right into her comforting arms.

Lugh hugged his mother. He felt Rhiannon's heart beating with what he perceived to be maternal love.

She sized up the youthful tautness of his pectorals and recalled the night that she made love to him in her mind, through the eyes of Bryn. As she felt the hardness of his powerful thighs against hers, she became so aroused that she had to step back and break the embrace before she would compromise herself.

"The time is not right to make my move," her brain kept repeating as it struggled with the impulses it synchronically sent to the arms to tighten around his shoulders, and her mouth to part in a sultry motion towards his. She longed to penetrate his mouth with her tongue and to feel his, then lock in the most passionate kiss she would ever experience.

"...But the time is not right," she kept thinking resentfully, regretfully. She went to bed early because she could not stand to see Lugh looking so vulnerable and so tempting, and not being able to comfort him in the way she longed to. Lustful thoughts raced inside her head and kept her awake with desire that she knew she could not fulfill.

At one point, her eyes reddened and wide open, Rhiannon sat in her bed and, under the crushing weight of sleeplessness, she felt aloof. She felt the reality of her surroundings crumble and become dream-like. She saw the walls close in and move back as though they were breathing with her, and her heart began to pound much too fast, much too loud. She could feel it in her ears, and she brought her shaky hands over her closed eyes and cried.

She had never felt like that before. Nothing had scared her before, much less the workings of her mind and of her heart, and now she was their victim. She realized that she had fallen in love with Lugh, and that he might never love her back, not the way she knew she loved him.

Constant thoughts of Lugh had haunted her mind for too long to keep denying to herself the fact that she was obsessed with him, that she no longer had full control over her life.

"He must love me too...he must love me!" She whispered as she noticed, like in a dream, that she was shaking. She wiped the tears off her face but they kept coming with more force than ever, faster than before, calling up a desperate sequence of sighs which obstructed the passage of breath in her throat.

She slid off the bed and stumbled to the mirror of her vanity table and gasped at what she saw. Her angelic-looking face appeared flushed and puffy; her blue irises were disappearing into a fine network of tiny ruptured blood vessels. She sank her whole head in the basin of water that she kept in her room at all times to freshen up, and she found more comfort in the coolness of that water than she ever had in the arms of any man.

"This is what it would feel like all the time, if you loved me Lugh, if you just...." She broke down again and kept her face in the basin and cried there, lifting her head up briefly and frantically, at intervals, to catch her breath, and then, again, sank her face into that water which was her saving grace, in a night full of new and old pain.

Just when the thought of ending it all flashed through her mind, so at ease in the water which could take her life, she found the strength to pull her head out of the deep basin to take the longest, deepest breath she was capable of.

She seized a cloth and dried her soaked hair and face, then walked back to the mirror and spoke to the image of herself that looked worn, still, but refreshed, and she saw her eyes sparkle with renewed hope.

"I am going to live to make you love me, Lugh. I am going to live to love you," she said aloud, finding the ruthlessness that just instants before she thought she had lost forever. But it renewed itself, like her youth did, every time she slaughtered the innocents for it.

Chapter Forty-one

Another pain-filled day went by for Lugh, as he saw a change in Clodagh's condition and realized that it was a deterioration which brought her closer to death.

"If I could overcome the stubbornness of my hope I would release you myself, my love," he said under his breath while running his fingers up and down the dagger's sheath that hang on his belt.

Rhiannon stood behind and watched the motion of his fingers on the knife and knew what he was thinking. She put her hand on Lugh's shoulders and whispered in his ear, "Do you love me enough to want to take my life if I were languishing in pain?"

"But you are not! Why do you keep comparing yourself to Clodagh, some way or another? You should know already! I love you, and, yes, I love you enough that I would want to put you out of your misery if you were agonizing. The fact is, here you stand healthy, lucky for me, but she, she's dying!" Lugh retorted with much annoyance in his cracked voice.

Lugh's emotional response, so defying, so uncharacteristic, took Rhiannon aback. Her heart beat furiously, being her feelings torn between rage, at the way Lugh protected Clodagh's status of martyr, and hope, at the thought that, after all, he had said that she should know that he loved her.

"I am sorry," she said feigning humility. "I did not mean to sound callous. I realize that she is dying and that you are in pain but, I guess, having lost Urien's love I need constant reassurance that I still have yours."

"I love you, mother," he said as he hugged her. "I am so sorry for snapping at you. I shouldn't have. I think myself fortunate to still have you here, healthy, and to still have your love. It is your love which nourishes my hopes, my will to go on living. I beg of you, be patient with me. I am trying to accept the fact that there is no longer a chance to see Clodagh recover. I have not yet readied myself to accept her death, and you must help me." His voice, broken by tears, quivered in such a manner as to strike a chord of tenderness in Rhiannon.

How skilfully did Rhiannon play games with her own mind, convincing herself of the fact that Clodagh was fated to die to serve a higher purpose rather than to satisfy the lust she felt for her son. But Rhiannon believed that she was meant to be Lugh's great love, and the attainment of such love was the reason for which she justified destroying lives.

**

Clodagh, who was usually either sleeping or delirious, came to moments of consciousness, on and off, over the following days. She knew she was dying, she knew nothing could save her but Rhiannon's magic. She was convinced of that.

"I would not be dying if she willed me alive..." she feebly breathed in Lugh's ears as she watched his pupils dilate in the disbelief that she would say such a thing. Yet, he did not dare argue with Clodagh at the point of her death.

"She is a very powerful magician. My... my mother..."

"...You remember your mother?" Lugh interrupted in astonishment as he squeezed her hand and kissed it fervently, unwilling to let her go.

"I saw mother up there, when I travelled outside this body while you thought I slept, and she told me things ..." Clodagh, her beautiful dark hair looking thin and faded, tried to sweep it away from her pale face while she painfully attempted to sit up in her bed and failed, collapsing back flat in it, as Lugh suffered all through it trying to help her, to comfort her. But her comfort was at hand, and her only hope for happiness in the world beyond was to warn Lugh about Rhiannon.

"Believe my words: you must run away and find your sister. She will be your only salvation. Only dark, deep waters here, Lugh, and you are going to drown in them if you stay." She punctuated her last words with a look in her eyes, and a touch of Lugh's hands that ran through the boy's body with the power of lightning, and he felt all her love pervade his mind, his body and his soul, and he knew that their love would be rooted in the deepest layers of his being forever.

"...This body is dying, but I live, and so does my love for you. Look for me, and you will find me. But you must run away from here, for my soul will only dwell where the light lives," were Clodagh's last words.

As Lugh sat on her bed holding Clodagh's limp body, he drew her to him and rested his head against her chest and cried out at the loss of her heartbeat and wept, as his mind demanded, "...Take me with you...take me with you!"

***

The morning following Clodagh's death, which Rhiannon had felt happening during the night, she found Lugh asleep, lying next to Clodagh's cold and stiffened body, and she gently awoke him, pretending that she had just learned what had happened.

When Lugh opened his eyes, in his heart he cursed Rhiannon for being the one who awakened him to the devastating reality of having to live without Clodagh. As his eyes opened abruptly and he jerked into a sitting position Rhiannon saw the usual clarity of his green irises clouded by pain and by doubt.

She extended her hand to caress his face but he drew back. She parted her lips to impart words of support, but his eyes would tell her not to speak and she found herself unable to articulate a word. There was more than pain behind those eyes, which now looked charged with the intensity of the wisdom that a man three times his age might have.

"What were her last words?" Rhiannon uttered.

Lugh, partially groggy and partially disoriented by the depths of his desperation, looked at her coldly.

"'Beware of your mother'" she said. He articulated as if those were the only words of truth he knew.

"She was delirious Lugh, you cannot take the words of the dying as being the truth. There is no lucidity, no reality in them!" She said softly, fighting very hard with her demons within so that they would not erupt and ruin the plans she had made and that, up until that instant of doubt in Lugh's eyes, had turned out as successfully as she could have hoped they would.

Lugh stood up and got very close to her, the tip of his nose almost touching the bridge of hers.

"You are violating my space," she said with a tone which carried the warning that he better not test her patience further.

Lugh felt anger at thinking that what Clodagh had said might, even if remotely, be true, yet part of him wanted so desperately to believe that his mother was innocent, that she had been honest with him and Clodagh all along, so he left himself open for whatever defence of herself Rhiannon was going to present to him. He needed to believe in her innocence and in her love for him, the love that was going to lend him comfort, and the courage not to slash his own throat.

Lugh stepped back from his mother, and she watched the fire of anger and doubt burning in his eyes magically transmute into tears that begged for her acceptance. Moved and reassured, she took his head in her hands and kissed his forehead. He was crying like he did when he was a child and had run to her upon waking from a nightmare.

"You need me, Lugh. Trust in me. I love you. I loved, and love, Clodagh; did you really think that I could hurt either of you?" She asked.

Like a child, he nodded negatively.

"...She must have been delirious. You are right. What reason would you have for hurting either of us?" He said trying to convince himself above all.

Rhiannon smiled, attempting to break the drama and to infuse new hope and renewed trust of her in Lugh.

"I see you are coming to your senses," she said merrily, bringing her forehead close to his. "Who's your best friend in the whole world?"

"You are," he said with all the conviction in the sound of his voice that he needed to hear to pacify himself. "You are, mother."

Clodagh was buried on Caer Balor's grounds with a very simple and brief ceremony. Urien had been warned to keep away: Lugh held him responsible, aside from Morrigan, for all that had happened to Iweridd, to Clodagh and to himself. He also felt very protective of his mother's feelings, and he blamed all her misery on Urien as well.

Urien watched the burial from his chambers' window, feeling nothing but relief at the thought that both Iweridd and Clodagh were now finally out of his life.

"Good-bye, sweet nothing...my lowly, little peasant..." he uttered under his breath, twisting his lips into an expression of simulated "feeling" which gave shape to the intensity of his mockery of her death, and of her life.

Chapter Forty-two

As summer approached, the people of Iona were readying themselves to celebrate its coming by preparing for the festival of Lugnassadh.

Morrigan and Haakon spent most of their time by the sea, the waters of which, now warmer, were more inviting than ever. For both of them the pull to the water was a compulsion of their natures. Water was the source and the shelter of their souls.

Haakon looked at Morrigan with tenderness, especially when she was staring at the sea as if in waiting of being embraced and lulled by it. She, secure in the warmth of his hold, could feel his heart beating, and each beat sent a shiver of love through her body.

Morrigan, coming out of her aquatic trance, turned her head towards Haakon's face and her love-filled eyes met his, and they both felt like they did the first time they saw each other at the fair of Beltane. She leaned closer to his shoulder and let her head shift on his chest to hear the rhythm of his breathing, and rejoiced in feeling the life-force coursing through his being. He cupped his hand around the curvature of her face and she heard only the sound of his voice, punctuated by the drumming cadence of his heart.

"The beloved, Freyja, eternal Mother of Life, became Wodan's bride. To her the spindle's wheel was consecrated and keys she had, hanging from her belt.

"She spun to complete the cloth of existence; the source of babies and every seed were her most cherished secret. Ur-Mother she was, of the deep: from It, all life came into the secret of birth, and in It, it vanished into the secret of death.

"Gracious was Freyja above any apparition, and her gentle grace lifted the heart of each god and man to the sun. She did not belong to anyone when the sky and the earth embraced. In the happiness of the dawn and the golden flame of the evening, Moon and Stars drank the light of her love and took her with them, into the black secret of the night....

"...He came to see his beloved, whom, within the shining radiance of the waters, within the silent state of the maturing stems, within the depths of the turgid calyxes revelled in the bliss of his impetuous love."

When the melodious sound of his voice stopped, Morrigan felt it should have never; life seemed to lack completeness without that wondrous, sublime poetry that had held her spellbound all through Haakon's heartfelt and breathless narration. Poetry the beauty of which had been so deep, so touching, that she was shedding tears for it, as she looked at her lover and saw the most secret and most enchanting facet of his personality uncovered.

The movement of her head lifting off of his chest called him back to reality; he too had had his turn of staring into the sea and at the fiery sky of the sunset. They said nothing to each other, at first. They kissed sweetly, more tenderly than voraciously.

"What was that beautiful poetry? Where did it come from?" Morrigan burned to know.

Haakon looked into her eyes and sized the ancientness of her soul. Like Freyja, Morrigan had an ancestral power and loveliness about her, which she radiated and tried to conceal at the same time.

"That was a passage from the Norse book of the Ur gods. You inspired me to recall and recite that passage. My father knows all of the narration, if you wish to listen to the genesis and downfall of the Norse gods," Haakon said with a teasing smile.

"I would love to hear more of that poetry; it is the most enchanting I have heard, and this is a land of poets," she said, and he kissed her forehead softly.

The sun was growing warmer each day and, each day Morrigan and Haakon watched it reflect and shimmer on the surface of the sea, and then break into millions of light-reflecting particles.

Morrigan's dreams were growing more complex and more disturbing each night. Haakon watched her toss and turn and murmur bits of unintelligible phrases in which only the name Lugh was clear. Haakon knew that the time of Morrigan's journey to the mainland was approaching, and she did too.

On a breezy summer evening at the cabin, Haakon asked Morrigan to go and walk down to the beach together.

"Tonight I'm supposed to teleport myself, body and soul. You go down to the beach and watch for me. I will attempt joining you, but do not be alarmed if it takes me a while to get there," Morrigan said smiling.

"You must be sure it's time. Are you nervous? Can I help?" Haakon asked. She hugged him and kissed his cheek.

"I know that it is time; I feel it, I'm ready. I am not any more nervous tonight than the night I projected to Airmid. You can help by waiting for me to join you by the seashore and then we shall go visit Airmid and your parents."

They kissed deeply and soulfully and, in silence, Haakon departed without turning back, leaving Morrigan to accomplish the work she was supposed to.

The new moon resplendent silvery in the darkening sky, bearing a good auspice for Morrigan's new magic undertaking. Morrigan, wearing an unobtrusive, body-hugging green tunic and leather strap sandals, stood motionless in the wind, establishing her balance by focusing her attention on the area of her body right beneath the navel, and grounding herself still on her legs, positioned slightly apart, with the right one forward in respect to the left. She stood steady in the wind which blew warm and powerful, and she attuned her mind to it, making the wind her focus and the vehicle which would help her actualize teleportation.

The wind blew more intense in progression with her growing concentration and it caressed her body, shaping it as though it were a sculpture in the process of being perfected and, as it became perfect, the molecules which made up her body came apart and dissipated in the darkness, airborne, and held together by the force of her will and by the power of the moon.

Haakon waited, looking up towards the woods, yet unsure from which direction she would come. Standing in the perfect balance that she had maintained throughout the teleportation, she materialized as Haakon watched her come together. He enveloped her into a warm hold.

"I know now how you must have felt when you watched me turn into an eagle, and then back to my own self," he said as she, relieved that her task had been accomplished, smiled.

They strolled their way to Airmid's dwelling, where the old Druid was expecting them and had invited Haakon's parents to share in the evening meal. Airmid welcomed Haakon and Morrigan with a hug. The house smelled of burnt aromatic herbs which Airmid had gathered and blended for the occasion, to help celebrate Morrigan's progression into the fulfilment of her destiny.

Sitting on the floor around a short oval table, they dined and enjoyed one another's company. There was a gap of silence which Umma broke.

"Morrigan, Lugh is calling you," she announced.

"I know," Morrigan said, looking into Umma's eyes with the warmth of love and reassurance. She could feel the pain in Umma's concern for her safety, and for that of her son.

Gunar felt and understood the uneasiness of the situation, and did not try to comfort those present with platitudes. Instead, he recited The Speech Of The High One, the Norse people's account of how Odin, the ancestral father of the Nordic Gods, achieved wisdom through constraint:

"I know I hung on that windswept tree,
Swung there for nine long nights,
Wounded by my own blade,

Bloodied for Odin,
Myself an offering to myself:
Bound to the tree
That no man's knows
Whither the roots of it run.

"None gave me bread,
None gave me drink.
Down to the deepest depths I peered
Until I spied the Runes.
With a roaring cry I seized them up,
Then dizzy and fainting, I fell.

"Well-being I won
And wisdom too.
I grew and took joy in my growth:
From a word to a word
I was led to a word,
From a deed to another deed."

***

The night came, its deep darkness weighed with eventfulness which Morrigan could feel. She tossed and turned in her bed next to her sleeping lover, weary of the fact that her stirring might wake him.

She rose from her bed, walked to a wooden cabinet and pulled out of it the bowl containing the sleep stones. These were pebbles that she had gathered long ago from every bit of land on Iona, from the seaside, from the quiet grounds of the woods, and from the bottom of the river's bed.

Once, she had half-filled with the stones the special bowl that she herself had crafted from the red clay vibrating with the spirit of the earth. She lit candles in the night, bowed her head over the bowl and whispered quiet incantations for the stones to absorb and later release, to herself, during a sleepless night. Morrigan walked slowly and quietly back to her bed, set the stones bowl next to her and blew on them to revive the power of the incantation, then lay in bed awaiting sleep.

The sleep the stones had summoned was deep and yet, Morrigan stirred and babbled, waving her arms through the darkness. Lugh was calling her. He had reached a point of such rage over Clodagh's death that, spurred by Rhiannon to do so, he had tapped into his negative inner-energy powerfully enough to reach his sister's subconscious mind.

"Come to me, sister," the voice in the darkness requested, unmistakably filled with such longing and sorrow that Morrigan's mind writhed upon hearing it. "Come save Lugh, your own brother, from the hell he is trapped in. Am I forgotten? Have I no place in your heart?"

Morrigan, still asleep, sat up in the bed and opened her eyes, haunted by the blurred vision of a young, dark man standing before her, suspended in the obscurity, pleading for her help and her love. Her hands reached out to the image but grasped emptiness, as she watched the gaunt figure of Lugh retreat and disappear.

"Come to me, to Caer Balor where, my soul imprisoned, I live my daily death at the doing of Urien and Rhiannon." His words echoed through her consciousness and woke her, as if they had been thunder. Her tumultuous waking sigh woke Haakon abruptly as well.

Haakon put his arms around Morrigan's shoulders. "You feel so cold," he said.

She turned her head towards her lover. "He is calling me to my death," she said. "I felt such anger and such pain directed at me; I love him, yet, I must accept the fact that he wants me dead," she said as she cried feebly.

"You knew this time would come. You also know that his hatred has been planted inside of him by Urien and Rhiannon. Knowing this should be of comfort to you. He will come to love you once he discovers the truth," Haakon said while she still looked upset, her eyes glazed and tired, looking at nothing.

In the morning, preparations for Morrigan and Haakon's journey were made. They were given provisions of mostly dehydrated foods to last them one week, and especially made lightweight clothing.

"Within seven moons Morrigan should be able to tell Lugh the truth and to convince him of it, or perish in the attempt of doing so. You must leave at sunset," Airmid stated, looking at peace with herself and confident in Morrigan's and Haakon's ability to survive. Unbeknownst to many, Airmid had cried bitter tears of panic and rage at the thought that Urien and Rhiannon might, once again, take away from her the people she loved most. It was her duty not to show her anguish to Haakon and Morrigan, but she had shared her grief, privately, with Umma, who bore her same concerns.

"The prophecy must be fulfilled, for better or for worse," Umma had said. Airmid had looked into Umma's eyes and discovered that the Vittka had accepted what could not be avoided, and derived a sense of relief from it. If Umma had been able to find inner peace, she should be able to reach that state too.

At a public gathering, the people of Iona witnessed and shared in a blessing for Morrigan and Haakon's safety and success. It was established that Morrigan and Haakon would teleport themselves to Aileach, where Haakon would transform himself into the eagle, Erilaz, to accompany Morrigan everywhere, ready to spring to her aid, should the need arise.

It was agreed that it would be better if Lugh did not know about Haakon's existence until he could be trusted. If successful, Morrigan and Haakon would teleport Lugh and themselves back to Iona.

Chapter Forty-three

Airmid and Umma, clothed in ceremonial white gowns, each kissed Morrigan and Haakon on both cheeks, as Gunar and the rest of the people on Iona mentally bid the two a heartfelt farewell, full of hope and good wishes. As the reddish disk of the sun began to break the pink-blue line of the horizon, Morrigan, holding Haakon's hand on one side, and their minimal luggage on the other, summoned all the energy she could muster to vanish from their world and materialize into another which was unknown to them, and filled with danger.

Haakon and Morrigan materialized in a patch of countryside surrounding Caer Balor just as the evening had begun to veil everything in dimness.

"How are you feeling?" Morrigan asked Haakon.

"Dizzy, a bit dizzy..." he replied looking rather lost.

"It's perfectly normal," she said smiling as she caressed his face.

In the darkness, Morrigan felt her brother searching for her, as much as he felt her presence. The connection between them, when fully conscious, was more intuitive than telepathic.

Morrigan turned towards Haakon. "It's time for you to become Erilaz; he is drawing near," she said. They kissed warmly, then she watched him transmute into the eagle, which rested on her right shoulder.

Lugh's heart was pounding with anticipation, due partially to curiosity and partially to anger. Morrigan felt nervous and hyper excited. "I can't believe I'm about to meet my brother," she kept thinking, while the pain of sensing his anger lurked behind the excitement.

She discerned the light of a torch in the distance and had to stop to take a deep breath and think her heart quiet. Her body was having a hard time catching up with her tumultuous emotions.

Soon Lugh realized how close he was to her and for a brief moment he forgot his rage, and longed to see his sister's face. Within a few instants their eyes met in the light of Lugh's torch, and there was silence. Each noticed the resemblance between them, although minimal.

Surprisingly to Lugh, as he gazed into his sister's eyes he felt the warmth of a wave of inner peace which made it easier for him to bring himself to smile to greet Morrigan, whose eyes were brimming with emotion.

"Welcome, sister," Lugh uttered while reaching for her luggage.

She extended her hand to his face and had to touch it.

"I cannot believe that you are real" she said, and then introduced him to Erilaz.

"It's a fine bird, majestic," he commented. "I bet it weighs on your shoulder."

"It does, but I am accustomed to it," Morrigan replied.

Lugh experienced an instant of doubt about all which Rhiannon had told him about Morrigan and Airmid.

"You have to help me, sister. Stay with us at Caer Balor and watch Urien and Rhiannon. Only if you get to know them as I do, we will be able to devise a plan for me to break free."

She nodded, knowing full well that he was lying, that he was trying to trap her, and she played along for a while.

"How are you going to explain my presence to Urien and Rhiannon? I had planned of dwelling elsewhere for the time being," she said.

"I made a deal with them. I promised I would fulfill their wishes of making a warrior out of me, in exchange for letting me meet my only sister. You see, I am not cut out to be a fighter; that is the very thing from which I want to run away, and the main reason I summoned you here," Lugh explained.

She gave him a look so fierce and so tender at once, that he found himself gasping for air.

"You want me dead," she stated in cold blood, startling him.

"It is you who has been hurting us; it is you who wants to see us dead, in your misguided belief that Urien and Rhiannon murdered our birth parents! You seek to destroy us!" He shouted with the accusatory conviction of his implanted beliefs.

"I mean you no harm," she replied serenely. "Why should I walk with you to my death?"

"Because if you do not, I will slay you right here, right now," Lugh answered, trying hard to feel the viciousness of his threats in his heart as he knew he could not actually kill her.

"Why don't you, then?" She shouted, defiant.

"Because Urien and Rhiannon have always wanted to meet you. After all the harm that you've caused them, it's only fair that they would at least have their curiosity satisfied."

"They want to skin me alive personally," Morrigan interjected.

"They don't want to harm you, but they will have to do it if you don't stop using your magic to our detriment."

Morrigan felt her blood boil with rage. "They've told you the story backwards, you fool!" she yelled. "But I'll come, and I will prove to you that I have done nothing to harm any of you, especially you!"

"We must follow our destiny Lugh," she said, simmering to a state of sedation. "Let me show you the truth, let me tell you who they are, what they've done, and what they still do. That is why I came to you and I won't leave without my brother."

"Don't lie to me, Morrigan. I know you hate me. I always knew you would come after me and my parents some day, so I called for you to cut short the agony of waiting," Lugh replied coldly.

"How can you be sure that they haven't lied to you?" She asked.

"Let's go," Lugh said, pondering with puzzlement in his heart the memory of Clodagh's dying words of warning about Rhiannon, and the exhortation to develop trust in his sister. Still, he thought that, after all, he had known Urien and Rhiannon his whole life; Morrigan was a stranger to him.

At one motion of Lugh's torch, soldiers gathered around them. They all walked to the nearby Caer Balor in silence, while Erilaz hovered low above Morrigan's head.

Chapter Forty-four

The entrance corridors of the castle looked gloomy and bare. Morrigan felt an unprecedented sense of dread and oppression and, as a divertive, she tried to concentrate on the light of the torches which hung high on the walls, set between the cracks of the rectangular stone blocks.

The corridors, narrow and cold, branched out maze-like, leading to different wings of the castle and to a multitude of rooms.

"Why do they need all these rooms?" Morrigan pondered, not used to such wastefulness, as she passed by dark chambers and closed doors.

Lugh stopped in front of the entrance to the conference chamber, broadly lit and sumptuous when compared to the surrounding squalor of the palace.

Morrigan stopped also; Lugh was staring into her eyes.

"Urien and Rhiannon awaited your coming. Try to show them their due respect; after you caused the death of Clodagh I was set on hounding you myself and to slay you. It's thanks to my parents that you stand here, still breathing."

"Ah!" Morrigan uttered sarcastically, leaving Lugh feeling unsure of whether or not that "ah" had been an expression of jest.

As Morrigan stepped into the large and luminous room, Urien and Rhiannon sat, as regal-looking as they could possibly manage, in their chairs of authority, holding glassed filled with warm cider. Urien was so excited at the sight of Morrigan that he could hear the blood rushing to his head.

Morrigan's vision was filled with the bright light of the room and, for the first few seconds, all she could see through the vapour-like cloud of brightness were two figures sitting very still and quite far from where she was standing. As she walked forward, her vision finally cleared and, once she was close enough to the sitting figures, she blinked quickly and put their faces into focus.

It struck her how young and beautiful Rhiannon looked in person, and she was assaulted by a choky feeling, realizing that those were the tangible results of many sacrifices of children.

"Welcome to Caer Balor," Urien said standing up, and motioned a servant to prepare a chair for their guest.

"Beautiful eagle," he added.

"Am I truly welcome?" Morrigan baited. Lugh, who stood behind her, came forward and motioned her to stop it, by running his hand horizontally under his chin. Rhiannon motioned him to cease his intimidations and spoke.

"We love Lugh and, if you turn out to be as wonderful a person as he is, I am certain we'll come to love you too. After all, you are his only sister."

Food was fetched for Erilaz and a frugal dinner was served, but quiet reigned through the meal, after which Morrigan was showed to her room by Lugh himself. He found that he was very curious about her, whether he liked it or not. He felt strangely at peace in her company. She had a sedating, but not numbing, effect on his anger. He experienced a kind of completeness around her.

"It must be her wicked magic," he rationalized.

"I'm not out to get you," she said while entering her room, as if she were responding to his thoughts.

"Come in, talk with me," Morrigan said while setting Erilaz up on a perch protruding from the wall, placed next to yet another of the many owls that she had noticed at Caer Balor.

In defiant silence, Lugh obliged her request and sat himself down on an armchair facing the one in which Morrigan had seated herself.

"Who was Clodagh?" She asked with empathy which he misconstrued as flippancy.

"How dare you ask that question? I told you I know it was you who caused her death! Don't insult her memory by pretending that you don't know who she was!" Lugh blurted out bitterly.

Morrigan stood up, walked to the door, opened it and motioned him to get out.

"Until you give me a chance, the benefit of the doubt at least, I see we won't be able to communicate and, believe me, for our people's sake and for your own good, we need to. No time for games."

Lugh blushed with embarrassment and wondered who "our people" might be. It was true; he realized that he had not given her even the benefit of the doubt, yet, he knew that, as much as he had been trying to deny it to himself, he had good reason to doubt Rhiannon.

"Please, please forgive my close-mindedness, my arrogance. This place is all I have ever known and my parents' words the only truth. Let me stay and talk with you." He appealed to her soulfully and she knew he was sincere.

Morrigan closed the door, smiled at Lugh and walked in front of the owl, then began staring very intensely into its eyes.

"What are you doing?" Lugh asked intrigued.

"I am admiring this lovely bird," she answered automatically, barely moving her lips and without turning her head in Lugh's direction.

"It looks more like you're studying it; why?" He probed, a bit alarmed by her physical stillness, and the far removed sound of her voice. As she saw and felt him walk towards her, she flattened her hand against the air in front of him as a signal to stop there, which Lugh obeyed. He looked in the direction of the owl and noticed that it had stopped blinking.

"Is it dead?" He asked anxiously.

"I would not hurt a living thing, an innocent creature," she replied as she finally blinked and looked, smiling, towards Lugh. Her smile radiated such happiness and earnestness that he felt its warmth sink into his bones, and he found himself smiling back with her same sincerity.

"What is it with the owl?" Lugh asked again.

Morrigan put her arm around his shoulders and walked with him to the edge of her bed where they both sat, as he looked at her inquisitively.

"All these owls I have seen at Caer Balor, they're not ordinary. Did you ever notice, sense, anything particular about them?" She asked.

"No, not really. The owl in my room, Bryn, is practically my best friend; I have had it since I was a small child. I love Bryn."

"There is nothing wrong with the birds in themselves, nothing evil at all. They are peculiar creatures because they have been tampered with." Lugh looked at her in puzzlement. "Somebody has surgically linked their visual and auditory centres in their brain to her own...." She clarified.

"You said her own, right? You said her...are you referring to my mother?" Lugh interrupted.

"I am referring to Rhiannon," she answered dryly.

"Why would she do that? I know that she possibly could have; she is a powerful sorceress and has a vast knowledge of human and animal physiology," Lugh reasoned aloud.

"She did it to be aware of everything that happens in this castle, every corner of it since, as powerful as she may be, she cannot be in several places at once.

"The owls see and hear what goes on in every room, especially yours I would assume and, when she wills it, she establishes mental contact with any owl, and she sees and hears what it does. I had to neutralize this one; I made it temporarily blind and deaf, so that all she sees and hears is nothingness."

Lugh realized that it all sounded plausible. Rhiannon did always have the ultimate control and run of the domestic as well as the political business at Caer Balor.

He felt that Morrigan was not lying. At the same time, he felt the staggering weight of the implications in the matter: in light of Morrigan's discovery, and his, Bryn had not been a gift of love to him, to be a companion to him, but was made into a spy, a spy which relayed to Rhiannon all words and deeds that he had always thought happened in the privacy of his chambers.

He looked stunned and pale, bitten by the first, tangible sign that made him see that his whole life might have been a cruel lie. He said nothing for a few instants, bowed his head down and began to cry, but could not sort out whether the source of those tears was rooted in pain or anger.

He told Morrigan about his lover, Clodagh and Urien's rape of her. She did not appear surprised. Morrigan gently stroked his cheeks; she was crying too, because she could feel his anguish.

"Look at this as the beginning of a new,   richer life. What was before has not been wasted time, but precious experience. You are the one who was lied to, not the liar. Have no regrets."

Lugh raised his gaze to her and realized that he felt no shame for his tears. "Tell me everything," he said.

Chapter Forty-five

The next morning the atmosphere was tense at the breakfast table. Rhiannon looked into Morrigan's eyes with intimidation and frustration.

"I know what you did to my owl," she kept thinking, while wishing that she could say so aloud and punish Morrigan accordingly, but she could not yet. Before revealing herself, she needed to pry out of Morrigan all the magical knowledge that she possessed, then, she could discard her.

Lugh looked at Rhiannon bleakly, distrustfully and with anger, having reason to believe Morrigan, and thus having accepted the fact that, just as Rhiannon had raised him amidst lies, she had caused Clodagh to die.

What truly disturbed him was having learned that Urien and Rhiannon were siblings and lovers, and that they had been instrumental in the murder of his birth parents and acted in all things with cunning and maliciousness.

Yet, although he knew that what Morrigan had told him was true, part of him still could not accept it and kept hoping that, Rhiannon at least, would have a logical explanation that would exonerate her from all the wrong doings she had been a part of.

"Maybe Urien made her do those things," he thought, at the same time being fully aware that he was getting entangled into wishful thinking.

"Why did you leave that regal bird of yours in you room?" Urien enquired as inanely as ever.

"It was sleeping. I will feed it later." Morrigan answered with annoyance, feeling that Urien's interest in Erilaz was inappropriate and intrusive, and it gave her the impression that, if and when Urien decided to make her suffer, he would start by torturing her beloved Erilaz.

"Does your palace have dungeons?" Morrigan asked rhetorically and provocatively, while looking into Urien's and Rhiannon's eyes, whose pupils dilated in full alertness.

"All there is down there is a bunch of old things, that's all," Rhiannon anticipated, stone cold.

Lugh did not know about Rhiannon's blood sacrifices yet. Morrigan had thought it best to tell him at a later time, since what she had already told her brother had been so psychologically overwhelming to him, and he needed to assimilate it all before dealing with further revelations.

She remembered that in one moon the summer solstice would be celebrated on Iona and a child would be slain by Rhiannon. She had to prevent that from happening, and she was going to need help to accomplish that.

The only way that she had to convince Lugh of Rhiannon's sacrifices was to show him. She hated hurting him further, but it was necessary to his growth and to her own. He must know the whole truth in order for the both of them to transform their lives.

Rhiannon appeared very tense, aware of the fact that Morrigan could sense her feelings of lust for Lugh. Morrigan herself was a bit taken aback from that revelation, but then reminded herself of where and amongst whom she was and it all seemed befitting.

"I wonder how much you know about me; how much you have told him," Rhiannon thought, and this time Morrigan intercepted the thought and gave Rhiannon a look that seemed like an answer.

"Not enough, yet," her eyes had said.

Rhiannon, flushed with rage and the feeling of powerlessness which comes when one has been stripped naked and exposed to the eyes of another - she got up and left the table. "I need to confer with you alone, in my chambers, as soon as you're done eating," she ordered Lugh as she left the room.

Lugh's heart raced: for the first time he was afraid of Rhiannon. He knew she would no longer be Mother to him. Morrigan looked into his eyes. Urien had left the table also, so Morrigan seized the moment to inform Lugh of the nature of Rhiannon's interest in him.

"She wants you," Morrigan said. "She has lusted after you for a long time, I could see it in her eyes, hear it her thoughts, feel it in her soul. It is her plan to rid herself of Urien and to share her power, and her bed, with you."

Lugh grew pale, stood up, walked up to an empty bowl and vomited in it.

"What are you saying?" He uttered among shivers that kept creeping up his back. "That is supposed to be my mother and, as horrible as she might be, I refuse to believe that she'd love me that way. It sickens me!" He shouted, turning to look at Morrigan.

"I told you so that you can prepare yourself for what she has in mind to tell you, in her private conference with you. She knows I have told you many unpleasant truths about her and Urien, so, she is going to use the offering of her body to you as a last attempt to keep you on her side."

"I will go talk to her and I'll prove to you that you are wrong about this, you must be!" Lugh said as he walked out of that room into his own, for grooming and composing himself before he paid a visit to Rhiannon.

Morrigan looked at him with tenderness and sadness into her eyes, for she knew that the anguish Lugh was about to walk into would not be his last. She would have to tell him of Rhiannon's blood sacrifices and after that, maybe he would become stronger and accept the reality of the situation. What crime could be more heinous than killing a child?

"Haakon!" she remembered suddenly, grabbed some food that she had saved in her plate for him, and ran to her room.

Urien was waiting there, seated on her bed, with Erilaz perched on his left arm.

Morrigan, stunned, stopped abruptly in his presence but tried to appear calm.

"Why are you here?"

"I won't play games with you," he said looking at her with hungry eyes. "I find you sexually desirable, very desirable, and I was hoping that I might have had the same effect on you...."

The very thought of his implications made Morrigan feel sick.

"I find you as attractive as the sight and the smell of a butchered swine," she dared.

"I expected you to be spirited; it's exactly that potential to be cruel that I have seen in you that excites me."

"You won't find me very exciting if I break a couple of major bones in your repulsive body," she warned, the tone of her voice growing deeper.

"You break my bones, I'll break this little one's," Urien said eyeing Erilaz. "I gather it's special, or should I say he? A shape-shifter, perhaps, this lover of yours?"

"How do you know about this?" Morrigan asked, irate and refusing to believe that Urien could be that perceptive.

"Rhiannon told me; she sees a lot, you know, almost as well as you do...."

Erilaz, having grown restless, was pinned down to Urien's left arm by his right hand and stroked forcefully, to intimidate rather than to pet. But Erilaz was able to break free and flew around the room, and then squawked and circled above Urien's head.

Urien, scared but not defeated, lunged at Morrigan, gripped her waist with one hand and tore the top of her gown off while attempting to kiss her.

Morrigan, surprised that she could, did shatter a few bones in his body by the strength of her will, and he stumbled and fell, whining in pain. Haakon, who had had time to shape-shift into himself while Urien attacked Morrigan, could not refrain from punching Urien hard in the stomach and was about to do a lot worse, when Morrigan stopped him and brought him back to his senses.

"You are not a killer!" She said, and he knew she was right.

Urien had passed out. Morrigan checked his vital signs and, transferring healing energy from her right hand to his body, mended the broken bones and quietly chanted a spell that would keep him unconscious at least until midday.

Haakon stood in front of Morrigan and looked at her tenderly, seeing that the skin covering her collar bone and her left shoulder had been scratched and bruised by Urien.

"Does it hurt?" He asked caressing her face.

"A little, but I can take care of that," she said kissing the knuckles of his hand.

"What do we do now?"

"We wait," she said. "Lugh is going to seek me out in a while. He is about to find out of Rhiannon's real feelings and intentions towards him; she wants him for her lover. He will be upset and come here, where I'll introduce the two of you, and we'll work on a plan to catch Rhiannon in the middle of her human sacrifice on the day of the Summer Solstice. The child must be saved!

"Afterwards, you, I, Lugh and the child will have to disappear. If captured, they'll put us to death, and we'll have to figure out what to do when and if it comes to that."

Haakon kissed her bruises and held her close to him.

"It's so good to hold you," he said.

Chapter Forty-six

In Rhiannon's bedroom, Morrigan's prediction was unfolding.

"You were not yourself at breakfast today," Rhiannon lamented. "Your eyes looked at me with a new sternness; what lies has Morrigan told you about me?"

"Did you kill Clodagh because you hoped to become my lover?" He asked bluntly.

"She killed Clodagh, she did it!" Rhiannon shouted, outraged that he had dared to take Morrigan's word over hers.

"...Liar! You and Urien made me believe that you were my parents, while you murdered my real mother and father and took me away from the only family I had left!

"You made me believe that you and Urien were just lovers, while the disgusting truth is that you are brother and sister, too. Do you realize how sick you make me? How sick you two are?" Lugh shouted back.

She, out of her mind with the panic of having lost any hope to enthral Lugh into her life and her bed, physically threw herself at him, dropped on her knees and wound herself around his legs.

"I did it all for us, I've always loved you! Aren't I beautiful enough, young enough, desirable enough for you?" She begged as she climbed up along his body to stand up, and he stepped back, in abhorrence and disbelief.

"How could you ever come to think of me that way? It's all true...all my sister has told me is true! You and Urien are greedy, murderous, lascivious monsters and I have been trapped here by you, all these years!" Lugh yelled. But words no longer frightened Rhiannon, who had made herself deaf to them and was frantically disrobing in a last attempt to make love to him.

"...How can you know the depths of my love if you don't make love to me? Love me!" She commanded as she clutched the leather tunic covering his chest and rubbed herself against him.

"Just make love to me once, just once, and then you will never have to see me again, I swear it! You will be free to go...."

Lugh had no choice but to push her away from him. She fell hard on her back and began to whimper in very visible pain, but could not scream, the pain was so intense.

Lugh was torn at that sight; she was an aberration, but also a human being. Should he help her? He could not just walk away. He kneeled down beside her and took her hand to reassure her of the fact that he'd get her help, but as soon as she had clutched his hand, he watched her canines grow into fangs which sank into the flesh of his chest before he had any time to react to what was happening.

He found himself with his back flat on the cold floor and the weight of Rhiannon on him, as she sat astride him. He shut his eyes and screamed louder than he ever had in his life, and a few instants later he heard people running towards him. He opened his eyes and saw Haakon and Morrigan grubbing Rhiannon by each arm and dragging her off his body, while she growled and salivated like a beast.

Lugh could finally breathe and he found the strength to stand up and watch Morrigan hypnotize the beast that Rhiannon had become, just as he had seen her hypnotize the owl in her room. But it did not work with Rhiannon, who fought Morrigan's power by invoking that of Balor, and strength came to her.

Haakon held Rhiannon's arms folded behind her back, as she struggled to reach out to Morrigan to hit her, to blind her, to destroy the one who had destroyed her only reason for living. It was a demon they all were seeing: her body looked shrunk and stringy, odd muscle clusters bulged and relaxed under the skin with each of her growls. Her skin looked gray and lifeless, like that of a corpse, but she had a wiry strength in her limbs, and Haakon found it increasingly harder to keep her arms bound and her torso still.

She tried to kick herself free but Lugh bound her legs with his arms while Morrigan tried to hold her gaze steady. The beast began to salivate acid as it tried to speak, and the sound of her voice now being that of Balor, it paralysed the three who were trying to fight her. The beast was free to scoot away, revealing the presence of a grotesquely gnarled backbone.

Morrigan, Haakon and Lugh were shaking and realized that they could finally move and speak.

"I have never encountered a force that dark before in my life," Morrigan said.

"Whoever you are," Lugh said looking at Haakon, "thank you, both of you, to have come to my help."

Haakon smiled in acknowledgment.

"This is Erilaz; his human name is Haakon, a shape-shifter, and he is my lover," Morrigan said. Lugh looked truly surprised.

"He's the eagle?"

Haakon laughed, "Yes, I'm the eagle."

"There is a magical world out there," Lugh realized. "A world full of good, wondrous magic and I have been kept prisoner here, ignorant of it all."

"No longer, my brother. You have powers which have not been allowed to develop. On Iona, we'll work together on identifying them and on bringing them to life," Morrigan reassured him.

"There are so many wonders for you to discover, so much to live for.

"We have to leave; it's not over with Rhiannon. She could have killed us, but she let us live. If I know her at all, it is just so that she may play with us and then kill us later," Lugh said.

"There is a child that we must save. The coming moon will bring about the time for Rhiannon to sacrifice a child," Morrigan said, shocking Lugh. She explained and he wept and trembled for a while, as she and Haakon tried to comfort him.

"She is resilient," Morrigan continued, frank but compassionate. "I believe that she will overcome her disillusionment over you," Morrigan said looking at Lugh. "All she has left is the pursuit of power and, now more than ever, she will try to achieve it at any cost.

"She is going to want to restore her youth, her beauty. Maybe she will be able to, maybe she won't, but I know that she is going to try. We have to stay, hide and watch her, see whether she'll go through with the sacrifice. I wonder if she holds a victim captive yet."

Just as they were talking, they heard the clunk of soldiers' gear and the heavy footsteps of many advance towards them. They grew silent as they watched Rhiannon and Urien get closer and closer to them, followed by what seemed to be their whole army.

Rhiannon looked as young and as beautiful as she ever did. Urien also seemed to have been restored to perfect health and consciousness. They looked refreshed but cold and far removed, and Morrigan screamed in terror.

"They have no souls.... Their bodies are empty shells!"

As Rhiannon advanced towards Morrigan, Haakon and Lugh cried out in fear: they could feel it too, but they tried to shield Morrigan from the beast.

One touch of Rhiannon's hand felt as cold as the most bitter winter to Haakon and Lugh, and they felt that they had to step aside.

Rhiannon was standing only a few inches away from Morrigan, who felt cold and was shivering. She was horrified in the presence of that animated shell of a human without a soul, and kept repeating words of peacefulness and courage to herself, but that force was too dark even for her to fight it.

"Here," Rhiannon's voice sounded metallic and hollow, "You have no power. Balor has taken our souls in exchange for limitless power within the walls of this castle. We still possess our minds, consciousness and will. Balor has taken away only what we never wanted: that remote potential to be weakened by any feelings of love, forgiveness, guilt. You know what I speak of, good girl; you are full of such weaknesses, and it shall be easy to destroy you, all of you!

"We no longer need the knowledge of your magic; it is useless to us, too unsophisticated for us, after having been blessed by the eye of Balor."

Morrigan turned helplessly towards her brother and her lover.

"I cannot fight this," she whispered.

"You can. We will, the three of us" Haakon said, shaking her gently, while Lugh begged her not to give up, not to believe that Urien and Rhiannon were unbeatable.

Urien stepped forward. "We could have such fun, torturing you, dicing you up alive; drinking blood out of your skulls. But, Balor says, you must die burning at dawn, in the presence of the rebellious people of Aileach.

"There has been unrest for too long, simmering among the people. Let your deaths be a lesson to them. After all, they'll see my son, Lugh, up there. What mercy could they hope for?" Urien said, his voice as hollow as if resounding from the bottom of a deep well.

One look from Rhiannon and the soldiers took Morrigan, Haakon and Lugh to the dungeons to lock them in a cell. They all walked in silence through the dark corridors, into the stench and coldness of the underground prison.

The captives huddled together once the heavy door was locked behind them. Lugh had been exposed to somewhat rough military training all his life, but Morrigan and Haakon had never known the restrictions of a cell, or those of total darkness; they panicked, tried to crawl their way up towards the door and began to scream and to pound and scratch at the cell's door until they felt their fingernails ache and bleed.

"We'll be out of here at dawn. In the meantime, we can at least talk. We are not alone, we have one another, and we can figure out a way to escape the execution," Lugh said.

"I feel ashamed. I have never felt so powerless, so hopeless..." Morrigan whispered.

"I thought I'd have more courage, but I disappoint myself. The soldiers took us away and I could do nothing," Haakon added.

Lugh felt angry. "Listen to yourselves: '...I have never felt so powerless...' '...The soldiers took us away, and I did nothing....' Who do you think you are?

"Morrigan, the way to prove yourself to your Self is by fighting back just when others have made you feel powerless. Find those inner-resources and fight like a warrior, if you cannot fight like a Druid.

"Haakon, no one expects you to be responsible for the fate of us all. It is human to feel fear. You may be scared and yet, be courageous enough not to let the fear paralyse you. Pull yourselves together, I need you!"

Morrigan and Haakon's silence let Lugh know that they were pondering his words.

"You are very wise for someone who has not had much experience on the outside," Morrigan said.

"If you have a plan," Haakon added, "tell us how we can help."

"You two can teleport, can't you?" Lugh perceptively enquired. "Could you teleport me also?"

"Yes, we can teleport you also. We no longer need to stay here to prevent the child's sacrifice; it's obvious that there is no child, and that Balor will provide all for Urien and Rhiannon from now on.

But I cannot dematerialize us right now while we are in Caer Balor. It is true, here my magic seems to have no power, but once out of the castle, once we are closely gathered together I shall attempt to will us to Iona. I'll need to make physical contact with both of you, perhaps holding hands," Morrigan said.

"I am sure that Rhiannon and Urien are aware of these facts, so they will keep us separated on the way to the stake, but I know that we'll be all tied around the same pole, so we'll be within a certain physical proximity. Is that going to be enough?" Lugh asked.

"It should be," Morrigan explained. "As long as we are close enough for our auras to blend, teleportation should be possible."

Charged up with new hope and confidence in themselves, the prisoners awaited the coming of dawn patiently, craving light and fresh air and the thrill of pursuing their freedom.

Lugh, deep in meditation, surprised himself by achieving telepathic contact with Corax and Tharan, and ordered the birds free and they obeyed, flying away from Aileach.

Chapter Forty-seven

When the sun lay low on the horizon, the captives heard the clunk and jingles of keys unlock the heavy door of the dungeons, and the first beam of light invaded their sight fields powerfully and painfully. Soldiers marched down the steps to the filthy basement floor and then to the cell and opened it. They grabbed Morrigan first, then pushed them all up the steps leading out of that tomb.

Once their eyes had adjusted to the incoming light, the three looked back and caught a glimpse of the statue of Balor, the monstrous god whose gigantic eye, at the moment covered by its heavy lid, quivered and moved as though it belonged to a live body. The sight chilled Morrigan's blood. "...Balor is alive in our palace...." Rhiannon's words reverberated in her mind.

When Rhiannon had called upon Balor's name, she invoked it with such energy of will that she caused the eye to become real. In its presence its gaze did not kill her, but restored her youthful appearance, her physical beauty, and Urien's health.

Once out of Caer Balor, Morrigan, Lugh and Haakon found themselves almost blinded by the light, and deafened by the screaming crowd. The people had been told about the prisoners and about the fact that they were being executed for trying to overthrow Urien and Rhiannon's reign. The crowd, far from being intimidated, cheered profusely and yelled words of praise at the captives, which they thought of as heroes. They were closing in on them.

Lugh was not used to finding himself in the midst of large crowds, so he felt the suffocating grip of claustrophobia take his breath away and, overwhelmed by panic, he yelled. Haakon and Morrigan looked at him with empathy.

"You won't suffocate, it just feels like it. Breathe slow and shallow," Morrigan whispered, and a guard struck her across her face with the back of his rough hand. Haakon and Lugh synchronically reacted to that act by kneeing the guard in the stomach and tried to free themselves, but they were punched down and doubled over in pain, their lips and cheeks bleeding.

"We are about to die; isn't that enough?" Morrigan yelled, and a soldier dug his elbow in her ribs. Morrigan vomited.

Urien and Rhiannon, in the fashion of the Roman emperors they had heard about, sat high in their thrones which were mounted on a platform built close to the stake, to ensure a better view of the execution.

The soldiers walking ahead and behind of the prisoners had to shove their way through the overexcited crowd by hitting and kicking the subjects out of their way, even spearing the most obstinate ones, and then tossing the corpses aside to be swallowed by the ceaseless swarming.

Once at the feet of the steps leading up to the stake, Morrigan realized how high the pile of wood logs was all around the wide pole to which they were going to be chained.

In proud silence, and almost relishing the salty flavour of their own sweat, the three let the soldiers chain them to the large pole without opposition. Morrigan tried to set her fear aside to concentrate on the teleportation spell which would deliver them from death.

Lugh faced Urien and Rhiannon. They sat, clothed in full royal attire; deep purple gowns rimmed with gold; crowns and jewels, and he was overcome with a feeling of freedom that he had never felt before.

"You shall be delivered from Evil!" Lugh screamed at the crowd, which cheered loudly and became agitated by the prophetic energy that they felt in his words.

Haakon was the one who had been chained to the pole rather removed from Lugh and Morrigan. She was growing increasingly worried and laboured hard to pacify her mind, and to positively channel her will into the escape.

A tall soldier carrying a torch approached the gigantic pile of resin-covered wood and lit it. Morrigan felt the intensity of the blaze in a hot waft of air which, of all things, reminded her of the pleasant smell and feel of the bonfires at home. Then, she was startled by the flames, high and menacing, but she couldn't scream. The survival instinct kicked in, and with it, a powerful wave of adrenaline, and she found her concentration.

She strained to extend her chained wrists towards Haakon's hands, but couldn't reach him. Her heart sank: if she could not get any closer they would not escape. Not without Haakon. Her mind went blank as she watched, panicked, the flames lick their way towards them.

She heard the crowd emit a sigh of awe and then saw Erilaz set on her shoulder, and her heart burst with renewed hope. They were ready, but it was hard to still her mind.

"Do it!" Lugh incited her. "Do not doubt your abilities!"

She breathed in mostly smoke and coughed, as a result breaking her concentration. Just as she had regained it and commanded the three of them to Iona, a far-shot spear coming from one of Urien and Rhiannon's best soldiers, pierced Erilaz' breast while they dematerialized, and the eagle had fallen in her arms.

**

They were on Iona in what appeared to them to be only a flash, and realized that Erilaz, now shifting into his human form, had been wounded to death. Morrigan emitted a cry so morbid that it made it clear to the forces of the universe that she wished to be struck dead too.

In Aileach the crowd sounded crazed. Urien and Rhiannon, shocked and defeated, quickly sought shelter inside the walls of their fortress and the guards were ordered to kill anyone who came anywhere near the castle grounds, and to impale their heads around the outer perimeter of the castle for the rest of the people to see.

Chapter Forty-eight

Morrigan, Lugh and Haakon had materialized in the middle of the village, where Airmid had figured that they would, and were welcomed by a silent crowd. Umma had felt the shot which killed her son; the village knew he was dead.

Following her scream of desperation, Morrigan cried bitterly, hunched over her lover's limp, cold body. His tunic was stained with so much blood.

Lugh wrapped his arms around his sister's quivering shoulders as she wept.

Airmid and Umma gathered close to them, looking at peace with themselves.

"Do something!" Morrigan yelled in her grandmother's face as she hugged her, then turned to Umma.

"You must revive him!" She kept screaming, her face distorted by pain and reddened by the profuse tears. Airmid and Umma spoke softly, caressing her hair.

"Haakon might be able to be brought back to life. The ritual has not been attempted on Iona for many years but we have nothing to lose by trying," Airmid said, as Morrigan realized that her grandmother and Umma had already thought of a way to restore the life of her beloved.

"How are you going to do it? Is there anything I can do? Tell me what must be done!" Morrigan uttered faster than she could think. Inside she felt like a tangled bundle of raw emotions.

"Morrigan!" Airmid commanded. "Calm yourself! We are going to do whatever possible to help him. We love him too. I cannot avail myself of your help unless you piece your mind together."

Umma hugged the girl and they both cried. Airmid, and Gunar, who was torn inside by a quiet grief, moved Haakon's body to the dolmen altar by the sea.

Morrigan, Lugh and Umma slowly followed, progressively finding the inner comfort they thought they had lost.

Haakon's body was laid on the dolmen inside the circle of stones where Amergin and Kalos had appeared to Morrigan. She still felt their presence there blow a soft breeze of hope through her heart. She realized that she could smell the cherished and missed aroma of Iona's sea again.

A violet, silk cloth covered Haakon's naked body, then Airmid ordered everyone but Umma to leave them alone for the recitation of the spell which would stop the decaying of Haakon's body, and which would put his soul in stasis until the time would come that the life-force could be available to fill that body again.

Lugh, Morrigan, Gunar and the crowd who had followed, slowly and reluctantly walked back to the village. Lugh huddled close to his sister, his arms around her shoulders as if he meant to protect her from everything. He was surprised and overjoyed by the welcoming presence of Corax and Tharan, which flew all around him. They had made it home too!

Gunar walked with his head bowed, oblivious to the content of the ritual, wishing he knew. He hoped that he could welcome his son's return to life with joy and feasting.

The weather became stormy. Airmid and Umma had raised the wind, called on Taranis, divinity of thunder, and invoked rain and lightning. In the distance, a bluish flame of light, not fire, could be spied burning inside the circle of stones and the remote and arcane chanting of the Druid and the Vittka, their voices carried close and far by the hissing wind, resounded as the evening approached and its darkness weighed upon Morrigan's heart as though it were the slab of the altar where her beloved lay.

Time went by and the moon appeared. Soon after, Umma and Airmid were at Airmid's dwelling, where Lugh, Gunar and Morrigan had been sitting and waiting.

"Haakon's body has been successfully put into stasis. In two moons, the Fomor will be called to the surface by Urien and Rhiannon. Morrigan and Lugh, the same ritual that the two of you will enact to call the Dannan's army from the sky will have the power to resuscitate Haakon," Airmid explained, while Umma, exhausted, had sat by the fire, and felt that she could finally grieve.

"I know nothing of your ways. I don't know about this ritual," Lugh lamented.

"Remember," Airmid said, "we must be ready within two moons. By then, you will have learned all you need to know. Now, grandson of mine," Airmid was visibly moved, "come hug this old woman, who's only waited a lifetime to meet you" she said, opening her arms and her heart to him.

Lugh eagerly responded; he hugged his grandmother and felt he was home. He intuitively knew that was what home was supposed to feel like. Morrigan joined in the embrace.

"Are you sure that the revival ritual will work?" Morrigan asked.

"The hard part was putting Haakon in suspended animation; the rest will unfold easily. Have faith in the goddess," Airmid said, caressing Morrigan's reddened face.

The embrace soon extended to Umma and Gunar, especially, who had been somewhat neglected and left alone to grieve, and was now given a chance to rejoice in the light of new hope.

Chapter Forty-nine

In Aileach Urien and Rhiannon, still trying to recuperate from the blow of defeat, awaited the night of the third moon, the full moon during which they would mate, teleport to Iona and call the Fomor to life.

Ragnar and part of their army were to remain in Aileach to keep control over the city and its restless inhabitants. The most ruthless, highly trained part of their army had set sail for Iona almost immediately after the captives escaped, so that they would be able to rendezvous with Urien and Rhiannon within three moons.

"I just did not anticipate that turn of events!" Rhiannon screamed at Urien, who had blamed her for her lack of foresight. "...It did not even occur to me that the eagle-man could shape-shift while chained up!" She yelled.

"So much for your smarts and for your Balor-enhanced second sight!" Urien sneered.

"You are the one to talk, seen and proved that you are totally useless, skilless and helpless without me," retorted Rhiannon, who made a dramatic exit out of their bedchambers and was directed towards her laboratory in the dungeons.

***

The night came over Iona, but not many could sleep. People too were being trained to be part of The Ritual: all souls had to become one, as it was when life first began, in order to survive the Fomor.

In the morning Airmid called yet another meeting to refresh the instructions that she had been giving the people gradually, during the time in which Morrigan and Haakon had been gone.

They practiced the attunement of all minds into one, a perfect state of communion with one another's consciousness and that of the cosmos. That is how they were supposed to fight back, with the power and the energy that the merging of their life-forces would generate.

The actual, physical battling would happen only between the Fomor and the Dannan, but Urien's soldiers were expected to be there and attack the local population. Airmid and Umma had taught the people to use their minds to control the aggressors.

"As long as you keep attuned to one another and maintain focus, you'll be able to manipulate Urien's men," Airmid had promised.

The most important function of the people was to prevent Urien and Rhiannon's men from disrupting the ongoing ritual in which

Morrigan and Lugh would be engaged and, of course, to protect themselves, until the Dannan would descend from the sky.

The young people were assigned the task to take the small children into hiding to the other side of the island, where they would go underground for the duration of the battle.

After the council Morrigan asked Airmid if she could go see Haakon.

"You may go, but do not touch him: his body is enveloped in an energy field which is dangerous to the living. I hope you are aware of the fact that it will be very painful to look at him, lifeless," Airmid said.

Morrigan nodded affirmatively and began her walk towards the dolmen by the sea. Umma, although starved for the sight of her son, would rather wait and look at him when he had come alive.

At the sight of Haakon's face, his skin now donning a blue cast, Morrigan burst into tears and felt the first of many pangs of pain.

"I love you. Wherever you are, wherever your soul is suspended. If you can see me, if you can hear me, know that I love you and that I will put all of myself into calling you back to me. I am sorry about Aileach; I was not strong enough, fast enough to get us away before they..." she swallowed hard and breathed deeply. "Before they shot you..." she thought, unable to speak.

She walked away abruptly because she could not endure being there any longer. It seemed so unfruitful and it hurt far too much. She found Umma half way between the dolmen site and Airmid's home. She was waiting there for Morrigan with a shawl and a cup of warm mead, but all the girl really needed was to be held, which Umma did, finding herself solace in that love, that bond with the woman who loved her son.

Gunar had cloistered himself inside his dwelling and did not wish to be disturbed or to be called to join the company of others, not even to meals.

"I wish that he unburdened himself to me, that he'd cry and scream and let his pain out," Umma lamented to Airmid.

"Some of us prefer to grieve in solitude."

Umma, Airmid, Lugh and Morrigan dined together. There was so much that Airmid wanted to know about her grandson, and so much he needed to know about them but most of all, he longed to know about his birth parents.

"...I was blessed with seeing them; their astral bodies," Morrigan said, alluding to the night, during the celebration of Samhain, when her mother held her in her arms.

"Did they ask about me?" Lugh enquired promptly.

"They love you; they are very much aware of the circumstances of your upbringing and they said that, if you wished it one day, they would appear to you too."

A smile and a wonderfully warm expression appeared on Lugh's face. He felt as happy as when he was with Clodagh.

"Tell us about Clodagh," Morrigan asked, catching his thought.

"She was wonderful. Small looking, fragile but very strong inside, very wise for her years. She was beautiful and I lost her, but before dying she told me to keep looking for her. I am not sure that I know what that means. I just thought they were the words of delirium that she was speaking." A wave of sadness passed through everyone.

"If I were you, I would take her words very seriously. Expect to meet her. In the body of another woman perhaps, but she'll come back to you," Umma divined, sure enough of herself and her dreams to know that she would not be leading Lugh to the pursuit of a false hope.

"How can you be sure of such things?" Lugh enquired, vexed with the burden of whether to let himself be hopeful or to dismiss that stranger's words.

"...I dream of things that come to pass, and so did my mother, and her mother before her. I've seen this creature of sweetness wander the earth lonely and lost, searching for you.

"Her astral body is only a pale reflection of the beauty she must have been when happy, nonetheless, she glows like the sun. She is a relentless predator of happiness; she never knew much of it in her life, up until she met you. She won't rest until she finds you. Look for her in the eyes of a fair-haired stranger," Umma uttered seemingly drifting in and out of ordinary consciousness.

Airmid and Morrigan, who knew the genuineness and accuracy of Umma's visions, both touched Lugh's shaky hands and smiled, full of hope. He, transfixed, looked with hope into his sister's eyes.

Chapter Fifty

The morning of the third day came. People on Iona seemed electrified, excited and confident that they would defeat the ancient enemy. No one felt fear, only anticipation, particularly Morrigan, for whom that night would not only transform the present but alter what had been, in Haakon's resurrection.

The children were reassured and prepared to be apart from their parents for a while. Food, water, candles, games, cots and blankets were taken to the semi-deserted part of the island.

They would stay outside, play, eat and nap on the green fields until sundown. After that time each child, holding a small torch, would enter the caves as they had practiced in preliminary excursions.

Morrigan looked with tenderness and love at the children lining up to follow their caretakers. Some of them did not look too happy to go; some of their parents did not look delighted by it either.

She saw mothers and fathers tenderly kiss their children, the little children of Iona who would inherit the new world with the coming of the new age of Danu, or the dread and violence-filled legacy of a Fomorian reign. But she did not allow herself to dwell on the negative: the Fomor would not win. It could not be.

"By the power of Danu and of all our life-forces in unison and communion, we shall overcome the Fomor and bring light to the world!" She thought as she walked towards the sea.

Lugh saw her walking away, followed her and caught up with her.

"Are you worried?" He asked, while a few steps behind her.

"No, just anxious to get it over with today. I'm looking forward to the joys to come, to all of us coming together, to you finding your lost love, and to me getting mine back."

"...Are you afraid it might not happen?"

"I am, a little, but I cannot let myself think negatively because it is that kind of attitude which precipitates negative situations."

Lugh smiled in agreement. "I'll fight as hard as I possibly can," he vowed.

"What will it be like to witness the clash of the Dannan and the Fomor?" Morrigan pondered as she imagined what sounds and sights colliding stars would generate. "Will the Earth tremble?"

***

Everyone in Iona had been meditating and stretching to prepare the body for higher functioning, and to ease it into the attunement of mind and spirit. Breakfast had been the first and last meal of the day.

A large bonfire burned at the centre of the village. People gathered around it, sat on the ground and watched Airmid, clothed entirely in silver, carrying the Druid's staff in her left hand and the owl of wisdom on her right shoulder, advance towards them.

She had been meditating all night and her face looked pale and withdrawn into a higher mode of being. She threw a fistful of herbs in the fire and the scent of wisdom filled the surrounding air.

She spoke in verse which lulled the senses of the people, who shifted into the other state of being, similar to that which they experienced during sleep and dreaming.

Airmid intoned a note and held it; her people followed suit and a surreal buzz came to life. Morrigan and Lugh participated as well, and so did Gunar. In that state, where no one felt separate from the other, the essence of happiness and the meaning of life were known.

Chapter Fifty-one

It was evening. In Aileach, Urien and Rhiannon prepared for their ritual. The altar where she had slain the children was still stained with their blood and stood under the gaze of Balor's vicious eye, waiting to become her and Urien's mating bed. The bride and groom of darkness disrobed.

The torches in the dungeons were extinguished by Ragnar personally, who was to witness the mating. Only a handful of candles was kept lit, and set by the altar slab.

***

On Iona, the people gathered on the vast plain by the sea, outside the cromlech where Haakon's body lay. Airmid was to be the only one to remain inside the circle of stones. Lugh and Morrigan, clothed in their black, form-fitting, one-piece body garments, stood on the shore, their feet immersed in the life-conducive water.

"Look into my eyes and you will know what to do," Morrigan told her brother, who had practiced stilling his thoughts and steadying his galloping heart.

The people around, all clothed in black as well, waited for Airmid's voice to intone the note to join her, and to create the cosmic buzz that would call the Dannan to the world of flesh and fire.

As the buzz began, Morrigan and Lugh levitated like Morrigan and Airmid had, the day that they saw the many faces of Danu. Lugh felt butterflies in his stomach; Morrigan enjoyed the feeling of weightlessness that her body was rediscovering and they both began to slowly revolve in space, side by side, one counter clockwise the other.

The collective mind of all people summoned their most sacred ancestors, those they called gods, and from the sky which they illuminated, they descended, fierce and proud, carrying the wisdom of the ages in their burning eyes.

The Morrigan, wild and dishevelled, lead the army of the gods, inciting them to fight and to win. Lugh's sudden and unexpected verse-weaving opened the gates of the ancient magic universe, and its powers.

Chapter Fifty-two

Balor's eye opened and lightning flashed out of it. Urien and Rhiannon looked steadily into the light until their minds became one with Balor's. Urien lifted Rhiannon onto the altar and she lay, waiting for her lover-brother to possess her.

Urien climbed mechanically on top of her and the mating, devoid of passion, took place and, thrust by thrust they teleported themselves to Iona.

Ragnar, the only special soldier who had been left behind, watched in awe of what he thought was high magic. He knew little of the world outside Caer Balor, and nothing about the higher power of love.

As Urien and Rhiannon's bodies landed on Iona, not too far from the site of the Ritual, the people sensed they had arrived, but they did not look for them. The two naked strangers looked around with dismay, noticing the absence of their troops and the clamour of the approaching Dannan.

Airmid and Umma had psychically intercepted Urien's crew and prevented them from reaching their island. They raised the winds, the winds raised the waters, and the vessel carrying Urien and Rhiannon's best fighters sank, killing all of them, as the Druid and the Vittka had intended.

As Urien and Rhiannon realized Airmid's intervention they, nude and crawling, felt as insignificant and as helpless as worms at the mercy of giants. Nonetheless their mating had called the Fomor to the surface of the waters.

A majestic gurgle, like an underwater thunder, was heard and shook the island. The people, still focusing on their task and vocalizing louder in the attempt to disperse the impact of the sound and the vibration that came from the Fomor, had to look upon the monsters, yet control their reactions, harness their fear and not let it distract them from being one.

The bull, hog and monster-headed marine warriors of Balor were heavily concealed in their amphibian armours, which shone in metallic tones of green and blue, blending into each other under the light of the moon. They advanced quickly towards the shore, but they could harm no mortal.

It was a sight the people of Iona would never forget. The Dannan, radiant, descended like eagles from the sky on the Fomor.

The two armies fought between sea and sky, not far from Morrigan and Lugh, yet, not harming them. It looked and sounded as if the stars were colliding and falling to be swallowed by the sea. Blood was not spilled: only energy was spent, and the Dannan were powered by the collective life force of the people of Iona. Urien and Rhiannon were no match for them, and were numerically nowhere near what was needed to feed the Fomor.

The battle was like lightning and thunder, the clank and crash jarred the bottom of the sea and the ground of the surface. Large waves leapt towards the shore as if to eat it. When Morrigan became the Morrigu and Lugh the Sun-God of the Dannan, they screamed, and their wild cries echoed throughout the heavens.

***

In the cromlech, Airmid cradled Haakon's head in one of her hands while opening his mouth with the other and there, in the presence of the overseeing spirit of the goddess, she breathed her life-force into the boy until she, drained, collapsed on his body now full of life, and unthawing from its state of arrested death.

Chapter Fifty-three

The Fomor were pushed back into the roaring waters and sank, mercilessly depleted of energy by the Dannan. Urien and Rhiannon yelled and writhed in the sand. Their minds could not stand to face the reality that the all-powerful Balor had failed them.

Morrigan and Lugh unexpectedly descended upon them like wild birds of prey. Morrigan had come to know the rage she could not fathom she would ever feel.

Rhiannon lay on her back, her beautiful body covered with sweat and sand, as she tried to crawl backwards, away from the Morrigan; it was pain which scared her, not death. She laughed as she backed away, but Morrigan, hovering above her, pointed her index finger at Rhiannon's heart and, as she did, in the place of the nail a thin blade grew, sharp, like that of a dagger.

"This is going to hurt!" the Morrigan chuckled as she traced a spiral with her talon onto the skin of Rhiannon's left breast.

"I like pain!" Rhiannon defied.

"You shall have it; see how it feels!" the Morrigan cried out, and pierced through Rhiannon's heart, slowly, but deeply in a cutting, back-and-forth motion which ripped through the tissues, rather than cut.

As she screamed loud and high to the sky, the beautiful alabaster skin of her chest and abdomen covered with blood, Rhiannon thought of Ragnar and the agreement she had made with him, unbeknownst to anyone.

"My soul is already here, in this cruet," she had told him before the mating ceremony had begun. "It already belongs to the Lord of Annwn. All you need is my life-force; when I die, the cruet will glow green, calling me to it. Breathe, drink the glow, and you and I shall be as one.

"Find a woman, a beautiful and young woman whose body you desire, render her unconscious, and once my life-force is inside of you, all you have to do is breathe it into the girl with a kiss and I shall come to life through her, within her, to be yours forever and forever to rule the world, together."

As Rhiannon's body was dying, the substance in the cruet glowed and Ragnar drank it. Seconds after, Rhiannon had taken full possession of his body, but his soul she banished to the Fomorian hell, enslaving it to its demons.

"...A man's body: the power of its musculature, the might of the bone mass...so many cruelties to perpetrate and savour; so many new carnal pleasures to sample. So much respect to be bestowed upon, in a man's body," Rhiannon thought.

***

Lugh, looking every bit the majestic and menacing warrior that Urien wanted him to be, leaped off his astral horse onto Urien's back as he was trying to get up and run to the shore, hoping to drown at sea, rather than sample Lugh's blade.

"There's nowhere to hide!" Lugh whispered in Urien's ear as he landed on top of the back of his shoulders, pinning him to the ground. "I can smell your fear," Lugh smirked.

"...I know I've been a dreadful bastard but I beg of you, spare my life; I was your father once!" Urien pleaded through the tears and tremors of his muscles.

Lugh stood off of him, grabbed him by the hair and had Urien on his knees, facing him.

Urien, whimpering, looked upward and squinted, half-blinded by the light of Lugh's dazzling astral body. There was a moment of eerie silence, and the last thing Urien saw was the twinkling of Lugh's blade in the crepuscular glow. Lugh's sword came down heavy on Urien's neck, severing his head.

"It's finished," Lugh said.

At that moment, the Dannan ascended to the sky and disappeared as suddenly and as spectacularly as they had descended.

Lugh and Morrigan, having re-entered their bodies, gradually stopped revolving and landed on their feet, disoriented. The people, fully out of their trance, cheered their return among them and began to celebrate the victory of the goddess, and the empowerment which, through Lugh and Morrigan, they had received and which would allow them to change the world. The children were cheerfully retrieved from their hiding places.

Chapter Fifty-four

As soon as her feet touched the ground, Morrigan ran towards the circle of stones to see Haakon, but he met her half way, standing, waiting for her, alive and radiant. She ran into his arms and they both felt immense happiness and relief. Lugh joined them soon while Umma, quietly knowing, entered the circle of stones and tended to Airmid's lifeless body.

Morrigan looked around for Airmid, but Haakon gently pulled her to him and she felt a strange emptiness within.

"...'You know that my heart is forever your dwelling. I say goodbye now, but I will never be too far from you,'" he uttered. Morrigan knew that those were Airmid's words and she fell to her knees and screamed loud and hard, mourning the loss of her mother, her teacher and her friend.

Haakon knelt beside her and tried to calm her, when Lugh appeared, shocked and bereaved, after having heard about the loss of Airmid.

When Morrigan was calm enough to listen, although still blinded by pain and tears, she felt Haakon put his hand on her stomach.

"'Raise the boy-child that Morrigan is carrying well,' she said," Haakon whispered.

Morrigan looked deep into her mate's eyes and she felt as though she was been torn in half by her emotions. She had barely had time to adjust to Haakon's re-birth, that she had to grieve for Airmid's death and now, she felt overcome by surprise and happiness as she had learned that she was with child.

"She gave us a great gift; her life was well spent," Morrigan realized as she uttered those words to Haakon, and then looked down at her still flat stomach in awe of the thought that she was carrying a human being inside of herself. She could not wait to see him, and to love him, and protect him forever, and to raise him well in a world which was destined for constant changes.

Lugh had ventured inside the cromlech and was shedding tears over the body of the newfound grandmother that he would not get to know.

"She loved you," Umma told Lugh while putting her arms around his shoulders. "A part of her, part of her memories, her thoughts, her feelings, will always be with Haakon and through him, with us. She decided to give Haakon her life-force immediately after we became aware that he had been killed; we felt it happen. She felt that she had lead a long and fruitful life and you, Morrigan and Haakon deserved the same chance. There is much work ahead of you, all three of you.

"It was the power of Danu, during the ritual, which allowed the passage of her life-force into my son's body restoring him to consciousness. I did not ask for that sacrifice; she chose to do it, and she was a very stubborn, wonderful and selfless woman," Umma said between the laughter and the tears which she shared with Lugh.

"I offered to give my son my life-force," she added. "But she said that I was younger, and that Haakon, Morrigan, you, my husband and the village need me to be your nurturer and Druid now."

Chapter Fifty-five

Airmid was buried in the same chamber that Sandda had been, and in the same ceremonial manner. Umma had been trained and instructed by Airmid all along, about her duties and tasks as Druid, a title which was destined to be passed on to Morrigan at Umma's death. At a council called after Airmid's burial Umma, wearing her traditional Vittka's gown and jewels, invested Morrigan with the title of High Priestess of Danu. They would co-operate, as Vittka and Druid, in sharing their responsibilities to the people. Then Umma gifted Morrigan with her dazzling and powerful crystals.

"Although everything is quiet on our beautiful island, what happened last night is changing the world," Morrigan told the people.

"People are readying themselves to welcome the New Age, but it won't come without effort. There will be much opposition by a new religion," she prophesied, Lugh and Haakon by her side.

In the privacy of their cabin Morrigan and Haakon had the opportunity to express their tremendous joy about her pregnancy, and to celebrate it with a small ritual under the light of the moon. The ritual was meant to let their child's soul know that he was loved, and very much wanted.

"What a wonderful time to be born; such an eventful time..." Morrigan said looking into Haakon's eyes with excitement and joy sparkling in hers.

"It is, my love, it is," he said as he pulled her to him and kissed her forehead, both of them feeling grateful and still amazed at the fact that he was alive and well.

"...My heart shall forever be your dwelling..." Airmid's words resounded through Haakon's and Morrigan's minds, whispered by the soft wind and by the trees, keepers of all knowledge like the stones and, as the stones, they looked majestic and solid, built to stand the test of time, to be there and to teach humans about the mysteries of life generation after generation, time after time.

THE END

Page 271; Haakon's narration of Old Norse poetry has been translated, from the Italian, (by myself) from the book La Magia Delle Rune, by Gebo Urdiz, Edizioni Mediterranee, Roma - Via Flaminia, 158 -where it was borrowed from K. Eigl's Deutche Goetter Und Heldensangen, Wien.

Page 274; Gunar's "The Speech Of The High One" has been taken from Ralph Blum's The Book Of Runes, Oracle Books, St. Martin's Press, New York, 1987.

Page 275; The "Sleep Stones" ritual is an idea borrowed from the book The Practice Of Witchcraft, by Robin Skelton. Porcepic Books, Victoria, Canada, 1990. I obtained his permission to use the sleeping stones before he passed away.

LaVergne, TN USA
23 December 2009
167898LV00001B/12/A